FOREVERMORE

Warren could not remember the last time he felt this way about a woman. He wasn't sure if what he was feeling was infatuation or just plain love, but he knew it was intense and he knew it felt good and it felt right. He wanted to take care of her, to protect her, to do anything that would make her happy.

He pulled Alexandra closer and began touching her, moving his hand up her thigh, caressing the soft flesh through the silk that covered it. "Alexandra," he moaned.

He began kissing her face. He ran his tongue along the soft line of her neck, up to her ear, and gently nibbled her lobe. Warren wanted to make love to her, but he didn't want it to be meaningless. He needed to be sure that her feelings for him were as genuine as his were for her.

"I'm crazy about you, Alexandra. I want you, but on a permanent basis. I want you to be my lady. I don't want to share you with anyone. Are you ready to deal with that?"

"I'm not looking for a fling. I'm not into flings," she said resentfully.

"Baby, I'm not trying to insult you. I just want to know how you feel before I put my heart on the line."

Alexandra studied his face. She could see he was very serious.

"I want you, Warren," she said sincerely. "I want you to be my man and I don't want to share you with anyone, either."

She hugged him tightly and he returned her warm embrace. Warren could feel her heart beating next to his and he knew his feelings for her would grow stronger with each new day.

D1711610

*A*T *F*IRST *S*IGHT

Cheryl Faye

PINNACLE BOOKS
KENSINGTON PUBLISHING CORP.

PINNACLE BOOKS are published by

Kensington Publishing Corp.
850 Third Avenue
New York, NY 10022

First Printing: August, 1996

Printed in the United States of America
10 9 8 7 6 5 4 3 2 1

For my sons, Michael and Douglas II (I love you both); PopPop (I miss you); Mommy and Daddy (Barbara and James Smith, Sr.—you're the best!!); my sisters Jackie, Mamie (Lou) and Stephanie and my brother "all in the kool-aid . . ." James, Jr. (who could ask for better blood). And Mr. Moe

Acknowledgments

First, I'd like to thank God. I know without the love of the Father and your son Jesus Christ, none of this would be possible.

Douglas Tiburcio, Sr., if it were not for our bet, my first saga might have stayed in my head.

To those who were there at the beginning, the sisters at Met Life in the Pensions department, Sharon, Gwen, Didee, and Mary. You gave me the encouragement to keep writing.

Thank you to my good friend and hang-out partner, Charisse Bellamy. You were my first "editor."

To the ladies on the sixteenth floor at Hughes Hubbard & Reed, Doris McPherson, Michele Kimbrow (all the best for you with your writing), Edwina Battle (fifteenth floor), and Peggy Dixon. Thank you for your time, your cheers, and your great spellchecking. (Your Majesty, I told you I'd mention your name.)

And last, but certainly not least, my sisters of SHADES OF US. We all need a shoulder to lean on sometimes. I'm glad I've got you!!

PART ONE

One

Alexandra Jenkins was sitting facing the door at a table near the back of the restaurant when he walked in. She was having dinner with her older brother, David, who had just completed a two-year tour of duty overseas in the Marine Corps.

David was in the middle of a story about himself and some of the guys in his company when she spied him.

He was tall, well over six feet, she guessed, and his skin was the color of semisweet chocolate. He wore a very neatly trimmed mustache and his jet-black hair was long, and wavy.

His posture was perfect. That was the only way she could describe it, and it made him appear taller than he actually was. He was wearing an olive-green double-breasted suit, white shirt, and a reddish print tie.

David, curious that she was no longer paying attention to what he was saying, snapped his fingers.

"Earth to Alex, earth to Alex," he said.

"What?" she said, as she slowly came out of her trance, and "he" disappeared from her line of vision.

"You're not listening to me."

"Yes, I am, Davey," she fibbed.

"Oh, yeah? What did I just say?"

She blushed and lowered her eyes. "I'm sorry," she said softly.

"What were you looking at?" he asked, turning to see for himself.

"Nothing. I just thought I saw someone I knew."

"Well, since you're not paying me any mind, I won't bore you with any more of my stories."

"You're not boring me," she said, though he was.

"Yeah, right. So anyway, you're still seeing Gerard, right?"

"Yeah," she groaned.

"How're y'all doing?"

"All right, I guess," she said, with little enthusiasm.

"Well, damn, Alex, don't sound so excited."

She shrugged and tried to explain.

"It's just that Gerry . . ." She paused for a moment. "He's boring! He never wants to do anything except go to these tired poetry readings in the Village or to the ballet. If I ask him to come with me to see a movie, he complains if it's not a foreign film with English subtitles."

"Gerard?" David said, with an astonished look.

"Yes, Gerard. You haven't seen him in a long time. He's changed since he started working at that brokerage house. I think he's trying to impress those white folks he's working with since he's the only black guy in the whole office."

"Yeah, but why's he acting like that with you?"

"Don't ask me. I'm really getting tired of him."

"But he's making money, right?"

"Oh, yeah. He's making close to seventy-five thousand a year."

"Whoa! Really?"

"Yeah. Mommy's like 'You'd better marry that man,' but I couldn't see myself married to him, no matter how much he's making. Besides, I'm making a pretty decent salary on my own."

Suddenly Alexandra beheld again the man who had

captured her attention a few minutes earlier. He had been wearing shades when he entered the restaurant but he had since removed them so she could now see his dark and intense eyes.

He was walking in the direction of their table. She was struck speechless, watching as he paused briefly and spoke to a couple seated a few tables away from them. He smiled at them and his smile brightened his dark eyes.

She did not realize that she was staring at him until he looked over at her. The corner of his mouth curled into a subtle smile and she blushed and looked away quickly. She could not help smiling.

"What are you grinning about?" David asked.

"Nothing."

Within the next few seconds, as quickly as she had turned her face away and back, he was moving toward their table.

"Oh, my God," she sighed breathlessly.

"What?" David asked.

"Good evening, folks," he said, as he stood over them.

He was boldly looking at Alexandra with that same soft, subtle smile, but his eyes sparkled. He thought she was beautiful, her light-brown complexion, flawless. She wore her thick shoulder-length brown hair in curls that were combed away from her face. Her small slanted eyes and pug nose fit her oval-shaped face perfectly, and when she smiled, her cheeks were punctuated by a deep set of dimples.

"Good evening," Alexandra said, softly.

David looked up and was about to return the greeting when he recognized his friend from college.

"CB? Oh, wow, Cool Breeze!" David exclaimed.

Immediately shocked by hearing the nickname he

had been called during his college years, he turned his attention to David, noticing him for the first time.

"David Jenkins? What's up?"

David rose from his seat and the two men embraced.

"How you been, man? It's good to see you," David said happily.

"I've been all right. How 'bout you? Long time, no see. You look good," CB said.

"You, too, man. What's up? What you been up to?"

"Yo, man, working hard, that's all."

Alexandra sat in stunned silence as she watched her brother and this beautiful black man carry on the way friends do who have not seen each other in years.

Finally, David said, "Yo, Cool, let me introduce you to my sister."

"Yeah, I was wondering when you were gonna get around to that," he said, smiling at Alexandra.

"Alex, this is Cool Breeze," David said.

"No one's called me that in ten years. My name is Warren. Warren Michaels," he said, offering his hand. "I'm pleased to meet you."

His smile turned her to putty.

"Hi, I'm Alexandra," she said timidly. "Nice to meet you, too."

"We went to school together, Alex. CB was the quarterback on our football team. He could've played pro ball. He was unstoppable," David boasted.

"Not true. I was very stoppable. It just took a while," he said with a smile.

"You shoulda seen him play, Sis. Barely broke a sweat, that's why we called him Cool Breeze."

"Your brother has always had a tendency to exaggerate," Warren said.

"I know," she said, grinning.

"So what you doin', man? You havin' dinner? Are you by yourself?" David asked.

"No, man. I own this place," Warren said.

"Get outta here!"

"Yeah. How's your dinner?"

"Hey, it's great. You've got a nice place here."

Michaels was a fairly large restaurant. The decor was very modern. A small lounge furnished with cocktail tables and equipped with a bar was separated from the main dining room for the convenience of customers waiting to be seated. In the dining room, the tables were all covered with wine-colored linen tablecloths, fresh-cut flowers and a single candle adorning each. The lighting was atmospherically dim. On the walls were pictures of famous African-American entertainers, past and present. The standard cuisine was a variety of soul food and Caribbean specialties.

"Thanks." Warren acknowledged the compliment. "So what the hell are you doing?" he asked.

"Hey, man, I'm home on leave. I'm a career man in the Marines."

"Yeah? I remember when you went in. It's been that good to you, huh?"

"Yeah," David said.

Alexandra sat quietly and finished what was left of her meal as her brother and Warren spent the next few minutes catching up.

As she watched them together, reminiscing about old times, she noticed, for the first time really, how handsome her brother was. The Marines had indeed been very good to him.

David was just slightly taller than Alexandra, five feet nine, but he was very muscular. He was darker than she, having taken his chocolate brown complexion from their father. His face was more round than oval but he had small, slanted eyes, a trait he and Alexandra had inherited from their mother. He had what Alexandra had always called an "aristocratic nose," and a small mouth with very kissable lips. His ever-ready smile was punctuated by dimples that ran in the family on their father's side. His hair was cut close, military style.

While he was in college, he played the running back position on their team. Back then he was a lot stockier, but now he had slimmed down and firmed up.

He and Alexandra were their parents' only children and, growing up, they had been very close. She had always looked up to him and he had always been very protective of her. Though they had not seen each other in two years, they corresponded often and spent as much time together as they could whenever he was home on leave.

Suddenly, a young woman walked over. "Excuse me, Mr. Michaels," she said. "You have a phone call."

"Thanks, Sally, I'll be right there."

To David and Alexandra he said, "This is probably the call I've been waiting for. Let me go take this. And, David, don't leave without seeing me, okay?"

After David agreed, Alexandra watched Warren as he walked away from their table. He was even better looking up close, she thought.

"I can't believe you know him," she said in awe as David returned to his seat.

"Yeah. Is that who you were looking at?"

"Yes. He's gorgeous, David. Is he married?"

"He was. Whether he still is or not, I really don't know."

"He's so fine. Was he always that fine?" she asked.

"Well, Alex, I really couldn't say, you know," David laughed. "He's never struck me like that."

"I know, but when you were in school, did he have a lot of girlfriends?"

"Oh, man, when we were in school, girls used to go crazy over this guy, especially after a game. They used to mob him," said David.

AT FIRST SIGHT   15

"I can see why."

"Hey, why all the questions about Warren? Have you forgotten about Gerard?"

"Of course not. But just because I'm seeing Gerard doesn't mean I'm dead. I can still appreciate the beauty of a man who looks as good as that."

They had finished dinner and David was pulling bills out of his wallet to pay the check when Warren came back to their table.

"Put your money away, David," Warren said.

"Hey, you know you don't have to tell me twice," David said as he immediately closed his wallet and put it back in his jacket pocket. "Hey, CB, are you and Marge still together?"

"Naw, man, we've been divorced for almost seven years. She's about to get remarried, as a matter of fact," Warren answered.

"Oh, yeah? What about you? Are you gonna get remarried, too?"

"No, I don't think so. Once is more than enough for me," he said.

"I heard that. Y'all have a kid, right?"

"Yeah, a little girl. Well, she's really not that little anymore. She'll be nine years old in a couple of months."

David and Alexandra rose from the table and the three of them started toward the door.

"So CB, is this the only restaurant you own?" David asked.

"No, I have another place in Queens. It's bigger than this one. It's more of a night club scene, you know. There's dining on one level and then downstairs there's dancing, and occasionally we have live entertainment," Warren explained.

"Yeah? How long have you been in business?"

"I've had this place for almost five years. The one in

Queens is newer. It's been open for about two and a half years."

"That's great, man. So you're doing all right, huh?" David asked.

"Yeah, I'm doing all right." Then, "Hey, what are y'all doing this Sunday?" Warren asked suddenly.

"I'll be in Virginia on Sunday," David said.

"Virginia? For what?"

"That's my new command. I'll be down at Quantico."

"Aw, man, I'm having a big cookout on Sunday for my birthday. I'd really like for you to come," he said.

"Sorry. Can't make it."

"Go to Virginia on Monday."

"I've been on leave for a month, man. I'll be working on Monday. Besides, my wife and I have to go down and get our house settled and everything."

"Where is your wife?" Warren asked.

"She's in the Bronx visiting her sister who just had a baby. I'm gonna go get her later."

"Well, Alexandra, *you* won't be in Virginia, will you?" Warren asked, smiling as he gently touched her arm.

"No, I'll be here."

"Then why don't you come? I'd rather have you there anyway," he said with a wink.

She blushed and said, "I'll try."

"Well, I hope you can make it. Here, let me give you my address and phone number."

He reached into the breast pocket of his jacket and removed a business card holder and took out one of the cards. He leaned over the mâitre d's station and began writing on the back of the card.

As he was writing, he said, "If you like, Alexandra, you can bring a friend. The more the merrier, and make sure to bring your bathing suit."

"Where're you staying?" David asked.

"Huntington. Out on the Island," he answered.

When he handed the card to Alexandra, she noticed that aside from the address and telephone number of the restaurant, he had put his home address, phone and beeper numbers on the back of the card.

"Thank you. I'll try to make it there."

"I hope you can," he said as he boldly looked into her eyes.

"Hey, CB, man, we've gotta run. We're supposed to be catching a seven o'clock show at the theater down the street," David said.

"All right, man. It was great seeing you again," Warren said sincerely as he shook David's hand and they embraced again. "Alexandra has my number so keep in touch. I wish you were gonna be around a little longer, we could've played catch up."

"Yeah, I know, but since I'll only be in VA, I'll probably be coming up here a lot more often. We'll get together on my next trip up," David said.

"Definitely." He turned to Alexandra and said, "It was a pleasure meeting you, Alexandra. I hope to see you Sunday."

He leaned over and kissed her cheek.

"It was nice meeting you, too, Warren."

"All right, y'all have a good night. David, take it easy, man."

"You, too," said David, and they left the restaurant.

Once they were outside, David turned to Alexandra and asked, "So are you gonna go Sunday?"

"Hell, yeah. I wouldn't miss it for the world."

Two

Warren Michaels was having breakfast in bed Sunday morning, August tenth. It was his thirty-fourth birthday, and he had made up his mind that on this day he would not lift a finger to do anything that he did not want to. His lady friend, Susan Mitchell, had gotten up and made him a breakfast of French toast and bacon, orange juice and maple-walnut coffee, his favorite.

"What time are you expecting your guests to arrive?" Susan asked.

"Starting about one," he answered.

"What time are the caterers coming?"

"They're supposed to be here by twelve. What time is it now?"

"A quarter after ten."

The telephone rang. Warren sat where he was. He knew Susan would get it.

She got up and walked to the other side of the bed and picked up the telephone on the nightstand.

"Hello."

"Good morning." The voice was female. "May I speak to Warren, please?"

"Who's calling?" Susan asked in a proprietary tone.

"Alexandra Jenkins."

Susan hesitated for a moment, looking over at Warren. Then she handed him the phone.

"Who is it?"

"Someone named Alexandra," she said with a frown.

"Oh!" he said, a hint of surprise in his voice as he took the phone from her. "Hello."

"Hi, Warren. This is Dave's sister Alexandra."

"Yes, hi. How are you?"

"I'm fine, thank you. How are you?"

"Great. What's up?"

"I was just calling to get directions to your house," she said.

He set his breakfast tray aside. "Oh, good. So you're coming?"

"Yes."

"Great! Do you have a pen handy?"

He gave her very specific directions. "Will you be coming alone?" he asked after she had finished jotting down the directions.

"No, a girlfriend of mine is going to come with me. What time should we get there?" she asked.

"Anytime after one. We'll be going all day, probably. Oh, and don't forget your bathing suit," he reminded her.

"I won't. So, I'll see you later," she said.

He smiled as he hung up the telephone. He was glad she was coming.

"Who was that?" Susan asked, noticing the grin on his face.

"Oh, remember the other day I told you I'd run into a guy I went to school with in the restaurant downtown? Well, that was his sister."

"Is he coming, too?"

"No, he had to fly to Virginia today."

"You seem awfully happy that she's coming. Is something going on with you and her?" Susan asked.

With a grimace he said, "I just met her the other day, Susan. If you think you're going to have a problem with any of my guests today, though, maybe you shouldn't be here."

"Well, you just seem extremely happy that she's going to be here," she said indignantly.

"I'm no more happy about her coming than I am anyone else. It's my birthday and I'm having a party. It would be a real bust if no one came, now wouldn't it?" Warren said.

"Just forget I said anything," Susan said sourly.

Warren got up from the bed then and went into the bathroom to shower. He was developing a sick feeling in his gut.

They had been together now for over two years and he was fed up with the way she always assumed there was another woman in the background.

As he turned on the shower and stepped into the stall, he reflected on the past two years. They had met soon after he opened Michaels Too. He had been quite taken with Susan when she walked into the club wearing a skin tight black catsuit. Aside from her beauty, once they got to know each other he had also been impressed by her intelligence. He had fallen for her quite hard and went out of his way to do whatever he thought would make her happy.

His only problem with her was her insecurity. He could still remember their first argument. Now that he thought about it, it had been more like a scene out of a B movie.

A woman he had known vaguely from college had come into the club and, to his surprise, greeted him like they were old friends. Always having considered himself a gentleman, if not a bit of a flirt, he had been very charming, and though their conversation had been completely innocent, he had gently kissed her hand when they parted.

Susan had pounced on him almost immediately, accusing him of blatantly disrespecting her. He remembered how embarrassed he had been at the way she yelled at him in front of the hundreds of people present at the club. But his feelings for her then were so strong that he apologized for doing whatever it was he had done to make her think he was being unfaithful.

Despite the love he felt for her and the way he tried to prove to her that she was the only woman in his life, on many more occasions, Susan had caused scenes in his club, accusing him of sleeping around.

In the last year or so, Susan had often brought up the subject of marriage. She had often said if he really loved her, he'd make her his wife. He reasoned, however, that if they were married, her scenes would only get worse. Besides, he had been married once already and it had not been great. Though he and his ex-wife were basically kids when they wed, he was in no rush to do it again.

He had never been able to understand why it was so difficult for her to see that he loved only her and had never cheated on her. As far as he was concerned, if she really loved him the way she claimed to, she would trust him. In the past few months, Warren began to resent her accusations.

It had gotten so bad that he could now tell, simply by the way she would look at him, if she was about to attack him. If they were in public, his stomach would tighten in anxious anticipation of her anger. He hated being put on the spot that way, and though he had always tried to appease her on prior occasions, it had finally reached a point where he would more quickly ignore her than try to pacify her. Her constant insinuations had caused his interest in her to wane, and his love for her was no longer as sure as it had once been.

As he washed up, he prayed that she would not ruin this day for him.

* * *

When he came out of the bathroom a half hour later, Susan was still in bed.

"Get out of bed and get dressed, Susan. The caterers will be here in a little while."

Susan got up without a word to him. She was getting sick of being treated like nothing more than one of his "numbers." He knew she wanted to get married. After two years, she felt she was due. She was thirty-seven years old and her biological clock was ticking off the wall. She wanted to have a baby. Whenever she brought up the subject of marriage and children, Warren became uncommunicative.

She did not believe him, either, when he told her that he had just met this woman Alexandra the other day. Why would he be so excited about seeing her if there was nothing going on between them?

Well, Susan thought, when this Alexandra showed up, she would let her know that she would not sit idly by and let her try to move in on her good thing.

She was sure he slept with other women, even though she had no solid proof. But it seemed that lately, he did not care if she knew or if she liked it or not.

When Susan went into the bathroom, she slammed the door and locked it, then turned on the faucets in the shower stall. She took off her nightgown, stepped over to the sink to brush her hair and stared at her reflection in the mirror.

It did not matter to her that he was well-off or that, until recently, he had always treated her like a queen. She was a beautiful black woman; she was supposed to be treated like a queen. She deserved to be.

Suddenly, her thoughts went to Jeff Foster. He had asked her to marry him on more occasions than she could count and she had turned him down each time.

The last proposal had been just last month when he was in town playing a gig at Westbury.

Jeff was a musician. A drummer who, though he had never really made it in the big time, played with many big-name performers and in all parts of the world.

They met when Susan was still in high school. She had gone to a night club with her older cousin Andrea against her parents' wishes. Jeff was playing that night with her favorite group, the Duprees.

Susan had always been more grown-up than her classmates. She was wearing makeup in the eighth grade and would not be caught dead in a pair of sneakers and jeans.

When the band was finished playing that evening, Jeff came straight to their table and sat down, though there had been another young man sitting with them who was trying to talk to Susan. He introduced himself and told her that he thought she was the most beautiful woman in the place.

She was taken in by his big brown puppy-dog eyes and wide smile.

He was twenty-one at the time, and she was seventeen. She started to lie to him about her age, but for some reason she told him the truth. He told her that when she turned eighteen, he was going to make a woman out of her. When she and her cousin left the club that night, he walked her to their car. He put his arms around her and kissed her good-night. In that instant she fell in love with him.

When Susan went away to college, he would visit her occasionally, spending weekends with her when he could, taking her to the different clubs that he played at in her college town. He would tell her stories about the many different places he traveled just to play his drums. One day, he promised, he would take her with him.

He had even written a song for her.

Though she did not see him often because he traveled so much, Susan floated on his cloud for almost eight years until she realized, painfully, that he would never be the settling-down type. For as much as he claimed he loved her, she knew that music was his first love.

When she finally told him that she could not continue their long-distance romance, he asked her to marry him and travel with him. But she turned him down. She was trying to get her interior design business off the ground and that was more important to her than his love.

Almost against her will, though, she saw him whenever he came to town. He would call and tell her he was coming on a certain date and, true to his word, he always did. He had never broken a promise to her in twenty years.

After tying her long black hair up in a bun, she stepped in front of the full-length mirror and examined her body. *You've still got it,* she thought. For a thirty-seven year-old woman, she looked better than a whole lot of twenty-year-olds. Her stomach was flat, her breasts were still firm, and her behind did not sag. Most of her friends her age had become victims of gravity. She still turned heads wherever she went, so it was not even a matter of a lack of suitors.

She sometimes wondered why she even put up with Warren. She was an intelligent woman and a success in her own right. The interior design company was now lucrative and she did not have to wait for anyone to give her anything.

As she stepped into the shower, she decided that

maybe she should consider Jeff's proposal a little more seriously. She knew she could count on him, no matter what. After twenty years, he had more than proven he was as good as his word. She made up her mind that if Warren wanted to continue to play games, he would have to find himself another toy. She would be out of there.

Three

Twenty-nine-year-old Alexandra lived alone in a two-bedroom apartment in the Park Slope section of Brooklyn, just three blocks away from Prospect Park. She was a CPA and worked as the Controller in the accounting department of the same law office where she had been employed for seven years. She had been promoted to this position ten months ago, a major accomplishment since she started there as an accounting clerk. It was also significant because in this office of twenty-five attorneys, only one was black, and of her accounting staff, there was only one black out of the ten individuals who reported to her.

Alexandra was in excellent physical condition because she was somewhat fanatical about physical fitness. She got up every morning, and without fail, rain or shine, jogged around the park. She was a member of a health club she visited at least three times a week, and her spare bedroom was used for working out. She did not smoke, though she did occasionally drink, but never in excess. She ate healthy foods and drank eight glasses of water every day.

Because she lived such a healthy lifestyle, she had a beautiful complexion and always received compliments.

She considered herself pretty as opposed to beautiful, and one quickly picked up on her self-confidence, though she was by no means conceited or arrogant. She was simply pleased with herself and her life.

She was about five feet seven and she was stacked, with an hourglass figure and very healthy legs. She wore a size seven, in clothes and shoes.

As she got dressed in a pair of red spandex shorts and a white midriff top, she thought about Warren. She also thought about the woman who had answered his phone when she called him. Since he told David that he was not married, Alexandra wondered who she was.

Her telephone rang, interrupting her thoughts.

"Hey, girl. What's up?"

"Hi, Shari."

Shari Bennett and Alexandra had met when they were both on the cheerleading squad in their junior year at high school. They ended up going to Medgar Evars College in Brooklyn together as they had become very close friends. Shari was currently the Personnel Manager at a prestigious brokerage house in the Wall Street area of Manhattan.

"You're still coming with me, right?" Alexandra asked hopefully.

"Oh, yeah. I was just calling to see if you thought we should bring anything. I was thinking about running down to the store and, if you want, I could pick up something."

"Well, he didn't say anything about bringing anything. I don't think we have to worry," Alexandra told Shari.

"Yeah, right, he's probably got everything covered himself," Shari said. "Are you wearing your bathing suit or are you gonna carry it?"

"I'm wearing it."

"Which one?"

"My hot-pink string bikini," Alexandra said, smiling wickedly.

"Ooh, you slut."

"Thank you very much."

They laughed, then Shari asked, "What time are you coming to get me?"

"I should be leaving here at about one o'clock. Oh, you know, I called him this morning to get the directions and his woman answered the phone," Alexandra said as she stood in front of her bedroom mirror brushing her hair.

"How do you know it was his woman?"

"Because she sounded upset about me calling. I doubt seriously if his maid would sound so territorial."

"Well, he invited you, so I wouldn't worry about it."

"Oh, I'm not. I'm gonna go out there and have myself a ball."

"Yeah, right. Maybe I can find me a husband," Shari said, laughing.

"Look, let me get off this phone," Alexandra laughed. "I'll see you in a few."

Four

Warren was very proud of his two-story, four bedroom, three-and-a-half-bathroom house. It was situated in a cul-de-sac on a very quiet street in Huntington, Long Island. The driveway leading up to the front door was semicircular and forked off to a three-car garage. Inside, the first thing one noticed was the white marble floor leading straight back to the dining room. Directly off the foyer was the living room to the left and the den to the right. The living room was sparsely furnished but very elegant, with a fireplace and a fully stocked wet bar. Warren collected African-American art and had a number of beautiful pieces displayed. In the den, a state-of-the-art entertainment center equipped with a wide-screen television and compact disc player, turntable, cassette deck, and a reel-to-reel tape player stood opposite a rust-colored calfskin, L-shaped sectional sofa. An avid music lover, he owned a large collection of albums, tapes and CD's.

The dining room was large. A glass-and-brass table seated ten, and there was a glass and brass étagère which displayed beautiful lead crystal glassware. A chandelier hung from the ceiling just above the dining-room table. The kitchen could be entered from the dining room or the hallway. Warren was an amateur chef, and the room was a cook's kitchen filled with the most modern equipment available. A full bathroom was situated just off the kitchen. An exit led to a patio and an enormous back-yard, with a kidney-shaped swimming pool and a bath-house.

The lawn was professionally manicured. A high wooden fence surrounded the grounds in back, and in one corner of the yard was a garden where he grew his own vegetables, including collard greens, tomatoes, and cucumbers. A small rose garden was located a few yards away.

Warren, sitting alongside the pool, looked to the sky. Perfect, he thought. It was a beautiful sunny day with not a cloud in the sky. The temperature was in the high eighties. There were about twenty-five people already present. The music was playing and everyone was either eating, swimming, or mingling. As Warren talked with two of his guests, he noticed Alexandra and another young lady enter the yard from the gate.

Although her friend was attractive, Warren thought Alexandra looked captivating in her revealing outfit.

"Excuse me, fellas, I see a couple of incredibly gor-geous women that I must give my attention to," Warren said.

Susan was sitting on the other side of the pool and observed Warren as he got up and started toward the women who just arrived. She had never seen either of them before and surmised that one of them was prob-ably that Alexandra woman who had called earlier.

Alexandra noticed Warren walking toward them and nudged her friend.

"There he is, Shari."

Warren was wearing off-white linen Bermuda shorts and an off-white cotton tank top that exposed his well-defined arms and chest. On his feet were brown huara-che sandals. His hair was pulled back in a ponytail.

"Oh, Alex," Shari said, turning her back to Warren. "He's gorgeous."

"I know," Alexandra said. Then, with a big smile, "Hi, Warren."

"Hey, lady," Warren said, kissing her cheek as he greeted her. "How are you? I'm glad you could make it."

"I'm fine. Happy birthday," Alexandra said.

"Thank you."

Alexandra introduced Shari and Warren.

Shari was taller than Alexandra and built like a brick house. She was dark-skinned and wore her hair cut short and natural in a fade which complemented her very African-looking features. Her breasts were large and her waist small in comparison to her large bottom. She was wearing stretch denim shorts and a gold-colored body suit that defined her every curve outstandingly. He thought she was a very beautiful black sister, but as far as he was concerned she was still not as beautiful as Alexandra.

"Nice to meet you, Warren. Happy birthday," Shari said.

"Thank you," he said, with a charming smile.

"Is today your actual birthday?" Alexandra inquired.

Warren confirmed that was the case.

"So, how's your day going so far?" she asked.

"Great, and since you ladies are here now, I'm sure it'll only get better. I hope you brought your bathing suits."

"We did," Shari said with a devilish smile, admiring his handsome features.

"Good. You can change over there in the bathhouse," he told them, pointing in that direction.

"Oh, I have mine on," Shari said.

"Me, too," Alexandra added.

Warren leaned back and looked Alexandra up and down before he said, "Do you really? Well, like I said, I'm sure the day will only get better."

Suddenly, another woman appeared beside Warren.

"Warren, your brother's on the phone," Susan announced, giving Alexandra and Shari the once-over.

Warren did not miss the look.

"Yeah, all right," he grumbled without looking at Susan. "You ladies help yourselves to whatever you like. Make yourselves at home."

"Aren't you going to introduce me to your friends?" Susan interrupted.

With that, she grabbed him possessively around his waist.

"Of course," he said, as he put his arm around her shoulder. "This is Shari and Alexandra. Ladies, this is Susan."

"You're the one whose brother went to school with my honey, right?" Susan said to Alexandra before she or Shari could respond to the introduction.

"Yes."

"Well, like I was saying, make yourselves at home. There's plenty of food and drink and the water's great," Warren said, gesturing toward the pool.

"Okay, thank you," they said in unison.

"Let's go," he said to Susan as he led her away from them.

"That's the woman who answered the phone when I called this morning," Alexandra told Shari after Susan and Warren had walked away.

"I figured that. You know she's not going to let him out of her sight with you here," Shari said.

"I get the feeling she doesn't dictate his movements as much as she'd like to," Alexandra said, matter-of-factly.

"I get that feeling, too."

"Come on, let's get something to eat. Or would you rather get in the pool first?" Alexandra asked.

"Let's eat," Shari said. "I see a really fine brother over there near the grill."

* * *

Later in the afternoon, after swimming a number of laps, Alexandra toweled off, went to the bar and got herself a drink, then sat in one of the lounge chairs to relax. She caught sight of Shari sitting across the yard speaking to one of Warren's friends. Warren, himself, seemed to be having a great time.

She noticed Susan was sitting on the opposite side of the pool and seemed to be paying an awful lot of attention to her. Though Alexandra was very attracted to Warren, he, in turn, seemed to be having too much fun to pay much attention to her. But she really did not expect anything from him, particularly now that she knew he was involved with someone.

Suddenly, someone approached her from her blind side.

"Excuse me, miss, but I'm going to have to arrest you for looking so good."

Alexandra looked up at the stranger with the corny come-on and smiled. He was cute, she noticed, but looked old enough to be her father and had a stomach that protruded even though he was thin.

She decided to play along with him anyway, just for fun.

"But, Officer, I have a license," she said coyly.

He laughed, not expecting her quick return.

"Touché," he said good-naturedly. "Would you mind if I sat down?"

"Hey, it's not my chair."

He slid the lounge chair next to hers a little closer and got comfortable.

"My name is Tommy," he said, extending his hand.

"Hi, Tommy. I'm Alexandra," she said as she shook his hand.

"Pleased to meet you."

"Likewise."

"I noticed you swimming laps in there like a professional. Are you?"

"Oh, no," she said with a vigorous shake of her head. "Far from it. That was just my exercise for the day."

"Have you known Warren long?" Tommy asked.

"Actually, I just met him last week. He and my older brother went to college together. It was the first time they had seen each other in years."

"Oh, really? Is your brother here?"

"No. He couldn't make it today."

"Well, I'm glad you could," Tommy said.

She did not see Warren as he came toward them and was surprised when she heard his voice behind her.

"Alexandra, is this man bothering you? Tommy, are you bothering my guest?"

"Now, Warren would I do something like that?"

"Yes."

The three of them laughed together.

Warren sat down in a chair on the other side of Alexandra.

"How are you, Alexandra?" Warren asked with a warm smile.

"Fine."

"Yeah, that I can see. Are you having a good time?"

"Oh, yes. Very nice. You have a lovely home."

"Thank you. Would you like a tour?" he asked.

"Sure. A little later, okay?"

"Say the word."

"I was just asking her if she was a professional swimmer," Tommy said to Warren. "Did you see her doin' those laps?"

"Yes, I did. Were you in the Olympics?" Warren asked jokingly.

Alexandra giggled.

"No. I did swim on a team when I was in college, though. But it was no big deal."

"Well, I'm sure you have trophies to show for it," Warren said.

"Yes, a couple," she answered honestly.

"I knew it," Tommy said.

"Well, they're not for any real competitions, they're more for achievement. When I started college, I couldn't swim at all. Once I learned, though, there was no stopping me. I wish I had a pool that I could swim in every day, though," she added.

"Yeah, it's nice," Warren conceded.

"I haven't seen you in there, Warren," Alexandra challenged.

"I was in earlier today, before anyone got here. Believe me, if the weather permits, I go in every day. That's why I had it built."

"Well, I envy you," she told him.

"Hey, anytime you want to come out and use the pool, let me know. You're more than welcome," he told her sincerely.

Tommy could see that although he had initiated the conversation with Alexandra, he was now the crowd in "three's a crowd."

He excused himself and walked away.

"Have you eaten?" Warren asked her.

"Oh, yeah, but I'm not finished. I just had a little snack."

"Well, there's plenty left. Did you get any lobster?"

"Yes, that was my snack," she said with a chuckle.

"It's too bad that David couldn't come out today. It was good seeing him."

"I know. I hadn't seen him myself for two years. He was in Europe the last couple of years. I'm glad he'll be here in the States now," said Alexandra of her brother.

"He never told me he had such a gorgeous sister."

She smiled. "Well, when you guys were in college, you wouldn't have thought so. I was just fourteen."

"I'm sure I would have noticed the potential for greatness, though," he said, grinning.

She just laughed.

"You work out, don't you?" At her nod, he continued. "I can tell. What do you do?"

"I run. I also belong to a health club and I work the machines," she told him.

"I've got to show you my gym."

"Warren!"

They both turned.

Susan was standing on the patio.

"Your brother's here!" she yelled in an impatient tone.

He stared at her for a moment, then turned to Alexandra, giving her a look of disbelief.

"Why is she yelling?" he asked, speaking more to himself than to her.

Alexandra did not answer.

He sighed, made a face, then rose from the chair. "Excuse me, Alexandra."

She noticed that the look on his face was one of enormous displeasure.

He confronted Susan when he reached the patio. "Why are you yelling?"

"I was trying to get your attention. You're acting like you have no other guests besides that female in the skimpy bikini," Susan said nastily.

"What are you talking about? I'm not giving her any more attention that I am anyone else here. I really don't feel like having to defend myself to you every time you see me talking with a female guest. This is a party, Susan, and I won't let you ruin it with your jealousy," Warren said, then walked past her to greet his brother.

* * *

Alexandra got up from her lounge chair threw on a T-shirt, then walked over to the buffet table and fixed herself a plate. She sat at one of the tables on the patio. As she was eating, Shari and the man she had been talking to came over and joined her at the table.

"Hey, hon," Shari said.

"Hi."

"Vernon, this is my girlfriend, Alexandra. Al, this is Vernon," Shari said.

"Hi, Vernon. Nice to meet you."

"Likewise. Do you mind if we join you?" he asked.

"No, of course not. Sit down," Alexandra offered.

Vernon sported a bald head though and a small mustache and beard. His eyes were dark, his skin was a smooth coffee-and-cream color and his smile was beautiful and bright as the morning sun. Alexandra smiled as he pulled out a chair for Shari.

"Are you having fun?" Vernon asked Alexandra as he took the seat opposite her.

"Yes, I am. And the food is good, too," she said with a smile.

"Warren and Vernon grew up together," Shari interjected.

"Really? My brother went to school with Warren. That's how I met him."

Alexandra sat with Shari and Vernon for a while after she had finished her meal. She got the feeling Shari really liked this guy. She could understand why. He was very good-looking and seemed like a genuinely nice person.

After a while, Alexandra excused herself.

Warren was standing just off the patio speaking to a couple who had just arrived.

She stepped over to them and politely interrupted,

saying "Hello," to the man and woman standing with Warren. Then to him, "Excuse me, Warren. Can you tell me where the bathroom is?"

"Oh, I'll show you. I have to go inside anyway," he said to her. "Bill and Marcia, help yourselves to whatever you like. There's plenty of everything."

He turned away from them and led Alexandra into the house.

"Ooh, what a nice kitchen," she said as they walked through the room.

"Thanks. Here it is."

"Thank you," she said, smiling at him.

When she came out of the bathroom, Warren was in the kitchen talking on the telephone.

As she moved to the door, he reached for her hand to halt her.

"Hold up a second," he whispered to her.

She waited until he ended the conversation.

As he hung up the phone, he asked, "Would you like that tour now?"

"Oh, sure."

Warren walked her out of the kitchen and showed her his living room, den, and dining room. "Upstairs is just a couple of bedrooms and my office, which is a mess, so I won't subject you to that," he said as they returned to the kitchen. "Come on, I'll show you my exercise room downstairs."

"That I want to see."

When they got downstairs, she was surprised to find such a large room. He had told her he had a lot of equipment, but it seemed as though he had just about every piece of Universal equipment ever made, aside from the standard free weights, weight benches, sit-up platforms, and the like.

"Wow! Man, you've got everything down here."

"Yeah, just about."

"This is great. I could go crazy down here," Alexandra told him.

They stayed downstairs for almost fifteen minutes talking about their respective exercise routines.

Warren was delighted to be able to talk to her about his workout. He had never known a woman so dedicated to physical fitness as Alexandra. He found, too, that the more he talked to her, the more he wanted to know about her.

"You have a serious exercise room here," she told him.

"Anytime you want to use it, give me a call," he said sincerely.

Alexandra noticed that he was looking at her very intensely. Quite suddenly and inexplicably, she began feeling guilty about being down there alone with him.

"We should probably go back upstairs. They're probably looking for you," she said, speaking of his girlfriend.

"Yeah, I guess."

Warren really did not want to lose this moment with her. He was enjoying her company tremendously.

She turned toward the staircase and had taken two steps up when he reached for her hand. She turned back to him and noticed immediately the questioning look in his eyes. *He wants to kiss me*, she realized. In truth, her curiosity was piqued as well, but there were too many obstacles in their way. They stared into each other's eyes for a moment that seemed to go on forever. Finally Warren broke their silence.

"I'm really glad you were able to make it today," he said softly.

"So am I."

The current of sexual energy that passed between them was more intense than anything either of them had encountered before.

Were it not for the fact that Susan had already accused him of paying too much attention to Alexandra, Warren probably would not have hesitated to take her in his arms and kiss her the way he wanted to. Thankfully, his conscience got the best of him. He had never been unfaithful to Susan before. He would not start now. As strong as the yearning he felt for Alexandra was at that very moment, to give in to it would be tantamount to admitting that Susan's constant accusations were justified.

"We'd better go," she sighed.

Reluctantly, he agreed.

When she reached the top of the stairs and opened the door to step out of the staircase, Susan was standing just on the other side of the door.

When Warren appeared behind Alexandra, Susan immediately jumped on him.

"What the hell is going on here, Warren?" she yelled.

Alexandra was shocked to hear her speak to him in this manner and she turned back and looked at the furious woman.

Warren was surprised, too.

"Excuse me, Susan? What did you say?" he asked, knowing she could not possibly be speaking to him in that tone of voice.

"I said, what the hell is going on? What the hell are you doing in the basement with her?"

Guilt suddenly overwhelmed Alexandra, though their time together had been completely innocent. She quickly turned and walked out of the house. Warren, on the other hand, was simply embarrassed by her outburst.

"I want to know what you think you're doing?"

"Well, if you want any information from me about anything, you don't speak to me like that. I don't yell at you, Susan. I expect the same respect from you."

"Respect? You've got a lot of nerve talking about respect. Ever since she called you this morning to tell you she was coming, you've been walking around with your head in the clouds," Susan yelled.

Thoroughly disgusted by her dramatics, Warren said, "Get out of my face."

He started to walk past her, but she grabbed his arm and halted his movement.

"Don't you walk away from me, Warren!"

He looked at her as though she had lost her mind.

"Look, woman, I don't have time for this."

"What the hell were you doing with her in the basement?!"

"What do you think I was doing?" he yelled, no longer able to control his anger. "What did you see me doing? I was showing her around, all right? Is that all right with you? I didn't realize I had to ask your permission to talk to anyone in *my* house! I didn't realize that I had to ask your permission to show anyone around *my* house! What is your problem, Susan? You've got nothing better to do than give me a hard time about stuff that you're making up in your head. I don't have time for this! Since you're having such a lousy time because your imagination is working overtime, why don't you take your behind home?"

"If I leave now, Warren, you won't ever see me here again," she threatened.

The anger in his chest burned away any sensitivity for her feelings.

"Is that a promise?"

She was seething. *He thinks I'm joking,* she told herself. Knowing that he would give in as he always did, she threatened him again.

"I'm serious, Warren. If I leave, I'm not coming back."

He had already started past her and was at the door

leading onto the patio when he turned back to face her.

"Then why don't you leave," he said with indifference, then turned and walked outside.

Susan stood where she was, not believing he would let her go so easily. *Who the hell does he think he is? Well,* she thought, *I'll show him.*

She stormed up the back stairs and hurried to his bedroom to get her things. She went into his closet and pulled out the overnight bag she used whenever she stayed over with him. She put it on the bed and went to the bureau where she had a drawer of her own that was filled with lingerie. She grabbed a handful and carelessly tossed it into the bag. When she had emptied the drawer, she walked into the bathroom and began removing all the toiletries she had there. All the while she cursed him, knowing he would be coming up there at any minute to stop her. But she had already decided that he could beg and plead all he liked. She was through with him.

When Warren stepped outside, he immediately looked for Alexandra. She was at the other end of the yard, sitting at the edge of the pool with her face turned away from him. He started to walk over to her to apologize, but Shari got to her first.

"Yo, Warren, you wanna get in on a game of bid whist?" one of his friends suddenly called to him.

The voice startled him for a second, but he recovered quickly and turned to the speaker, "Naw, that's all right, man."

He absent-mindedly strolled over to an empty chair near the bathhouse and sat down. Susan had ruined everything. It was his birthday. He was supposed to be having a good time. He was not supposed to be arguing over this stupid nonsense with her. He was tired of her jealous rages. She was supposed to be his woman, but she gave him more grief than anyone else. Though he had to admit, this one time she had been on the mark about his attraction to Alexandra, she still had no foundation on which to base her accusations. Yes, he was extremely attracted to Alexandra, but he had not acted on his desire, specifically because of Susan. He reasoned, too, that if he had not been subjected to her unfounded fits of jealousy for the past two years, there would probably be no chance of Alexandra—or any other woman—turning his head.

He had never disrespected Susan; had never treated her other than as a jewel. He knew he did not deserve to be constantly attacked by her, no matter what she thought. And the way she was always creating a scene turned his stomach.

The more he thought about how she had acted, the angrier he became. He rose suddenly from his chair. He wanted her out of his house and out of his life.

Susan had her bag packed in fifteen minutes, but instead of leaving like she told him she would, she sat on the bed and waited for Warren to come to her.

In truth, she did not want to leave Warren. He was everything she wanted her significant other to be: successful, stable, handsome, classy, stylish, and charming. She knew he would do anything she asked. He always did. She knew she made him angry by accusing him of sleeping around, but lately he did not even deny it anymore. Though she had never caught him cheating on her, she was sure he had taken advantage of the many opportunities thrown in his face.

On many occasions at his night club, Michaels Too, she had witnessed women literally throwing themselves at him. Granted, she could clearly understand their actions. She had been instantly attracted to him herself. She got angry, though, because he never seemed to discourage their advances. She had watched him smile and talk with the women, and it did not seem to matter if she was there or not.

He always told her she was being overly insecure and that he was faithful to her. He used to say if he wanted to sleep with someone else, she would be the first one to know. Well, she did not care how much he denied it, there was no way he could tell her there was nothing going on with him and that Alexandra.

"I thought you were leaving," Susan heard Warren say from the doorway of the bedroom.

She smiled to herself. *I knew he would come,* she thought. When she turned to face him, she was surprised, however, to see the coldness in his eyes.

He took a couple of steps into the room but not in her direction. He seemed to be purposely trying to keep his distance.

"I can't take this anymore, Susan. I don't think I should have to explain why I've invited anyone to my house on my birthday to help me celebrate. Do you really think that I would invite someone here that I was involved with while you were here? I've never disrespected you in that way. I would never do that to you. Why do I have to constantly justify my friends and acquaintances to you? We've been together all this time, and no matter what I tell you, you still believe what you want. You still have no faith in the love I've given you. I've had enough. I can't take any more of this," he said, calmly but firmly.

They stared at each other across the room. The coldness in his eyes was gone, replaced by sadness, but he had made up his mind. Tears welled in her eyes as the realization that she had pushed him too far dawned on her. She realized then just how much she loved him.

"I want you to leave."

There were so many things she wanted to say to him at that moment, but the words would not come. She stared at him for the next few seconds, praying instead that he would take back his words. *He could not really be putting me out, could he?* After all they had been through. As he stood there, she noticed that his gaze did not waver. She realized then that he was serious and that they were through.

As difficult as it was to concede, she held her head high as she picked up her overnight bag and pocketbook and, as proudly as possible, walked past him and out of the room. She refused to cry in front of him. She walked straight to the staircase and descended deliberately but without looking back.

Warren followed her out of the room but stood at the top of the stairs and watched as she opened the front door and walked out.

He breathed a sigh of relief when the door closed behind her. At one time he had cared for her very much, but her constant accusations and performances had become a burden he could no longer endure.

For a brief moment he felt a twinge of guilt because, in all honesty, he could not deny what he felt for Alexandra, and her being there made it less difficult for him to end it with Susan.

Finally, Warren descended the stairs and walked to the front door and locked it. She was out of his life. Despite his feeling of relief, there was also a very real emptiness in his heart.

"Hey, Al, where you been? I was looking for you to see if you wanted to play a hand of bid whist," Shari said as she walked over to where Alexandra sat brooding.

"I was inside," Alexandra said, barely above a whisper.

"What did you say?"

Shari sat down next to her.

"I was inside." Alexandra pointed toward the house. "Warren was showing me around."

"Oh. I think his girlfriend was looking for him."

"Well, she found him."

Shari noticed that Alexandra appeared very solemn. "What's the matter?" she asked her friend.

Alexandra sighed before she answered, telling Shari all that had transpired.

"Well, I might wonder what he was doing in the basement with another woman if he was my man," Shari pointed out when Alexandra concluded the story.

"I might, too, but I wouldn't just jump on him like that without first trying to find out what was happening," Alexandra said. She noticed Warren coming out of the house then. "There he is."

Shari turned. "He looks angry."

"You should have heard the way she was talking to him."

"I wonder where she is," Shari said.

"I feel really bad for him. I feel kind of guilty, too," Alexandra confessed.

"Why should you feel guilty?"

Alexandra did not answer right away. She looked down at her hands in her lap.

Shari studied Alexandra closely, then smiled wickedly.

"What were y'all doing down there besides looking at his equipment? Or were you really looking at his equipment?"

Alexandra feigned shock as she exclaimed, "Shari!"

"Well, what were y'all doing down there?" she insisted.

"Nothing," she said.

"Then why do you feel guilty?"

"Because he wanted to kiss me and I wanted him to."

"But you didn't, right?" Shari asked.

"No."

"Then you didn't do anything wrong. There's no harm in having lustful thoughts if you don't act on them. Everybody has them once in awhile."

"That's what I keep telling myself, but I still feel guilty."

"He's going back in the house," Shari observed.

"Hey, Shari!" a voice called suddenly.

Both girls turned. Vernon was walking toward them.

"Wanna be my partner in a game of whist?" he asked.

"Maybe later, Vernon," Shari said as she looked at her friend sympathetically.

"Go on and play," Alexandra said with a wave of her hand.

"You sure?"

"Yeah, I'm okay."

Shari did not rise immediately. She continued to look at Alexandra questioningly.

"Go on. Vernon needs a partner," Alexandra smiled.

Shari smiled and gently touched Alexandra's cheek before she rose from her seat. "Okay, Vernon. Who're we playing?"

"Eddie and Tom. They're on a roll. No one's been able to beat them."

"Well, their winning streak's about to end. Come on," Shari said confidently as she took Vernon's arm. "See ya later, Al."

Alexandra sat where she was for the next fifteen minutes. She almost wished she had not come today. She knew that what was happening with Warren and his girl-

friend was not her fault—after all, she could sense
Susan's animosity toward her when they first arrived—
but in her heart she still felt responsible. She could not
deny how attracted she was to him. She had wanted
nothing more than to feel his lips pressed against hers
when they were in the basement together. He stirred
feelings in her that she had not felt in a long time. Even
with Gerard.

"Hi."

She looked up in surprise and saw Warren standing
over her.

"Hi."

"I'm sorry about what happened inside."

"I am, too."

"Do you mind if I sit?" he asked.

"No."

She was stretched out in the lounge chair, but sat up
and and wrapped her arms around her knees as he sat
on the end of her chair.

They sat in silence for the next couple of minutes.

"Where is she?" Alexandra finally asked.

"She left," he answered. "I asked her to leave."

"Oh God, Warren, I'm really sorry. I didn't mean
to . . ."

He reached over and touched her knee gently, reas-
suringly.

"It's not your fault, Alexandra. I don't want you to
feel as if any of this was because of you. It wasn't. This
was a long time coming," he explained.

"But . . ."

"Alexandra, listen. Susan and I had been going out
for two years. She's a very jealous woman, always has
been. I've put up with it for two years. And you know,
today of all days I didn't want to hear that. I mean, as
soon as I hung up the phone with you this morning,
she started."

"It's a shame that it had to happen on your birthday, though. Maybe in a couple of days you guys can get together and talk, maybe work things out," Alexandra suggested.

"No. It's over. It's too much work. Besides, what else could I do to convince her that I haven't been doing for two years?" he said with resignation.

"I'm really sorry, Warren."

"Yeah, me, too."

They sat again in silence for a few minutes. Alexandra broke it when she asked, "Do you usually wear your hair in a ponytail?"

He looked over at her, surprised by her question.

"Usually."

"Oh, 'cause I know when we met, you had it out," she said.

He cracked a smile and asked, "Which way do you prefer?"

"I think it looks nice loose," she said returning his smile.

He reached up and pulled his hair out of the rubber band.

"Is that better?"

She blushed and said, "Yes."

"As long as you're happy . . ."

They stared at each other for a moment before she said, "It's nice to see you smiling again."

"Well, you seem to have that effect on me."

She blushed again, but made no response.

"You have cute dimples," he said. "And you blush a lot. I know you're not as shy as you pretend," Warren said, looking at her out of the corner of his eye.

"I never said I was shy."

"Where's your boyfriend?" he asked suddenly.

"I don't know," she shrugged.

"Does he know where you are?"

"I told him I was going to a cookout on Long Island, and that's where I am," Alexandra said lightly.

"He couldn't make it, huh?"

"I didn't invite him."

"Didn't he wonder why?"

"I told him I didn't want him to come."

"You did?" Warren asked, eyes wide with surprise.

"No, I didn't," she said with a chuckle. "I told him that he wouldn't have a good time, so he might as well stay home."

"You didn't tell him that," Warren said, not believing her.

"Yes, I did tell him that, because he wouldn't have had a good time. This isn't the type of function he enjoys."

"Excuse me?"

She sighed.

"It's a long story. I'd rather not go into it."

"Okay."

They talked for the next few minutes about a variety of subjects and learned that they had many common points of view.

After a while Warren asked, "What are you doing tomorrow?"

"Working."

"After you get off of work."

"I'm not sure. I don't even know what time I'll be getting off tomorrow."

"Why not?"

"Well, I work for a law firm. I run the accounting department and we're having an audit that's to start tomorrow. I have to go in early and I'm really not sure what time I'll be getting off," Alexandra explained.

"I was going to ask you to have dinner with me."

"Well, I'd like to but . . ."

"Well, call me. I'll be downtown all evening tomorrow."

"Okay."

"As a matter of fact, why don't you give me your number? I mean, if you don't mind me calling you."

"No, I don't mind. I'll give you my number before I leave."

"Don't forget."

"I won't forget," she said somewhat seductively.

He looked into her eyes at that moment and the urge to taste her was stronger than before.

"I don't want you to think I'm some sort of insensitive creep, but I can't think of anything I'd like to do more than kiss you right now."

"I don't think you should."

"I know. You're right and I'll be cool but I just wanted you to know. I think you are a beautiful woman, Alexandra, and I'd really like to get to know you."

She did not answer him right away, so he continued.

"I understand if you don't feel the same, I mean, you've got a man and I'd be the last person to try and come between you, but I can't deny how much I'm attracted to you."

"I'm attracted to you, too, Warren, and I guess that's why I feel somewhat responsible for your fight with your girlfriend."

"You shouldn't feel responsible. I've had to deal with scenes like that for too long. I don't know many men that would have put up with it for as long as I did, but at one time I really loved her. It hurts that she never had any faith in me. What happened today was inevitable I think, regardless of who she zeroed in on."

"She probably cares for you very much."

"But not enough to believe in me. How long can anyone stay in a relationship like that?"

She considered his response and had to agree with

what he was saying. She did not believe she could have
tolerated being with a man who did not trust her.

"I'd like for us to be friends, Warren, but I'm still
involved with Gerard."

"I understand." He reached over and took her hand.
"I'll never disrespect you or him."

They were so caught up in this moment of emotional
intimacy that neither of them noticed his brother's approach.

"Hrrmph. Excuse me, folks."

Warren was slow in looking away from Alexandra. She
noticed his irritation when he turned away from her.

"What do you want?"

"Hey, man, the last thing I want to do is interrupt
you, but your guests want to know when you're planning
on cutting your cake. They want to sing 'Happy Birthday' to you."

Alexandra looked up at the man standing over them.
She was amazed. He looked as if he could be Warren's
twin.

"This is my brother Will," he said to Alexandra. "Wil-
lie, this is Alexandra."

"Hi, Alexandra. Pleased to meet you," Will said, with
a charming smile.

"Hi," she said with a smile as she shook her head.
"You guys look so much alike. You're not twins, are
you?"

"No, we're not twins," Will said. "He's older. Can't
you tell?"

"But I'm better looking," Warren said with a smile.

Alexandra thought so, too, though Will was extremely
handsome in his own right. He was thinner than Warren, but like Warren was tall and dark-skinned, and,
except for his eyes, was a mirror image of his older
brother. Unlike Warren, Will's hair was cut short and
he wore a diamond stud earring in his left earlobe.

"You would be better-looking if you tried cutting this mop you've got on your head," Will said, pulling at Warren's hair. "Alexandra, don't you think he needs a haircut?"

She smiled at Warren then looked up at Will and said, "Actually, I like his hair the way it is."

Warren smiled smugly and said, "Case closed. You can't argue with that."

"Nope, I'm not going to touch that," Will said. "So, when are you going to cut your cake?"

"Hey, we can do it now," Warren said. "Come on, Ally."

He rose from the chair and took Alexandra's hand and helped her up.

Alexandra was still wearing just a T-shirt over her bikini and as she started walking back toward the patio, Will halted Warren in his tracks.

"Damn!" Will sighed. "Where'd she come from?"

Warren smiled as he looked after Alexandra, then turned to his brother. "You've heard of the proverbial pot of gold at the end of the rainbow, haven't you?"

By eight-thirty that evening, Alexandra had long since changed back into her shorts and midriff top. Shari and Vernon were sitting in a corner by themselves talking quietly when Alexandra went and told her that they would have to start making preparations to leave.

Warren was sitting on the patio with his brother and another friend when she approached him from behind.

She put her hand on his shoulder and said, "I'm going to have to get ready to go."

He quickly rose from his chair. "No, don't tell me that."

"I have to."

"But it's so early," he said, almost whining.

"I know, but I have to get up very early tomorrow morning. I have to be at work by eight-thirty and I still have to take Shari home, and she lives in Manhattan," Alexandra explained.

"I don't want you to go," he said, taking her hand.

"I don't want to go, either, but I have to."

He looked at her with sad eyes and pouted like a child.

"Don't look at me like that," she said to him.

"I might as well tell everyone to leave then," he teased, then after a few seconds, softly said, "I'm glad you came."

"So am I. I had a very nice time today," she said with a smile.

"You've made my birthday very special by being here," he told her.

"I'm glad."

He nodded his head toward the gate. "Come on. I'll walk you out."

Shari and Vernon were already in front of the house, standing by Alexandra's silver Prelude.

Warren and Alexandra stopped near the rear of the car. She looked up at him and smiled.

"You've really made the day special," he told her again.

"I'm glad you feel that way. I had a great time. You have a lovely home."

"And I hope you plan on coming back."

"If you invite me, I will."

"You have an open invitation. Whenever you're ready, I'll be here. My door is open to you anytime," he said, reaching for her hand.

"I'll remember that."

"Make sure you do. And besides, we have a dinner date tomorrow."

"But I'm not sure what time I'll be getting off."

"I don't care. I'll be at the restaurant all night. Call me."

"Okay, I'll call you even if I can't make it. I promise."

"All right. I'm gonna hold you to that."

"I won't break my promise," she said.

Warren tried to prolong her leaving. The urge to kiss her overwhelmed him, and he asked, "Can I have a kiss for my birthday?"

She pointed a finger and cut her eyes at him. "All right, but just a little one."

"Hey, I'll take what I can get."

She stepped closer to him and tiptoed to kiss his cheek. He turned his head, though, so the kiss landed on his lips. She did not pull back immediately because her feeling matched his. The kiss lingered for a moment before their lips parted.

Alexandra moved away from him and got into the car.

He squatted down beside the door, his arms resting on the window frame. He stared at her as Shari got into the car from the other side.

"Good night, Warren," Shari said with a smile as Alexandra started the car.

"Good night, Shari," Warren said. "It was a pleasure meeting you."

"Likewise, I'm sure. I hope to see you again and I hope you enjoy the rest of your birthday," she told him.

"Thank you. I'm sure you'll see me again," he said, looking at Alexandra. She smiled at him and in a whisper said, "Good night, Warren."

"Good night, Alexandra."

When he rose from his squatting position and stepped back, she looked out of the window at him and he blew her a kiss.

"Call me when you get home," he said.

"You probably won't even hear the phone ring," she said with a wave of her hand.

"Yes, I will. I'll be waiting for your call. Call me when you get home, so I'll know you made it safely."

"All right."

Five

On the ride back to the city, Shari and Alexandra discussed Vernon and Warren.

"So, Al, when are you gonna see him again?" Shari asked of Warren.

"I'm supposed to have dinner with him tomorrow at his restaurant but I have an audit. I could be at the office late."

"Yeah, so? I saw the way you guys were checking each other out. There was some serious electricity flying through his backyard this evening, so don't tell me you're not going to make it your business to see him tomorrow."

"I'm gonna try, but I don't know. If I do it'll be just a friendship kind of thing anyway. I told him about Gerard," Alexandra then said.

"Well, Vernon and I are gonna hang out Tuesday. He has to go to Connecticut tomorrow morning for a job," Shari said.

"He's cute. What does he do?" Alexandra asked.

"He's an electrical consultant in business for himself. And he's single, never been married, has no kids and lives alone. It doesn't get any better than that."

"Yeah, right. Warren has an eight-year-old daughter."

"So, Al, what happened with his girlfriend? When did

she leave?" Shari asked as she turned toward Alexandra in her seat.

"He told her to leave. They broke up."

"Wha-a-at?"

"Yeah. He said he couldn't deal with her jealousy anymore. They had been going out for over two years."

"Get outta here! You know, it's a shame that someone so attractive would be so insecure."

"Yeah, 'cause he said he never cheated on her."

"And you believe that?"

"Yes, I do. When we were downstairs, Shari, I could tell he wanted to kiss me. It was all over his face, but he didn't. There was nothing to stop him. In all honesty, I don't think I would have stopped him if he had tried. I mean, I was curious, too. If he had, though, I might have a hard time believing that he was faithful to her. But like I said, he was a perfect gentleman. I really believe he was telling the truth."

Shari chuckled and said, "He could probably tell you anything and you'd believe it."

Alexandra laughed, too.

"Probably, but I think he just got fed up."

"Well, I know how that can be," Shari said.

They drove a few minutes in silence.

"I like him, Shari," Alexandra finally said. "He's really sweet. We talked for a long time. If I weren't seeing Gerard, I wouldn't think twice."

"Well, you and Gerry haven't really been spending a lot of time together lately. What's up with that?"

"I don't know. It's . . . There's no excitement with him anymore. I actually dread seeing him sometimes."

"So why don't you just break it off with him?"

"I probably will real soon."

"Hey, don't do it because of Warren," Shari warned.

"Oh, it has nothing to do with Warren. I think the only reason I haven't already told him it's over is because I haven't seen him. I don't want to hurt his feelings, I mean, he is a nice guy and all, but there's just nothing there anymore."

It was almost eleven by the time Alexandra got home that evening. She called Warren as soon as she got in.

A male voice answered the call, and she asked to speak to Warren.

She heard a lot of noise in the background. Obviously, they were still going strong.

"Hello!"

"Hi, it's Alexandra. I see you didn't send everybody home after I left," she said in a playful manner.

"I tried, Alexandra, but they wouldn't leave."

"Yeah, right."

He laughed.

"You just got in?" he asked as he took a seat on one of the stools in his kitchen.

"Yeah. There was a real bad accident on the Long Island Expressway. We sat there for almost twenty minutes."

"Yeah?"

"Yeah, but once we got past it, it was smooth sailing." She sat on her bed and pulled off her sandals. "Now I'm about to go in here and take my clothes off and get in the shower, then get my butt in bed. I'm exhausted."

Warren instantly visualized Alexandra's naked body covered with soap suds and water. A chill went down his spine. He wanted to say, "I wish I was there with you. I could help you wash your back." Instead, he said, "That sounds appealing."

She yawned then. "Oh, I'm sorry," she said.

"That's all right. You go on and do what you've gotta do. I'm gonna try to get these folks out of here, too, 'cause I'm kind of tired myself."

"Are there still a lot of people?"

"No, not that many, but they're the ones that never want to leave."

She chuckled. "Oh, yeah, I know them."

"So listen, sexy, you get yourself some rest. I'll give you a call tomorrow, all right?"

"All right."

"And I'll see you tomorrow night."

She smiled at his confidence.

"All right."

"Sleep tight, Alexandra."

"Thanks. Happy birthday," she said softly.

"Thanks to you, it was."

When she hung up she decided that, hook or crook, there was no way she was going to get stuck at her office so late that she would not be able to meet him for dinner tomorrow.

Six

The next day was indeed a hectic one for Alexandra. Because she wanted to get to work by eight-thirty that morning, she had to get up a half hour earlier so that she could take her morning jog around Prospect Park.

From the time the auditors arrived at her office at nine, until six-thirty that evening, she had not had a moment's rest.

Warren had called her at eleven, but she had been so busy, she could not take his call. She did not get the opportunity to go out for lunch, so by the time she left work, she was very hungry.

She called Warren at his restaurant at six forty-five.

"Warren Michaels here."

"Good evening, Mr. Michaels. This is Miss Jenkins."

"Good evening, Miss Jenkins. How are you?"

"Whipped."

"I'm sorry to hear that. Are you still at work?"

"Yes. I'm leaving right now," she said as she checked her hair and makeup in her compact mirror.

"Good. Take a cab. You know where I am, right?"

"Yes. And, Warren?"

"Yeah?"

"I'm starving," she groaned.

"Well, you're coming to the right place."

When Alexandra arrived at Michaels, she told the

cabdriver someone would be coming out to pay him
and got out of the car.

Warren was standing just inside the door of the restaurant, speaking to his mâitre d'.

"Hi, gorgeous," he said and kissed her quickly on
her forehead, then immediately stepped outside to pay
the driver.

When he came back inside, he grabbed her, gave her
a big hug and a soft kiss on her lips.

"Hi," he said breathlessly.

"Hi." Alexandra felt herself blush under the heat of
his stare.

"It's good to see you," Warren told her in a soft tone
as he held her hands. His cool demeanor belied the
excitement coursing through his body.

"It's good to see you, too. How are you?"

"Much better now. You look beautiful."

Alexandra was wearing a sleeveless cream-colored
linen dress that buttoned down the front, though the
bottom three buttons were left open exposing her
shapely legs. She wore very sheer off-white pantyhose
and cream-colored three-inch pumps on her feet. Her
hair was pinned up on top of her head but spilled down
over her forehead in a soft cascade of curls. She wore
pearl cluster earrings and a triple-strand pearl choker.

"Thank you. You look quite handsome, yourself."

Warren was impeccably dressed in a blue-green wor-
sted silk double-breasted suit, white cotton shirt with
French cuffs in which were personalized gold cuff links,
and a navy-blue-and-red print silk tie. Navy-blue eelskin
loafers completed the outfit.

"Did they wear you out today?" he asked as he slowly
walked her into the dining area.

"Like you wouldn't believe."

"Well, you can relax now. I have a very special dinner
lined up for you, my dear, if you'll just follow me."

Warren led Alexandra to a secluded table near the back of the restaurant. The lighting was very dim and there were two lighted candlesticks and a bud vase with two long-stemmed red roses resting in the center of the table. A bottle of chilled champagne cooled in a bucket. Two stemmed champagne flutes set off the place settings for two.

He pulled her chair out and seated her, then filled their glasses with champagne before taking his seat.

"Here's to you, Alexandra," he said, raising his glass in a toast.

She smiled and said, "To friends."

They sipped from their glasses, all the while gazing into each other's eyes.

"I hope you don't mind, but I took the liberty of ordering dinner for you."

She shook her head then took another sip from her glass and sighed, "This is very nice."

"You're a special lady. I wanted to make this evening special for you."

She smiled at him and thought to herself that he was a dream come true.

During the time she and Gerard had been dating, he had never done anything as romantic as this. She was quite enraptured by his thoughtfulness.

Warren was delighted that she was there with him, and though she was being somewhat reserved, he was positive she was as attracted to him as he was to her. He felt so good being with her that he could have screamed. He sat there, staring into her eyes, and she did not flinch, or blush, or turn her eyes away. He liked what he saw there.

"You are so beautiful," he said unpretentiously.

"Thank you."

One of his waiters appeared then, with their first

course. It was a hardy seafood chowder, filled with bits of lobster, crabmeat, calamari, and red snapper.

"Did you make this wonderful concoction?" she asked him, being a bit facetious.

"As a matter of fact, I did," he admitted.

She was genuinely surprised. "Did you really?"

"Yes."

"It's delicious," she said, smiling sincerely.

"Everything you're going to eat tonight, I prepared myself."

"I'm very flattered."

The rest of the meal was just as scrumptious. They had blackened snapper, seasoned yellow rice, and steamed vegetables. Dessert was chocolate mousse.

After dinner, over coffee, Alexandra said, "Dinner was excellent, Warren. Thank you very much."

"You're more than welcome."

"What time are you leaving here tonight?"

"When you leave. I'm going to drive you home, if you don't mind," he said. "Why?"

"Well . . . I was going to ask you if you could drive me home."

His heart leapt.

When they left the restaurant that evening, Alexandra was even more taken with Warren than when she arrived earlier.

His Infiniti Q45 was parked in the small lot behind his restaurant, and they drove to her apartment in relative silence.

She replayed their dinner conversation in her mind. He seemed to be a genuinely caring man. She noticed how attentive he was as she told him about her childhood and what it was like to be the younger sister of an overprotective big brother. He admitted that he was guilty of being a bit overprotective of his younger sister, too. He also talked about his daughter Crystal and his failed marriage. His eyes shone with pride as he spoke of his little girl. He told her that he had been married for eight years, most of which time had been fun but that his last year of marriage was filled with nothing but strife. His divorce had been less than amicable, but, after a year, he and his ex-wife Marge had been able to put aside their differences for the sake of their daughter. He told her that they had been high-school sweethearts and then went to college together. He said his marriage ended because he and Marge had simply outgrown each other, as they were both only nineteen when they got married. When they stopped blaming each other for their breakup and began to talk, they became good friends once again, as they had been in their teens.

When he pulled up in front of her apartment building, Alexandra said, "Thank you again for a lovely evening, Warren. I had a great time."

"I'm glad you did. I hope we can do this again."

"I think so," she smiled.

"Would you like me to walk you in?"

"Oh, no, I'll be fine."

"Well, then, I had a wonderful evening, Alexandra, and thank you for your company."

"It was my pleasure."

She leaned over and kissed him softly on the lips before she got out of his car.

Warren did not pull off until she was safely inside her building. As he drove back uptown to his restaurant, he smiled as he thought about his evening with Alexandra. He had the feeling that this was the beginning of something very special.

Seven

Over the next three weeks, Warren and Alexandra had dinner together six more times, each time at a different gourmet restaurant. He was always the perfect gentleman, and Alexandra found herself looking forward to each new time they were together. They had long conversations on the phone on the weekends, as he usually spent them with his daughter. Until now, she saw him only during the week. She was pleased to find that he was quite thoughtful and very attentive. She noticed that he paid attention to even the most insignificant things she said. For instance, one evening he surprised her after dinner with tickets to a Broadway play that she had indicated an interest in seeing during one of their many conversations. He sent flowers to her office after each of their dates with thank-you notes that also expressed his interest in her, but he was never too personal or forward. They enjoyed each other's company and were never at a loss for words. They still had not shared a real kiss, though on many occasions they both seemed to be fighting the urge to run with their feelings.

During this time, she also broke off her relationship with Gerard. Though she had no doubts about her lost feelings for him, it had been difficult to end it with him. They had known each other since they were children. He had been one of her brother's friends when they were growing up. She could tell, though he tried to pretend otherwise, that he was genuinely surprised and hurt by her actions. She offered to still be friends if he wanted, but told him she could no longer offer him more than that.

Four weeks had passed before Alexandra invited Warren up to her apartment for the first time.

"Would you like to come in for a drink, Warren?" she asked as he pulled up in front of her building.

"Thank you. I'd love to."

A very comfortable-looking blue-gray sofa sat opposite the front door with a matching loveseat that formed a right angle. Two solid oak steamer trunks doubled as cocktail tables and rested on a pale-gray rug in front of her seating area. A uniquely styled five-arm sofa lamp stood between the two sofas. A mix of abstract and African art decorated the walls, and a collection of black dolls ranging from rag dolls to African-garbed models sat atop an oak-finished wall unit that also held a stereo, television, and various other mementos.

She immediately kicked off her shoes and asked, "What would you like to drink? I have spring water, lemonade, and Corona beer."

"I'll take a Corona."

She went to the refrigerator and removed a bottle of her favorite beer for him. She opened it and walked back over to give it to him.

"Thank you," he said, gazing up into her eyes.

"You're welcome."

"You have a nice place here," he said.

"Thanks. Would you excuse me for a moment, Warren? I'm gonna go take this stuff off and put on something a little more comfortable, okay?"

"Sure, I'll be right here," he told her.

As Warren waited for Alexandra to return, he removed his jacket and loosened his tie. He sat back and relaxed, taking a long swig from his beer bottle. He was hot, though it had nothing to do with the temperature inside the apartment, and the beer was very cold.

As he looked around the room, he noticed a picture of her brother David in his dress blues on a shelf in her wall unit. He guessed the picture was taken when David first joined the military, because he looked exactly as he had when they were in school together. He smiled and thought of his college days. That had been a fun time in his life.

"Did I take too long?" Alexandra asked when she returned.

"No," he said with a soft smile.

She had changed into a pair of lavender silk lounging pajamas and her hair was out, falling gently over her shoulders. On her feet she wore lavender and white peau de soie mules. Though her body was completely covered by the garment, Warren thought she looked sexier than he had ever seen her.

She went to the refrigerator and took out a beer for herself. She opened it and poured the golden liquid into a tall glass, then came and sat down next to him, one leg curled under her.

"Dinner was excellent, as usual," she said after taking a sip of her drink.

"Thank you. I'm glad you enjoyed it," he said as he looked into her brown eyes.

They had had dinner at Michaels and, the same as their first date, Warren had prepared her entire meal.

"Where'd you learn to cook like that?" she asked with a smile.

"My mother. She taught all of us to cook. My mother can cook. She can really burn," he said proudly.

"She taught you well."

He shifted his body on the couch to face her.

"She used to tell me and Will she was going to make sure that we were never in a position that we could not feed ourselves. And she told us she was going to make sure that we knew how to reciprocate for our women," he said with a chuckle.

"Go 'head, Ma," Alexandra cheered.

"Yeah. You've gotta taste some of her cooking. I can't even touch it," he said modestly. "You should've seen me when I was a kid. I was a fat little thing. My mother used to bake some cakes, pies. . . . Whew, you name it, she made it, and I was her taster."

Alexandra laughed. "I can't imagine you fat."

"Yeah, I was. I've got to show you some of my baby pictures."

"You must've been cute."

"Naw, I wasn't. I was a fat, ugly little child," he said, laughing.

"I don't believe you."

"Yeah, I was. But don't tell anybody."

They stared into each other's eyes without saying a word. Their thoughts were identical, however. They were happy to be together.

"Do you mind if I take this out?" she asked as she touched the rubber band that held his hair.

"No."

Alexandra reached up and removed the band, then ran her fingers through his hair.

"Your hair is so soft," she murmured.

"You'd better stop that," he said in like tones.

"What?" she asked, innocently, not realizing how much she was turning him on.

"That," he said as she continued playing in his hair.

"Why?"

"Because you are steadily breaking down my resistance and I'm trying very hard to be on my best behavior," he said, looking her square in the eye.

"Oh." She quickly removed her hand. "Sorry."

He sighed and said, "That's all right. I just want you to know what you're getting yourself into."

She sat back for a moment, but looked over at him devilishly. Incredibly wicked thoughts ran through her head for a brief moment. She held them at bay.

"Warren, what made you decide to go into the restaurant business?" she suddenly asked.

"Well, actually I started with an ex-friend about eight years ago. We pooled our money and opened a dance club. It was only open for about two and a half years, though. My friend was tapping the till. He had a cocaine problem. It was a small place, but we were doing well for a while. We rented a space three nights a week, Thursday, Friday and Saturday, and we used to pack the place, but like I said, he was tapping the till, so eventually we folded. But while we were doing all right, I was putting money away because we were turning a nice profit on the place. I'm very good at saving money. I lucked out with Michaels spot. It was already a restaurant. I just bought the owner out, with the help of a backer. I closed the place for about a month, renovated it and changed the name, and since it's in such a great location, it's pretty much sold itself. I've since been able to buy my backer out, so it's mine now, outright."

"That's great," she exclaimed.

"Yeah. The rent's a little steep, but my take in two weeks covers it. My place in Queens is actually cheaper to run 'cause the rent's not nearly as high as in the city. And I wanted to do something for the home crowd, you know, that's why I opened Michaels Too. The menu's the same but the prices are a little cheaper, and I wanted to give the people a place to party."

"I'd like to go out there," she said, once again, though unconsciously, playing with his hair.

"I'll take you. What are you doing Friday?"

"Nothing planned."

"I'll take you out there Friday, okay?"

"Okay."

She was turning him on so much by now that he could no longer resist her. He reached over and gently placed a hand behind her head and pulled her face closer to his. He touched his lips to hers slowly, tentatively at first, wanting to savor the sweetness of her. Her scent filled his nostrils and became an aphrodisiac to him. He parted her lips with his tongue and was overjoyed when she opened up to him willingly.

Suddenly, Alexandra reached up and put her arms around his neck and returned his kiss with eager abandon.

He began caressing her neck, slowly moving his hands down her back as he pulled her closer. Her skin felt good underneath the silk garment that covered her.

Warren was causing a flame of desire to burn inside Alexandra, so much so, that before long she gave herself up to the passion that raged in her heart and lost herself in the tenderness of his kiss.

They were interrupted by a sudden knocking on her door.

Alexandra frowned as she pulled away from Warren. Her heart was racing from the intensity of the kiss they had just shared, and she felt a bit breathless. Warren noticed the swelling of her lips. The sight was intoxicating to him.

"Are you expecting anyone?" he asked her.

"No. It's probably just one of my neighbors, though," she said as she slowly rose from the couch.

"What makes you think so?"

"Because anyone else would have to ring the bell to get in from outside."

"Oh. Well, get rid of them," Warren said with a smile.

"Don't worry, I plan to," she said, smiling back at him.

When Alexandra opened the door, she was stunned to see Gerard standing on the other side. She had come home twice in the last week to find messages from him on her answering machine, but he had not asked her to call either time, so she hadn't.

"Hey, Al," he said.

She had not seen him since they broke up two weeks ago.

"How'd you get in?" she asked right away.

"Miss Young was coming in," he answered. "How you doin'?"

"I'm fine. What are you doing here?" she said, standing in the doorway.

"I wanted to see you. Is that all right?"

"Why didn't you call first?"

"I didn't realize I had to call you before I came to see you. I thought we could talk."

"I have company."

"I won't take up much of your time."

"I wish you had called first. I could have saved you a trip."

"Come on, Alex, I promise I won't be long."

Alexandra did not want to let him in, but when she saw he had no intention of leaving, she figured maybe if he saw Warren, he would be more apt to take her seriously.

"I'll give you two minutes," she said, as she stepped back and opened the door wider. Gerard walked into the apartment and was surprised to see the man sitting on Alexandra's sofa.

Alexandra introduced them.

Warren recognized the name immediately. This was her boyfriend, he thought. He sized Gerard up. Gerard was no more than five-feet-ten-inches tall, with a slight build. He was very fair-complected and wore wire-framed glasses. He had light-gray eyes, and was clean-shaven. He wore a white polo shirt and tan khaki pants.

"Let's go back here," Gerard said, and headed for the back of the apartment, not waiting for a response from her.

She looked over at Warren and sighed impatiently.

"Should I leave?" he asked her, hoping she would say no.

"Of course not."

"You all right?" he asked quietly.

She nodded her head and said, "I'll be right back."

Gerard stepped into her bedroom, and when Alexandra entered, he closed the door behind her.

"Who's that?" he asked immediately.

Alexandra ignored his question. "What do you want to talk to me about, Gerard?"

"You're dating someone else already?"

"Listen, if you came here to talk to me about something concerning you and me, then talk. I don't have to explain anything about my guest to you."

"I thought maybe we could give it another try. I really miss you, Alexandra."

"Gerry, it won't work. I don't want to date you anymore," she said nonchalantly.

His facial expression changed from one of humility to anger.

"Oh, and you just couldn't wait to start going out on dates and inviting guys home with you, huh, Alexandra?"

She did not answer, just turned away from him in annoyance.

"You're even sleeping around behind my back . . ."

"I'm not sleeping with anybody behind your back!" She quickly turned to face him. "What are you talking about? I'm not your girlfriend anymore, Gerard," she said angrily.

Gerard responded as though he had not heard her last words.

"Look at the way you're dressed," he said, holding his hand out to her. "You're going to tell me you're not planning to sleep with him?"

"It's time for you to leave."

She walked to the bedroom door and opened it.

"I thought what we had was special, Alex, but I guess I didn't mean anything to you at all, did I?"

"Good-bye, Gerard."

He stared at her for a long moment before he walked through the door. She followed him back to the front of the apartment.

When he reached the living room, Warren was standing, a book in hand, near her wall unit, which afforded him a view of her bedroom door.

They locked eyes for a moment, with Gerard looking away first.

He opened the front door to leave, but before he walked out, he turned back to Alexandra and said, "You won't be hearing from me anymore."

"Good."

She closed the door behind him.

"What a lot of nerve," she said.

Alexandra moved back to the couch and plopped down on it. Warren soon came and sat next to her. He put his arm around her and pulled her close. She rested her head on his shoulder.

"You all right?"

"Yeah," she said, without raising her head.

"What did he say?"

"He wanted us to get back together."

He kissed her lips softly.

"I can understand him not wanting to let you go."

She reached up to caress his cheek. She kissed him then, opening her mouth to taste the sweetness of his kiss.

Warren could not remember the last time he felt this way about a woman. He had loved Susan once, but this was different. He was not sure if what he was feeling was infatuation or just plain love, but he knew it was intense and he knew it felt good and he knew it felt right. He wanted to take care of her, to protect her, to do anything that would make her happy. There was a tenderness about Alexandra that he found only added to her physical beauty. His heart was full from the strength of his feelings for her.

He pulled her closer and began touching her, rubbing her softly, moving his hand up her thigh, caressing her soft flesh through the silk that covered it. She began to moan, and once again, her hands were massaging his scalp. She was driving him crazy.

Before he realized what he was doing, he had picked her up and placed her on his lap so that she was straddling him. She was firmly planted on his erection and began moving her hips, grinding against him. His hands traveled up her sides until they found her soft mounds. He fondled her breasts gently, carefully teasing her erect nipples with his thumbs. He moved against her, the urge to feel her sweetness strong in him.

"Alexandra," he moaned.

He began kissing her all over her face. He ran his tongue along the soft line of her neck, up to her ear, and gently nibbled her lobe.

"Oh, Warren," she sighed breathlessly.

He wanted to make love to her, but he did not want this to be a meaningless roll in the sack. He needed to be sure that her feelings for him were as genuine as his for her.

He pulled away from her suddenly, looking deep into

her eyes trying to read her thoughts past the lust that he could clearly see in them.

She tried to kiss him again, but he leaned away from her. She looked at him questioningly.

"What's wrong?" she asked, hurt that he had pulled away.

"Alexandra, what do you want from me?"

"What do you mean?"

"I mean, what are we doing? Is this going to be . . . ?"

"What?" she asked.

He looked deeply into her eyes. He did not want this to fail. He had to be sure where her head was at before he put his heart on the line again.

"I'm crazy about you, Alexandra. I want you. Bad. But I want you on a permanent basis. I want you to be my lady. I don't want to share you with anyone. I'm very stingy and very greedy. Are you ready to deal with that?"

"I want you, too, Warren."

"But are you ready to end one relationship and jump right into another?"

"My relationship with Gerard was over long before we broke up."

"But are you ready for another one?"

"With you, yes."

"Are you sure?"

"Yes! I'm not some mixed-up little girl, Warren, who doesn't know what she wants. You're here now because I want you here. I'm not looking for a fling if that's what you think. I'm not into flings," she said, with resentment.

"Baby, I'm not trying to insult you. I just want you to be sure about what you want. I have very strong feelings for you, and I want to know how you feel about me before I put my heart on the line."

She was becoming angry.

"What do you think, that I'm going to use you?" she asked as she started to rise from his lap.

He held her so that she could not get up.

"Alexandra, don't get angry. That's *not* what I'm trying to say. We haven't really known each other that long. The way I'm feeling, though, is like I've known you forever. We've both just ended relationships we'd been in for quite some time. I don't want to get hurt and I don't want to hurt you. I just want you to know what I want and what I expect from you if we're going to be together. That's all," he explained.

She studied his face and could see that he was very serious. Her anger subsided.

"I want you, Warren," she said sincerely. "I want you to be my man and I don't want to share you with anyone, either."

"You won't have to," he said, looking deeply into her eyes.

She had begun to feel as though he was doubting her intentions toward him, but now she could see that he was only trying to protect them both. She put her arms around his neck and pressed her forehead to his.

"I won't hurt you, Warren," she said softly.

He kissed her tenderly and said, "And I won't hurt you, Alexandra."

She hugged him tightly and he returned her warm embrace. Warren could feel her heart beating next to his and he knew his feelings for her would grow stronger with each new day.

"Will you stay with me tonight?" she asked.

"I'd love to," he answered.

"Let's go in the bedroom," she said as she began again to rise from his lap.

Again he stifled her movement, but this time he kissed her passionately, holding her tighter in his arms.

After a couple of minutes, she reluctantly pulled her

lips away from his and began to untie his necktie, though he had already loosened it. She pulled it off, then began unbuttoning his shirt. She ran her hands slowly across his muscular torso, savoring the feel of the downlike hair on his chest. Warren ran his hands up and down her back, underneath her tunic.

"I want you to make love to me," she whispered in his ear.

"I plan to. All night long," he muttered as he nibbled her neck.

She looked into his eyes and smiled before she hugged him again and kissed him.

As their tongues mingled, Warren ran his hands up and down her back and along her thighs, touching her gently, relishing the feel of the silk against her skin. He then raised her arms and removed her top, pulling it gently over her head. He bent his head and began nibbling her neck and shoulders. He extended her arms one at a time and kissed them softly, running his tongue up the length of her arm, inch by inch until he was in the delicate fold of her underarm. He caressed her body with his tongue along the line of her rib cage until his face was buried in her bosom. He sucked first one breast, then the other. Alexandra sighed in ecstasy. He continued kissing and sucking and licking her intermittently until she was kneeling on his lap and he was kissing her navel. Without stopping, or even coming up for air, he slid the bottoms of her pajamas down over her hips so that she was fully exposed to him. Alexandra held his head close to her body, loving the way he was making her feel. She ran her fingers through his soft hair, knowing that this was as much of an aphrodisiac for him as it was for her.

"Stand up, baby," he said in a husky voice.

He was so turned on by her that his voice had taken on an animalistic growl.

She stood over him, still on the couch, and he slid

the pants down her legs, all the while kissing the insides of her thighs. When she had stepped out of them, he reached up and cupped her behind in his large hands, sitting up so that he could position her just right. He eased her down slowly, pulling her legs over his shoulders, one at a time until he was smothering in her sweet cocoon.

Alexandra screamed when his tongue met her center of desire. She was slightly embarrassed by the sound of her own voice. No one had ever done this to her before and she had never before been made to feel so completely loved.

When she climaxed from his delicate ministrations, she cried out from the waves of sheer delight that coursed through her body.

Warren gently lowered her onto his lap, and when she looked into his eyes, they seemed to be clouded over as if his mind was elsewhere.

He kissed her softly, passionately, as he had never tasted anything so sweet in all his life.

When their lips parted, Alexandra squeezed him tightly, knowing that she had found the man of her dreams.

"No one's ever done that to me before," she whispered in his ear.

"Did you like it?"

She smiled shyly and said, "Yes, I did."

"Well, there's more where that came from. I'm going to love you all night, baby, like no one ever has."

He took her face in his hands and softly pressed his lips to hers.

"You are the sweetest woman I have ever known. I love the way you feel. I love the way you smell, and I love the way you taste. You'll never have to look anywhere else for love, Alexandra, because I'm going to give you all the love you need, whenever you need it, however you need it."

"Let's go to my room."

When they reached her bedroom, she sat down on the bed and slowly began to remove what was left of his clothes, drinking in the sight of his excellent masculine form. His shoulders were strong and broad. His chest bulged and his stomach was hard and rippled like a washboard. She loved the smooth dark-brown color of his skin and she told him so.

"You are the most beautiful black man I have ever seen."

He smiled softly and reached out to take her hand. He pulled her up from the bed and held her in his arms.

"I'm yours, if you want me," he said.

"I do want you," she sighed as she looked up at him.

"Am I dreaming, Alexandra?"

"Not unless we're having the same dream."

"I just want to hold you," he said. "I love the way you feel in my arms. I'm so afraid that if I let you go you'll disappear."

"I want to spend my life with you holding me like this."

He kissed her then, and it was like fireworks exploding in his brain. She made him feel so alive, so vibrant. He suddenly scooped her up in his arms and carried her to the bed. He laid her down gently and leaned over her, kissing her softly.

She reached up and held him around his neck and, as their tongues mingled, he moved onto the bed so that he was on top of her.

She moved her hips slowly beneath him, feeling his throbbing manhood against her thigh. Before long her hands were traveling down his back, and she sighed from the pleasure pulses that shot through her body just from feeling the strength of his back.

Her hands continued to caress him, finding their way to his firm backside until she grabbed hold and began pressing him closer to her until she was nearly controlling the dipping and swaying of his hips.

Warren loved the feel of her soft hands against his skin. He reached behind and took one of her hands and placed it between them. He wanted her to feel the effects of how much he yearned for her. He placed her hand on his manhood and she immediately began stroking him gently.

"Alexandra. Oh, yes. Yes," he moaned.

She was so hot for him that she could not wait any longer. She opened her legs to him and guided him to her warm, moist garden of love. She did not realize how large he was until he began to push inside.

"I won't hurt you," he gently assured her. "I won't hurt you, baby."

Though he wanted to plunge into her to immediately feel her warmth surround him, he took his time.

Alexandra continued to push up to him, and soon he had entered her billowy soft depths. She held him tightly as the feeling of him completely filling her caused her to explode almost immediately.

Warren could feel her walls contract on him with her orgasm, and he closed his eyes and sighed in delight. Soon she began moving on him, and what had started as a slow, mellow, and rhythmic dance of love soon turned into a frenzied battle of lust.

They made love in many different positions with Alexandra climaxing repeatedly before Warren gave in and released his warm seed into her welcoming canal.

They lay together, spent and exhausted until they both fell into a blissful sleep.

When Alexandra awoke the next morning, she smiled as she looked into the sleeping face of her beloved Warren. He looked like an angel with his hair tossed across his face. She gently moved the hair out of his face and kissed him softly on his cheek.

82   *Cheryl Faye*

She looked over at the clock on the nightstand. It read five fifty-two. She reached over and turned off the alarm so that its ringing at six A.M. would not wake him.

Alexandra got up from the bed and went to the bathroom. She washed her face and brushed her teeth, then came back to the bedroom and began making preparations to take her daily run around Prospect Park. She was dressed in a bright yellow print unitard with a short cut-off top over it. Her hair was tied back in a ponytail and she wore a sweatband around her head. She was sitting in her easy chair tying her sneakers when Warren woke up.

"Where're you going?"

She looked up and smiled at him.

"Good morning," she said.

She got up and walked around the bed to kiss him.

"How are you?" she asked him dreamily.

He did not answer but asked again, "Where're you going?"

"To run."

"So early?"

"Yeah. I always go this early."

"Are there many people out there when you run?" he asked, as he was worried about her running by herself.

"Oh, yeah, a lot. Don't worry, I'll be all right," she said, trying to reassure him.

He did not say anything but she could tell he was still worried.

"I'll run faster this morning so it won't take that long. I'll be back in about a half hour, okay?"

He frowned but reluctantly said, "Okay. Be careful."

She kissed him. "I will."

As soon as she left the apartment, Warren got up from the bed. There was no way he could sleep with her out there in that park at this time of the morning by herself. He decided he would bring a pair of running shoes and sweats to keep at her house so that he could run with her the next time.

He took a quick shower while he waited for her to return. He found an unopened toothbrush in her medicine cabinet and brushed his teeth.

When he was finished in the bathroom, he put on his underwear and his slacks and went to the kitchen and began preparing breakfast for her.

When Alexandra returned thirty minutes later, she was dripping with sweat.

"Hi. What are you doing?" she asked, still breathing heavily from her run.

"Making breakfast. How was your run?"

He thought she looked very alluring standing there in her wet unitard.

"It was great," she said enthusiastically. "You don't have to make breakfast."

"Yes, I do. Go take a shower. It'll be ready soon."

She walked over and gave him a kiss on his cheek.

"You're a dreamboat."

"No, I'm the love boat," he said with a smile.

Alexandra showered quickly and washed her hair. When she came out of the bathroom, she put on her robe and went back to the kitchen.

He had made bacon, eggs, and grits. Her plate was waiting for her when she came to the table.

"Do you want some toast?" he asked her.

"Just one slice, please."

As she said it, the toaster popped, and he placed a slice of wheat toast on her plate.

"Thank you. This is great. I don't usually eat breakfast at home. I'm usually running around like a crazy woman in the morning."

"Well, if I'm here, you're gonna eat breakfast," he said simply.

"Yes, Daddy."

He cleaned up the kitchen when they finished eating.

She was in her bedroom and partially dressed in a navy blue skirt and white bow blouse when Warren asked, "How are you going to fix your hair?"

"I'm just going to brush it back this morning."

"I'll brush it for you," he said as he picked up her brush from the dresser.

He stood behind her and gently brushed her thick hair until it lay tamely on her head.

She watched him in the mirror and smiled to herself. He looked so intense. When he was finished, he held her gently and kissed the back of her neck.

"Thank you," she said as she smiled at his reflection.

"My pleasure, sweet lady."

Warren drove Alexandra to work and told her he would pick her up when she got off that evening.

"Are you going home now?" she asked as they sat in his car in front of her office building.

"Yeah."

"What time are you coming back?"

"I'll probably just change and come right back."

"Are you going to stay with me tonight?"

"Do you want me to?"

"Yes."

"Then I'll stay."

She looked at her watch. It was eight-forty.

"I'd better go upstairs. I have a meeting at nine," she told him.

"All right, baby. I'll give you a call later."

He leaned over and kissed her, lovingly.

"Have a good day, beautiful lady."

"Thank you, Warren. You, too."

Alexandra was busy going over a client's account with her assistant, Christine, when a young man from the messenger department entered with a bouquet of red roses in his hand.

"For you, Miss Jenkins," he said.

"Thank you," she said as she took the flowers from him.

"My, you've been getting flowers delivered quite frequently, lately. Gerard must be trying to make up for some major boo-boo."

"Gerard and I broke up weeks ago, Chris."

"What?" Christine said in shock. "So who are all the flowers from?"

Alexandra smiled and said, "Warren."

"Who's Warren?"

Alexandra proceeded to tell Christine about Warren.

When she was finished, Christine smiled and said, "He sounds like a dream."

"I know, but he's real."

The attached card read: "The lingering sensation I get from the touch of your hand makes my pulse race. I yearn for the next time. Thank you for sharing your love. Forever, Warren."

"Oh, my God," she sighed upon reading the card, and her eyes began to water.

"What does it say?" Christine asked, anxiously.

Alexandra hesitated for a moment, then decided to show Christine the card.

"That's beautiful," Christine sighed after reading the card. "He sounds like a one-in-a-million man."

"He is."

Eight

Warren and Alexandra spent every evening together for the remainder of that week at her apartment. Their mutual adoration seemed to blossom with each new day.

On Friday, Warren picked Alexandra up at her office. They drove to her apartment, where he made dinner for her. While he prepared their meal, Alexandra packed a small overnight bag because she was going to stay with him at his house for the weekend.

After dinner, they showered together and got dressed for the evening. He was taking her to his club in Queens, Michaels Too.

Alexandra wore a sleeveless black spandex dress with a high collar. The dress was long, stopping just below her calf but was split off-center to mid-thigh. Underneath, she wore a thong panty and a pair of ultra-sheer black pantyhose. On her feet were four-inch black patent leather pumps.

Warren, having finished getting dressed, was in the living room putting a CD on the discplayer when she entered the room.

Regardless of the fact that he had seen her just about every day that week, he froze at the sight of her. She was more beautiful than ever. Her face was made up lightly and her hair was softly curled and gently rested on her shoulders.

"I'm ready whenever you are," she said as she adjusted the zipper on her purse.

He put the CD case on top of the stereo and took a step toward her.

"Come here," he said softly.

She moved over to him as he devoured her with his eyes.

"You look delicious," he said, enfolding her in his arms.

She giggled a "Thank you."

"You know, I'll probably be moving around a lot tonight. You're going to have your hands full trying to fight the men off."

"That's all right. I can handle it," she said confidently.

"I know you can," he said seductively.

"Shari told me that she and Vernon will probably come by the club tonight."

"Good. Then you won't be by yourself."

They arrived at Michaels Too at eleven-thirty. Warren was driving his brown Jaguar XJ6, what he called his "play car." Michaels Too had private parking for its guests and Warren had a space reserved for his exclusive use.

When they entered, they were greeted by his manager and best friend, Frank Edmonds.

The two men shook hands.

"What's happenin', Frankie? How're we doing?"

"So far, so good," Frank said, stealing a look at the beautiful woman on Warren's arm.

"Frankie, this is Alexandra. Ally, this is Frank. He manages Michaels Too for me."

"Hello," Frank said. "I'm pleased to meet you."

"Hi, how are you?" Alexandra said with a pleasant smile.

Frank was a big man. He was about the same height as Warren, but very broad, like a bodybuilder. He was light-skinned with a thick, dark mustache and looked as though he had Asian ancestry. He was bald and though he had a very unique look, she thought he was cute.

He was wearing a beige suit but had on a very close-fitting T-shirt underneath which exposed his massive frame.

"Frankie, if Alexandra comes in here and I'm not here, see that she gets whatever she wants," Warren said in all seriousness.

"You got it," Frank said.

"Are you hungry, baby?" Warren asked Alexandra.

"No."

"All right, let's go downstairs."

As Warren led her to the lower level of his restaurant/night club, he told her, "If you ever come here without me and you need anything, you see Frankie, okay?"

"Okay."

In the quick glimpse that she got of the restaurant, Alexandra observed that it was as elegant as his place in the city. She was surprised, however, at the size of the dance hall they walked into. There were two bars, the larger one taking up almost half of one wall. There was plush seating and cocktail tables against the wall on two sides of the hall and a large deejay booth on the wall opposite the entrance. The huge, sunken dance floor, which was enclosed by a brass railing with openings in four places to allow access from the seating area, was already packed.

As she and Warren walked over to the bar, she noticed that the majority of the patrons were mature adults, as opposed to the younger crowds at most of the city's dance clubs. She also took note of how spectacularly dressed everyone was. She was really not surprised to find that he owned such a classy place, though. Everything she had discovered about him in their first weeks together exemplified class.

There was an empty stool at the bar and he immediately seated her there.

"Hi, Warren," the lady behind the bar said.

"Hey, Sunni. How you doin', sweetheart?"

"Pretty good." She smiled at Alexandra and said, "Hi."

"Hi," Alexandra said, returning her warm smile.

Warren introduced the two women.

"Hi, Alexandra," Sunni said as she offered her hand. "Nice to meet you. What are you drinking?"

"A Cuervo margarita on the rocks. No salt," Alexandra answered.

"Warren, you want a Corona?"

"Yeah."

As Alexandra waited for her drink, she smiled at Warren and said, "You have a nice place here."

"Thank you, baby. I hope you enjoy yourself."

"I'm sure I will."

In the next hour, Warren introduced her to a number of his friends and employees. He seemed to be letting everyone know that she was his woman and that she was to be treated as royalty. He stayed close to her, though she knew he was probably used to moving around the club. She noticed how he interacted with the women that patronized his club, as they made no bones about letting their presence be known to him. He was very charming with everyone, and she smiled with satisfaction because she knew she would be going home with him.

It was just past twelve-thirty when she saw Shari and Vernon walk in. Warren also saw them and immediately went over to them.

"Hey, Vern, Shari. How y'all doin?" he said as he bent and kissed Shari's cheek.

"Hey, man. What's up?"

"Hi, Warren. Is Alexandra here?" Shari asked.

"Yeah, she's at the bar," Warren said, and pointed to her.

Alexandra waved and Shari left them and came over to her.

"Hi!"

"Hi, honey," Shari said as she and Alexandra exchanged pecks on the cheek.

"You look nice," Alexandra said, turning Shari around to check out her outfit.

"Thank you, dear."

Shari was wearing a bright orange spandex hip-hugging skirt and a black lace brassiere under a long-sleeved orange chiffon top with a wide-lapeled collar. The blouse wrapped and tied around the waist just above her hip.

"How's Vernon?" Alexandra asked.

"Excellent," Shari said, with a smug smile.

"How're you doing?" Shari then asked Alexandra.

"Fine. This is a nice club, right?"

"Yeah. Very nice. How long have you been here?"

"About an hour. Warren's been introducing me to everyone."

Warren and Vernon joined Alexandra and Shari at the bar. Vernon greeted Alexandra before Warren said to his bartender, "Hey, Al, give this lady and gentleman whatever they're drinking," gesturing at Shari and Vernon.

Warren felt more comfortable leaving Alexandra now that Shari had arrived, so that he could give more attention to what was going on in his club.

He went back upstairs to the door. As usual, there was a line outside waiting to get in. Frank came over from the restaurant and asked, "Yo, Warren, what's up with you and Susan?"

"Nothing."

"Damn, I go away for a few weeks and all kinds of things change. So, if she comes by here . . ."

Warren cut him off. "If she comes by here, she pays just like everybody else if she wants to come in."

"You're the boss," Frank said.

Alexandra had really loosened up since Shari arrived. Not only was she glad that her best friend was hanging out with her, but she had had two very potent margaritas before Shari got there.

"I have to use the ladies' room," she said suddenly.

"Come on. Where is it?"

"This way," Alexandra said, leading the way.

A few minutes later they were standing at the sink, touching up their makeup.

"Alexandra, that dress looks great on you," Shari said.

"Thanks," she said, smiling brightly. "Warren likes it, too."

"Excuse me." The words came from a woman who was about to leave the room.

Alexandra and Shari turned simultaneously.

"Is your name Alexandra?"

"Yes."

"You're with Warren Michaels?"

"Yes."

"Oh, hi! I'm his sister, Wanda," the woman said, extending her hand.

Alexandra said, "Hi!"

"How are you? I've heard a lot about you. It's nice to meet you."

Warren's sister was tall and slim, Alexandra guessed about five-ten. She was very pretty and had long black hair that she wore loose. She looked like a fashion model. Her resemblance to Warren and Will was uncanny. She was wearing black hipster bell-bottoms and a bright red midriff poet's blouse. A gold metallic belt hung loosely on her hips and black leather clogs were on her feet.

Alexandra introduced her to Shari and the three of them made small talk for a few minutes before they all left the ladies' room and returned to the dance hall.

The deejay had been spinning the latest tunes non-stop and the floor was packed for every song. Alexandra and Shari parted company with Wanda and were standing near the railing around the dance floor when two men came and asked them to dance.

Warren had since returned to the dance hall and was talking with a patron. He saw Alexandra dancing and smiled to himself as he watched her move to the beat of the reggae tune being played.

Though he played it very cool, he was quite aroused by the sight of her.

"She's cute, Warren," his sister said as she came up behind him.

"I know," he said with a smile.

"She seems nice, too."

"She is."

When Alexandra came off the floor, she walked over to Warren, who was now standing alone. "Hi."

"Hey, sexy."

"How are you?"

Though she was not holding him, she was standing so close that she could feel his swollen member straining against the fabric of his pants.

"Are you packing a gun?" she whispered as she looked up into his eyes.

"Yup. Fully loaded," he said, smiling down at her.

She kissed him softly.

"Are you having a good time?" he asked.

"Yes."

"I can't wait to get you home," he said.

"What are you gonna do?"

"You'll just have to wait and see."

"Ooh, I can't wait," she cooed.

She turned her back to him and purposely backed into him so that her backside was pressed firmly against the bulge in his pants.

"You're trying to hurt me, aren't you?" he said in her ear.

"I would never hurt you," she said. "Unless you asked me to."

He laughed.

Warren and Alexandra left Michaels Too at four-thirty in the morning when the club closed. Wanda was with them. Since her car was in the shop, she asked Warren to drive her home, about a mile from the club.

Once they had dropped her off, and as soon as Warren pulled onto the highway heading toward Long Island, he reached over and put his hand on Alexandra's leg, raising her dress as he did.

"Take these off," he said, meaning her pantyhose.

He knew that underneath her hose she wore only a thong and that fact, combined with the memory of her moving so seductively on the dance floor, had him aching for her love.

He slid his hand slowly up her dress and she moved closer to him in the seat to afford him a better opportunity to reach his desired destination.

He fondled her as he drove them home, never once taking his eyes off the road. Alexandra wiggled and moaned in the seat from his touch.

When they reached his house, he used the automatic garage door opener and drove straight into the garage.

They entered the house by way of the kitchen. Alexandra immediately made a beeline for the back stairs.

She wanted to get out of her dress as quickly as possible so they could love each other without restriction. But Warren had other plans. He stopped her before she reached the staircase and grabbed her, kissing her hungrily. He backed her into the island in the middle of the floor, holding her close with one hand as he unfastened his pants with the other. When his aching erection was released, he pulled her dress up and lifted her onto the island. She held him tightly. The force with which he was touching her was driving her insane. He pulled her panties aside and entered her, crying out loudly as he penetrated. She moaned in delight at the feel of him.

They made love in his kitchen with wild abandon.

Alexandra climaxed repeatedly from his thrusts and the many kisses and love bites he rained on her shoulders and neck. She cried out softly at first until he muttered, "No one can hear you, baby. Scream as loud as you like."

Afterward, they held each other quietly until their breathing returned to normal.

Warren took her face in his hands and tenderly kissed her lips.

"I'm sorry, Alexandra," he said, just barely above a whisper. "I just wanted you so bad that I couldn't wait until we got upstairs."

"Don't apologize, Warren," she said, staring into his ebony eyes. "I loved every second of it."

He wondered where she had been all his life.

"I'm falling in love with you," Alexandra uttered.

He held her tighter, kissing her lightly on her ear.

"And I with you, Alexandra."

Nine

They were awakened the next morning by the telephone's insistent ringing. By the time Warren realized he wasn't dreaming, the answering machine had picked up. He decided to listen for a moment to find out who was calling.

"Warren, this is Marge. I hope you get this message soon because I need you to watch Crystal for a couple of hours today, if you can. Danny's mother is in the hospital—"

He picked up the receiver when he heard his ex-wife's voice.

"Hey, Marge."

"Oh, hi. Did I wake you?"

"Yeah, you did," he said groggily. "What were you saying?"

"Danny's mother had a heart attack yesterday and we were going to go over to see her," Marge explained.

"How's she doing?" Warren asked of her fiancé's mother with genuine concern.

"Well, they said it wasn't a massive heart attack, but they want to keep an eye on her for a few days. She's already griping about being there, too."

"That's a good sign."

"Yeah, but Danny's really worried about her. Could you watch Chrissy for me?"

"Sure. You want me to come get her?"

"No, I'll bring her by. Thanks a lot, Warren. I'll see you about noon."

As Warren reached over to hang up the phone, Alexandra asked, "Who was that?"

"My ex-wife," he said, rolling over to face her, the better to relate details of the call.

"How's his mother doing?" Alexandra asked when he had finished.

Warren repeated the information Marge had given him, smiling at Alexandra's sensitivity.

"Is your daughter going to stay the night?"

"Yeah. You don't mind, do you?"

"Of course not. How could I?"

"Well, I know some women would mind but I'm glad you don't," he said.

"I'd like to meet her. Do you think she'll mind me being here?"

"Well, to be honest, I don't know. She was never really crazy about Susan, but then, Susan never went out of her way to be anything more than cordial."

"Well, if it's a problem, I'll go. Don't worry about it."

"I'd really like you to stay. Let's see how it goes, okay?"

"All right. So you're not going to go to the club tonight?"

"No."

"What time are they coming over?"

"About twelve."

She moved closer to him in the bed and gently brushed his hair back behind his ear. She then put her arm around his waist and pulled his lower body closer to her.

"So you think we have time to do the nasty?" she said in a beguiling manner.

He smiled at her and said, "I'll always have time with you."

It was a quarter after twelve when Warren's ex-wife, Marge, and her fiancé Danny Wilson arrived at Warren's house with Crystal.

He and Alexandra had gotten out of bed at around ten-thirty and went out to the pool and swam about ten laps together. Afterward, they went back inside, showered, then prepared a breakfast of homemade biscuits, fresh porgies, and grits.

Alexandra was in the kitchen washing the breakfast dishes when the doorbell rang. Warren was outside in the yard tending his vegetable garden.

When she informed him that someone was at the door, he walked back into the house, stopped at the sink and washed his hands, then proceeded to the front of the house to answer the bell.

Alexandra was slightly nervous about meeting Warren's ex-wife. Though he had already told her that he and Marge got along well, she knew a lot of women had problems with meeting their ex-husband's new girlfriends, regardless of their own status with the man.

When Warren opened the door to let them in, Marge rushed in immediately. "Hi, Warren!" she greeted him. "I have to use the bathroom."

She did not pause for a response but ran straight to the back of the house. Alexandra was just leaving the kitchen and entering the hallway leading to the front of the house when Marge reached the bathroom, which was adjacent to the kitchen.

"Hi!" she said quickly as she entered the bathroom and shut the door.

Warren, meanwhile, was greeting his daughter and Danny.

"Hi, Daddy!"

"Hey, sugar baby," he said as he picked her up and gave her a big hug and kiss. "How's my girl?"

"Fine. I'm gonna spend the night."

"I know. Hey, Danny. How ya' doin'?"

"What's up, Warren?"

The two men shook hands.

"I'm sorry to hear about your mother, Dan. How's she doing?" Warren asked.

"They say she's in stable condition, but they want to keep her there for a few days to watch her."

"Yeah. Well, I hope everything goes all right."

"Thanks."

"Come on in. Sit down."

They all moved into the den and sat down. Alexandra entered right behind them.

"Hello," she said.

"Alexandra, this is Danny and this is Crystal."

"Hi, Danny."

"Hi, how are you?" Danny said.

"Fine, thanks. Hello, Crystal. How are you?"

"Fine," she said, blushing.

"It's nice to meet you," Alexandra said with a smile.

She thought his daughter was a beautiful little girl, who favored Warren strongly. Just then, Marge entered the den.

"Marge, this is Alexandra. Baby, this is Marge."

"Hi, Alexandra. Excuse me for rushing in like that."

Alexandra thought Marge was a very pretty woman, but not really what she thought Warren's type to be. She was shorter than Alexandra by about two inches and looked sort of tomboyish. She was wearing a white T-shirt, blue jeans, and sneakers. Her hair was cut in a short bob and she seemed to be full of energy. She also gave Alexandra the impression of being very down-to-earth.

"How are you? It's nice to meet you," Marge said with an authentic smile.

She offered Alexandra her hand.

"It's nice meeting you, too, Marge," Alexandra said as they shook hands.

"Hey, Marge, do you remember Dave Jenkins who I used to play ball with?" Warren suddenly asked.

"Crazy Dave who used to mess with Andrea? Sure."

"Alexandra's his sister."

"Get outta here! How is he?" she asked, turning to Alexandra.

"Fine. He was just home about a month ago on leave," she told Marge.

"He's still in the service? Wow, I remember when he joined up."

"Yeah. He's still in there and he's doing real well."

"Well, that's good to hear. Give him my regards when you talk to him," she said.

"Okay, I will."

Warren turned his attention to his daughter. "So, how's my baby?" He tickled her gently.

"I'm fine, Daddy," she said with a tiny giggle.

"What do you want to do today?"

"Can we go to the zoo?"

"You just went to the zoo the other day," Marge said to her daughter.

"But I want to go again," Crystal responded.

"Well, if your father wants to take you, then have a good time," Marge said.

"Don't worry, we will. Right?" Warren said, tickling Crystal again.

"Right!" Crystal agreed with a chuckle.

"Well, we're going to get ready to go. Give me a kiss, Crystal."

Crystal stepped up to her mother and hugged and kissed her.

"Bye, Mommy."

"Bye, sweetie. See ya' tomorrow."

"Okay. Bye, Danny," Crystal said as she stepped to him and gave him a hug.

Danny kissed the top of her head and said, "Bye, Chrissy."

"Thanks again, Warren, for keeping her," Marge said.

"You don't have to thank me."

"I know, but thanks anyway. Alexandra, it was nice meeting you."

"It was real nice meeting you, too, Marge. Danny, I hope your mother gets well soon," Alexandra said.

"Thanks. Y'all take it easy," Danny said as he and Marge left.

Warren and Alexandra spent the day at the zoo with Crystal. Warren noticed that Alexandra and Crystal seemed to be getting along very well. He was glad to see Alexandra had so much patience with Crystal. The eight-year-old had a tremendous amount of energy and was quite inquisitive.

"Alexandra, are you my daddy's new girlfriend?" Crystal asked as she held Warren's hand while they strolled through the park.

As Alexandra looked over at Warren briefly, Crystal stared up at her with big innocent eyes waiting for an answer.

"Yes, I am, Crystal. Is that okay with you?"

Crystal shrugged and said, "I guess so. My mommy and Danny are gonna get married. Are you gonna marry my daddy?"

"Well, I don't know. We've only been boyfriend and girlfriend for a little while."

Crystal seemed to be considering Alexandra's answer.

After a moment she asked, "Do you like dolls?"

"I love dolls. As a matter of fact, I just bought myself a new Imani doll the other day."

"You did? I have Imani. I have a lot of dolls, and I have a big dollhouse at my Daddy's house. Will you play house with me?"

"Sure, I'd love to."

"Okay. I'll be the mother and you can be the daughter."

"Okay," Alexandra said with a big smile.

When they left the zoo, they went to Michaels Too for dinner, then headed back to Long Island and home.

As promised, Alexandra and Crystal played house in Crystal's bedroom for about an hour until Warren informed them that it was Crystal's bedtime.

Alexandra ran a tub filled with bubbles for Crystal and helped her bathe herself, then helped her get dressed for bed.

About fifteen minutes later, Warren tucked Crystal into bed. When he kissed her good night, she asked him, "Daddy, where's Alexandra?"

"I think she's downstairs."

"Can she tuck me in, too?"

"How about I go and ask her?"

Warren found Alexandra in the den watching television.

"Your presence is requested by the little lady of the house," he said.

"Really?"

Warren nodded.

Alexandra followed Warren upstairs to say good night to Crystal. She was delighted that she had asked for her.

"Good-night, Crystal," she said as she entered the room.

"Can you read me a story?"

Alexandra looked at Warren in surprise.

"Sure, sweetheart, I'll read you a story."

She made sure that Crystal was completely tucked in, then she sat on top of the covers, right next to her and began reading a story entitled *Amazing Grace*.

Warren sat in a chair across the room and listened as Alexandra read to his daughter. Watching her with Crystal made his heart swell with pride.

Alexandra was a dream to him. His love for her grew more and more every day.

PART TWO

Ten

Six weeks had passed and Warren and Alexandra were inseparable. They saw each other every day, usually spending the weekdays at Alexandra's apartment in Brooklyn and weekends at Warren's house on Long Island.

The week before, they had attended the wedding of Warren's ex-wife Marge and Danny Wilson. Crystal served as her mother's flower girl.

Warren smiled as he watched Marge walk down the aisle toward her new husband. She looked even more beautiful than she had the day they were married. Tears actually sprang to his eyes because he was so happy for her.

She had a good man in Danny Wilson. He knew, too, that though Danny had never tried to replace him as Crystal's father, he had always treated her as his own child. Besides, Crystal adored him, and that was good enough for him.

For a wedding present, Warren gave them airline tickets to Cancun, Mexico, to use whenever they chose. At the wedding reception, Alexandra caught Marge's bouquet. Marge teased Warren that Alexandra's catch was a sure sign from up above.

On this particular afternoon in the middle of October, as Warren sat in his restaurant in the city preparing the special dinner menu, a familiar voice took him away from his task.

"Hello, Warren."

He looked up immediately.

Susan Mitchell was wearing a red crepe suit trimmed with faux leopard at the collar and cuffs. On her head was a leopard print pillbox hat. She looked good, but that did not surprise him, because she always did. He was very suspicious of her reasons for being there.

He had not seen her since they broke up on his birthday. In the past month, however, she suddenly began calling him again. She had called him at least twice a week in the past three weeks. He had considered returning her calls once or twice, though he never did.

"What are you doing here?"

"It's nice to see you, too, Warren," she said sarcastically.

When he did not respond, she continued.

"I've tried to reach you on a number of occasions but you haven't been returning my calls."

"You didn't give me a reason to. You could have told me what you wanted."

"Well, since I'm here now, I will. You don't mind if I sit, do you?"

He did not respond.

She took the chair facing him. Very deliberately, she removed her black kidskin gloves and placed them on the table next to her pocketbook.

"How have you been?" she asked pointedly.

"Fine. What do you want, Susan?"

Her hardened expression softened and a plea slipped into her voice. "Can't we just talk?"

"Talk about what?"

"About us."

"There is no us," Warren stated.

"There used to be. Have you forgotten the two and a half years we were together?" she asked.

"Susan, that's history."

"Listen, there's no reason for you to speak to me the way you have been," she said angrily. "I'm just trying to be civil. After all, we're going to be seeing each other a lot in the next few years."

"What makes you think that?"

"Because you have a responsibility to bear."

"What are you talking about?"

She took a deep breath before she answered.

"I'm pregnant, Warren."

He paused then spoke. "Why're you telling me?"

"Because you're the father."

He laughed.

"Why are you laughing? I'm serious."

Warren looked at her. He could not believe that she would stoop so low.

"You're lying, Susan. Do you really think you can come in here and tell me something like this and I'm just going to fall for it?"

"I'm not lying! It's the truth. I'm three and a half months pregnant and the baby is yours!" she insisted.

Though she would not admit it even to herself, she knew there was a very real chance that the baby she carried was Jeff Foster's. In her heart, however, she prayed it was Warren's. After all, he was in a better position to support her than Jeff.

"We used protection, Susan, or have you forgotten?"

"Condoms aren't one hundred percent, Warren, you know that. Besides, there were times when you weren't protected."

"Yeah, but you told me you were. Were you lying to me then? I know how much you wanted to have a baby. Are you trying to set me up?"

"No, I'm not trying to set you up."

"Oh, and I guess you just found this out, huh?"

"No, I didn't. I've been trying to call you, to tell you but you wouldn't return my calls, remember?"

Warren felt as if he had been punched in the gut. A jumble of emotions coursed through his brain. He could not deal with this right now. He had to think.

"Susan, get out of here. Get out of my restaurant," he ordered.

She paused a moment, looking at him with a glint of humor in her eyes. She rose from the seat, as proud as she could be.

"You don't have to yell, Warren. I'm leaving," she said softly, "but no matter what you want to believe, you're going to be a father again in a few months, so you might as well get used to the idea."

She glided out of the restaurant with a very self-satisfied air.

After Susan left, Warren tried to focus on getting the special menu completed, but her accusation had totally ruined his ability to think straight.

He knew she was lying. She had to be. He figured she was probably trying to get back at him for the way he had cut her off and for ignoring all her calls.

Suddenly, he looked at his watch. He was supposed to pick Alexandra up from work in forty-five minutes.

He decided not to say anything to her about Susan's visit. Hopefully Susan would see that she was just wasting her time with this phony pregnancy story.

When Warren pulled up in front of Alexandra's office building, he was fifteen minutes early. He sat behind the wheel of his car and thought about the things Susan had said.

Could it be true?

Could she really be having my baby?

He prayed it was all a lie. He prayed that she would see there was no chance of them getting back together and that she would just leave him alone.

Warren was deep in thought when Alexandra finally

came downstairs. She had to tap on the window to get his attention.

When he saw her standing there, he smiled uneasily, but reached over to open the door to let her into the car.

"Hi," she said as she leaned over to kiss him. "You look like you've got some heavy stuff on your mind."

Warren pulled her close and kissed her passionately.

"I love you," he whispered to her.

"Ooh, I love you, too," she said with a big grin. "What a nice greeting."

"I missed you today," he told her.

"I missed you, too. How are you?"

"Much better now."

She caressed his cheek and looked into his eyes with love.

"Are you hungry?" he asked.

They were supposed to have dinner at Michaels.

"No, not really. At least not for anything on the menu at Michaels."

"Good. Let's go home. I want to make love to you real bad."

"Well, I hope you'll make love to me real good," she said, teasing him.

The following Friday, Warren and Alexandra went to Michaels Too as they usually did on most Friday and Saturday nights. Alexandra had, by now, become very accustomed to the club and was friendly with a number of Warren's friends and employees, so he was free to move around and manage the club without worrying that she was sitting by herself and not having a good time.

It was just after midnight and Warren was standing alone near the dance floor, his eyes on Alexandra as she danced. He loved watching her move, especially if she knew he was watching her. He was smiling to himself because at that particular time his sole thought was of taking her home and dancing with her to a beat of their own.

"Hello, Warren."

His heart hit his feet.

He turned sharply, shocked at seeing Susan.

"What are you doing here?"

"I came to party just like everyone else who paid fifteen dollars to get in here. And, by the way, Warren, I can't believe that you're actually making me pay to come in here," she said, one hand on her hip.

He glared at her. She was the last person in the world he wanted to see.

"You'd better not start anything, Susan!" he warned, at once reminded of the many scenes she had caused on previous occasions.

"I didn't come here to start anything, Warren. I told you, I came to party just like everyone else. Calm down. Don't get so bent out of shape. Don't worry, I won't tell Alexandra about us," she sneered as she sidled away from him.

He could not believe the gall of her. How dare she come there? He knew the only reason for her presence was to taunt him. He swore to himself that if she approached Alexandra and said anything to her, even so much as "Hello," she would rue the day she ever met him.

Alexandra had watched Susan approach Warren. She was very surprised to see the woman. As far as she knew, the last time Warren had seen her was at the cookout on his birthday when they broke up. She noticed, however, that not only was Warren surprised, but he actually looked horrified at seeing her. She wondered why he would react that way to her.

When she finished her dance, she went over to the

bar where Warren was standing against the wall. He had a deep scowl on his face, and though she approached him head-on, he appeared to not even see her.

"Hey, you," she said as she playfully struck him on the arm. "What's the matter?"

"Nothing."

"So why are you standing over here looking like you wanna kill someone?"

He shook his head and mumbled, "It's nothing. I just have a splitting headache, that's all."

"You looked fine until Susan showed up," she said, gingerly moving over to the bar.

"Sunni, could I get a margarita, please?" she asked the barmaid.

She turned back to face him. He was looking at her strangely.

"What? Did I say something I shouldn't have?"

He did not respond, just turned his face away from her.

"Here you go, Alex," Sunni said, placing a drink on the bar.

"Thanks, Sunni."

She took a sip from her drink then placed it back on the bar.

"Why'd you look so horrified when you saw Susan?" she asked Warren.

His head jerked back around toward her.

"What?"

"You heard what I said, Warren."

"What are you talking about, horrified?"

"I saw your face. That's how you looked."

"Surprised, maybe. Horrified, I don't think so."

"Has she called you lately?"

"No."

"And you haven't seen her?"

"No. Why are we talking about her?" he finally asked.

"It's just that your reaction to her seemed awfully strange, that's all."

"Yeah, well, let's talk about something else, all right. This is just making my headache worse."

She picked up her drink and started to walk away as she said, "Maybe I'm making your headache worse."

Warren grabbed her quickly to prevent her from walking away.

"Where are you going?"

"I wouldn't want to do anything to make your headache worse."

He took her drink from her hand and placed it on the bar.

"Come here."

He pulled her into his arms and held her close as he gently kissed her lips.

"I'm sorry, sweetheart."

She looked up into his eyes, then put her arms around his neck.

"Are you all right?" she asked.

"Yeah, I'm all right. I just . . . I don't trust Susan. I don't want her starting anything with you. She likes to perform, Alexandra. Preferably, for an audience."

"Why would she try to start anything?"

"I don't know. All I know is how she used to get with me."

"Well, don't worry about her, all right?"

She kissed him sensuously, putting her tongue in his mouth.

"Come on, baby. Let's dance."

Over the next four weeks, Susan appeared at Michaels Too almost every Friday and Saturday night. She knew Warren was there on those nights and she had every intention of letting him know that she was around to stay.

On most nights, Alexandra was also at the club and when she was, though Susan never said anything to her, she always made sure that Alexandra knew she was there, too.

Warren had not told anyone, not even his closest friend Frank or his sister and brother, about Susan's claim that he was the father of her unborn child. In all honesty, he really did not believe she was pregnant. She was at the club just about every weekend, and if she was pregnant like she claimed, he figured she would be showing. Besides, she had not mentioned another word to him about being pregnant since that first time she told him at Michaels, so he was sure the whole thing had been a ploy to try to win him back.

The Saturday afternoon before Thanksgiving, Alexandra was in the basement of Warren's house working out when he returned from having his Jaguar serviced.

"Hey, sexy."

She had just completed her fourth set of twenty-five sit-ups. Sweat was pouring off her but he pulled her up from the bench and hugged her close.

"Oh, baby, I'm all sweaty," she groaned.

"You know I love it when you sweat."

He nuzzled her behind her ear and felt her backside.

"Ooh, your face is cold. Is it that cold out?"

"Yeah. I was listening to the news on the car radio. It's twenty-eight degrees and it's very windy. It feels like ten."

"Damn. What are we gonna do when winter comes?"

"Stay in bed and work up some serious body heat."

She laughed as he kissed her on her neck.

"What do you want for dinner tonight?" she asked.

"No time. We have to get showered and dressed 'cause we have to be in the city by seven o'clock."

"For what?"

"We have a concert to attend at the Paramount."
"What concert?"
"Luther."
She screamed with glee.
"You have tickets for Luther Vandross?"
"Uh-huh," he said, with a self-righteous smile.
"Oh, Warren, why didn't you tell me?"
"Because it was a surprise."
"Ooh, come on, we've gotta take a shower and get dressed," she said, pulling him toward the stairs.
"That's what I just said."

After the concert, Warren and Alexandra drove to Queens to have dinner at Michaels Too. When they arrived, it was almost eleven o'clock and there was a line outside to get into the club downstairs. Frank greeted them at the door.
"Hey, y'all."
"Hi, Frank," Alexandra said as he kissed her cheek.
"Hey, man," Warren responded, shaking the man's hand.
"How was the concert, Alexandra?" Frank asked with a smile.
"You knew about it, too?" She playfully punched him in the arm. "You guys are real sneaky."
"So, how was it?" Frank asked again.
"It was great! But Luther's always great."
"Is my table set up?" Warren asked.
"Yup. Just like you wanted it," Frank said.
"Come on, baby. Let's go eat," Warren said, winking at Frank.
Warren had a table reserved for them in the back of the restaurant with roses, candles, and champagne, and had a special dinner planned for her much like their first dinner together.

She was so moved by his simple gesture of love that she sat there and cried.

Being the successful businessman he was and having the means to buy almost anything or go almost anywhere he wanted and being the object of so many women's desires, one would think that he would be arrogant and self-centered, but he was neither. He was the most sensitive and romantic man she had ever known.

"Warren, this is so beautiful," she said between sniffles. "You're always doing things to make me smile. I love you so much."

He reached across the table to caress her face and wipe away her tears.

"I love you, Alexandra. More than I've ever loved any woman in my life. You are the kindest, most generous, most selfless person I have ever known, and I would do anything if I thought it would bring a smile to your sweet face," he said tenderly.

"Will you promise me something?" she asked.

"Anything."

"Don't ever change and don't ever stop loving me, 'cause I'll always love you."

"I'll always love you, sweetheart."

It was almost one in the morning when they went downstairs to the club. The music was pumping and the dance floor seemed to be filled to capacity. Alexandra and Warren were both on Cloud Nine. She could not remember a time in her life when she had been happier. He walked with her on his arm with the air of a king escorting his queen.

Alexandra took a seat at a table Warren had reserved for a few guests who were visiting his club for the first time. She sat with them and danced with them, being the ever-cheerful hostess and making sure everyone was having a good time as Warren made his rounds in the club.

It was on nights like this that Warren was reminded of why he went into this business. He loved people and he loved entertaining his friends in high style.

He stopped near the door and surveyed his club. Everyone was having a great time. He had his lady with him, who always made everything all right, and he was feeling great. This was one of those rare perfect nights when he knew once he got home with Alexandra, they would be loving each other well into the next afternoon.

"Oh, there you are, Warren. I've been looking all over for you!"

Susan's voice sent a chill up his spine. *No!* his mind screamed before he even turned to her. *Not tonight, please, not tonight.*

She stepped in front of him, and when he saw her, his heart hit his feet with a big crash. He hated to admit it, but she looked beautiful. She was positively glowing. She was wearing a winter-white knit pant suit. The top was a turtleneck tunic decorated with gold sequins. The pants were straight-legged. Winter-white leather boots complemented the outfit. Her long black hair was styled in cascades of soft curls that fell down her back.

But that was not the reason for the feeling of dread that slowly crept up his spine.

His worst fear had been made manifest.

Susan stood before him in all her pregnant glory. There was no mistaking it; she was definitely with child.

"What's the matter? Why are you looking at me like that? You look like you've seen a ghost," she said.

"You're pregnant," he stated as if he were in shock.

"I told you I was. Did you think I was lying?"

All he could think about was Alexandra. What would he tell her? Why hadn't he told her already?

"Excuse me," he said, as he quickly moved past her.
"Warren!" she called after him.

He went in search of Alexandra. Where was she? She was not sitting where he had last seen her. He thought she might be in the ladies' room. *I've got to find her before she sees Susan,* he thought.

He walked slowly around the club, searching the dance floor, but it was so dark and crowded that he really could not see. His heart was beating wildly in his chest and he suddenly felt as though he was burning up with fever.

She's really pregnant, he thought. *She's really having my baby.* The idea gave him a lump in his throat. He felt as though he could not breathe.

Suddenly, he spotted Alexandra in a flash of the overhead lights. She was dancing on the far side of the floor away from him. He moved as fast as he could through the crowd, trying hard not to draw attention to himself.

Before he could reach her, Alexandra left the dance floor and headed out of the hall, he figured to the ladies' room.

As he headed toward the door to catch her, Susan, seemingly from out of nowhere, stepped through the door behind her.

There were a number of people milling around in the antechamber immediately outside the dance hall. Alexandra went directly to the ladies' room. She saw a number of women who she had met through Warren sitting in the lounge, and she chatted with them briefly before exiting to return to the dance hall.

As she was about to reenter the dance hall, she caught sight of Susan out of the corner of her eye, talking animatedly to a very good-looking man. She did a double take, as she thought her eyes were playing tricks on her. When she looked closer, however, she realized that what she was seeing was as real as the nose on her face.

Susan was pregnant.

She paused with her hand on the doorknob, not realizing that she was staring. The man gave her an en-
igmatic smile, causing Susan to turn to see what he was
looking at.

When she recognized Alexandra, Susan turned full-
face toward her. It looked to Alexandra as if she was
trying to poke her stomach out even more.

Alexandra felt as though the blood had been drained
from her face. She quickly pulled the door wide and
entered the dance hall blindly, not looking where she
was going. She collided with Warren.

"Hey, hon, watch where you're going," he said lightly.

She looked up at him, at first stunned by his presence.
She wondered if he knew.

Her heart was racing a mile a minute and she felt as
though she was on the verge of tears. But she had to
think a minute. She tried never to act without thinking
about what she was doing.

"Sorry," she said, quickly putting on a false face.

"How're you doing?"

"Fine."

He put his arms around her and hugged her close.

"I love you, you know," he whispered softly in her
ear.

She did not say anything but she held him tightly.
She was suddenly very afraid that she would lose him.

The deejay had slowed the pace of the music down
and was playing a love ballad.

"Dance with me, Alexandra."

He led her to the floor and wrapped her in a warm
and loving embrace. *How am I going to tell her about Susan,*
he asked himself as he held her. *It's going to break her
heart.*

Alexandra wondered if he could feel her heart racing.
Did he know about Susan? Was it his baby?

She figured he had to know, but why hadn't he told her? Did he really think she would not find out? Now she understood why his mood seemed to change so drastically whenever Susan was around.

She was becoming very angry, but she was not one for public scenes. She would wait until they were alone to confront him.

He had to know about her, she told herself. Alexandra figured from the size of her belly that she was about five or six months along. She and Warren had only been together for three months. How could he keep something like this from her? He claimed he loved her. Granted, he had always been very thoughtful and generous, and she could not deny that when she was with him, he treated her like a precious jewel. But why would he keep this from her?

"What are you thinking about?" he suddenly asked.

She looked up at him.

"Can we leave?"

"Sure, honey. Are you okay?"

"No, I'm not. I don't feel well."

Warren felt a sinking feeling in the pit of his stomach. He wondered if she had already seen Susan.

"Come on, let's get our coats."

Alexandra held her breath when they exited the dance hall, because she did not know if Susan was still standing outside. Besides, she did not miss the fact that Warren suddenly seemed to be in a rush to leave the club.

They ran into Frank on their way out, and he noticed the change in Alexandra's mood from earlier.

"Hey, Al, you all right?" he asked.

"I have a headache," she said, which was the truth. Her head was killing her.

"Well, I hope you feel better."

"Thanks, Frankie. See ya."

"I'll talk to you tomorrow, Frank," Warren said.

"All right. Y'all have a good night."

Warren held her hand as they walked to the car. Neither of them spoke.

They were seated in his car, and he had just turned on the ignition when she finally spoke.

"Is Susan having your baby?"

Warren froze. She knew.

He took a deep breath before he answered.

"That's what she says."

"What do you say?" she asked as she looked over at him.

"I don't think it's mine," though he had no doubts that it was.

"Why wouldn't you think it's yours? Who else's would it be?"

Warren closed his eyes and bowed his head in shame. *Why are you lying to her,* he asked himself.

"Why didn't you tell me?"

He did not answer right away. He was so nervous he thought he was going to be sick.

"I didn't know how to."

"How long have you known?"

He continued to look down at his lap, trying to remain composed, because he felt himself sinking fast.

"About a month."

She stared at him, but he would not look at her. Her eyes began to water and she felt a flood of emotions threatening to overtake her, but she tried to remain calm.

"How far is she?" she asked in a trembling voice.

He looked at her then. He wanted to reach over and touch her but he did not feel deserving enough.

"I think about five months."

She gasped loudly. Her fortitude had crumbled and she could not stop the tears from falling.

"Why didn't you tell me?" she cried. "How could you not tell me about this?"

"I'm sorry, Alexandra," he said, tears falling from his eyes. "I'm so sorry. I just kept thinking it couldn't be true. I thought she was lying."

His heart broke into a million pieces as he sat beside her, wanting desperately to hold her and comfort her and tell her that everything was going to be all right. But he would be deluding himself and blatantly lying to her if he did that. He felt as though his world was falling apart.

"I want to go home," she said through her tears.

"Alexandra . . ."

"Take me home. To Brooklyn."

"Alexandra, please stay with me tonight. Please. I know I should have told you, but I just didn't want to hurt you."

"So you'd rather me find out on my own, right?" she yelled. "Take me home, Warren! If you don't, I'll find my own way!"

She had her hand on the door, ready to throw it open and jump out. He reached over and grabbed her hand.

"All right, baby, all right. I'll take you home."

He had to compose himself before he could begin the drive. His eyes were wet from crying and his head was pounding.

Alexandra turned away from him in the seat. She could not believe this was happening. She knew he had been too good to be true. She knew things were just too perfect between them for it to have ever lasted. Deep in her heart she had always felt that one day something would happen to ruin the bliss she had experienced by loving him, but never in her wildest dreams could she have imagined it would be so terrible as this.

It was almost unbearable for Warren to listen to her sobs knowing that he was the cause of her pain and knowing that there was nothing he could do about it. As he drove from Queens to Brooklyn with just the sound of her crying, he had to wipe his eyes every few yards because he could not see through his own tears. She was everything he had always hoped for in a woman. She was his joy, his love, and his life and he was losing her. He could feel her slipping away from him, and no matter what he did or how he tried, he knew he could not pull her back.

When they finally pulled up in front of her building, Alexandra opened the passenger door as soon as he stopped the car.

"Alexandra, wait."

She did not pause, and he quickly jumped out and ran around the car to get her. He grabbed her and tried to put his arms around her, but she fought him, her fists swinging wildly.

"Leave me alone! Go away and leave me alone!" she cried.

"Alexandra, please. Please don't do this," he urged as he tried to hold her.

"No! No! Go away! I don't want to see you! Leave me alone!"

She broke free of his grasp and ran up the stairs and away from him. Her hands trembled as she tried to get the key in the lock. Finally, after what seemed like an eternity, the lock sprang and she was inside the house. She heard him calling after her, but she did not stop or turn back. She ran up to her apartment and, after gaining entrance, fell on her sofa and cried hysterically.

Warren stood at the base of her stoop, looking up at the door she had just run through. Tears welled in his eyes once more as he repeatedly breathed her name.

He stood there, impervious to the cold, for more than ten minutes. Finally, knowing that she was not coming back, he slowly lumbered over to his car, which was still running, and climbed in the open door, closing it with much effort.

He did not want to go home, not without her, but he had no place else to go. He knew he could not go back to the club. He felt that if he saw Susan now, he would surely kill her, though in his heart he knew he could not blame her for this.

He drove around aimlessly for hours, eventually finding himself in his own driveway at around six A.M. but not remembering how he had gotten there. For the first time in the three years since he had purchased it, the house felt cavernous. He had always loved the space he had there, but today it reminded him of how alone he now was without her.

He stood in the foyer looking up at the stairs, not sure whether he even had the energy or the will to climb them. He sighed heavily and slowly began the climb. When he reached his bedroom, he paused as he caught sight of her sweat pants thrown across his chair. He slowly trudged over to the chair and sat down, then cradled her sweats against his heart.

Eleven

It was two o'clock Sunday afternoon when Alexandra appeared at Shari's apartment. Shari knew something was wrong the moment she opened the door. Alexandra's eyes were red and puffy from crying and her clothes, which were always crisply pressed and well coordinated, looked as though they had been thrown on with no thought at all.

"What's wrong, Alex?" she asked with great concern as she pulled her into her apartment.

"Susan is pregnant."

She was crying and her voice trembled as she spoke.

"Susan? Who's Susan?"

"Warren's ex-girlfriend. She's pregnant."

"How do you know?"

"I saw her!"

"So?"

"It's Warren's baby."

"How do you know that?" Shari asked.

"She's five months pregnant, Shari. She was with him five months ago!"

"So what? Maybe she was playing around."

"Shari. She told Warren a month ago. If it's not his baby, why didn't he tell me then? *He* didn't even tell me. I found out last night at the club," Alexandra cried.

"Alex, calm down. What did Warren say?"

"He said he thought she was lying and that he didn't want to hurt me, that's why he didn't tell me."

"Of course he didn't want to hurt you. He loves you, Alexandra. You know that."

"But he should have said something."

"Yeah, he should have, but he didn't. So, what are you gonna do, turn your back on him?"

Alexandra did not respond.

"How does he feel about her pregnancy?"

"He said he doesn't believe it's his, but I think he just said that because he didn't have anything else to say."

"Maybe it's not. Maybe she's trying to set him up. I mean, didn't you tell me they had been going out for a couple of years?"

"Yeah."

"And he broke it off with her quite suddenly and right away took up with you. Did it ever cross your mind that maybe she might be trying to get back at him?"

"But that doesn't change the fact that she's still pregnant. It doesn't matter that he didn't want it or that he didn't know until it was too late. She's still having his baby."

"But you don't know that it's his," Shari argued.

Alexandra looked at Shari for a moment, then sighed and walked across the room.

"And what if it is? What then?"

"You won't know that for at least another four months. Right now, what you have to worry about is whether or not you want to give him up. He's a good man, Alexandra, and he loves you and I know you love him. I don't think you should just turn your back on him. I think you should try to talk to him."

"I don't know," Alexandra sighed.

"Is he at your house?"

"No. I made him bring me home and I told him I didn't want to see him anymore."

"Is that how you really feel?"

"I don't know how I feel."

"Do you want to stop seeing him?"

"I don't know. He lied to me."

They were both silent for a couple of minutes. Shari felt very sad for her friend. She knew that though they had only been together for three months, Alexandra's love for Warren was very strong.

"Do you still love him, Alexandra?" Shari asked, knowing she did.

Alexandra sat down in one of Shari's easy chairs and looked down at her hands folded in her lap.

"He hurt me."

"Do you still love him?"

She began to cry. "Yes."

"Then go to him and tell him how you feel."

"He knows how I feel."

"He knows that you're angry with him for not telling you about Susan. He doesn't know that you still love him. Maybe he needs to know that."

Alexandra did not comment.

"Do you think he did this to hurt you on purpose?"

"No."

"Then tell him that, too. Don't give up on him."

"Maybe I'll call him."

"No, don't call him. Go see him."

Twelve

Marge Wilson called Warren Sunday morning to find out if he would be attending their daughter's class play on Thanksgiving Eve. She immediately heard the distress in his voice when he picked up the phone. She asked him if he needed to talk. When he told her yes, she went right over.

She was shocked by his appearance when he opened the door. His hair was a mess, his clothes from the night before were wrinkled, as he had fallen asleep in them, and he looked as if he had been crying.

"Warren, what's wrong?" she asked worriedly.

He could not speak right away.

"Come on in here and sit down," she said, leading him into his den.

His eyes began to water, but he took a deep breath and was able to compose himself.

"What's the matter?" Marge asked again.

His voice trembled as he explained, "Susan came by Michaels about a month ago and told me she was pregnant and that I'm the father."

"What?"

"I didn't believe her. Last night, she came into the club and she's showing."

He had to take a moment before he could continue.

"Alexandra saw her last night."

"You didn't tell her when Susan first told you?"

He shook his head.

"Oh, no. What did she say?"

"She said she doesn't want to see me anymore." Against his will, a tear fell from his eye.

She sat down next to him and put her arm around his shoulder to comfort him.

"Why didn't you tell her?"

"I thought Susan was lying. I really thought she was lying."

Marge sighed. She felt bad for Warren. It broke her heart to see him this way. Despite his size and his somewhat foreboding appearance, she knew deep down inside he was a pussycat. He had always been a very sensitive man and, when he really fell in love, he put everything he had into it.

She remembered how he had been when he first realized that he was in love with Susan. He was like a little boy with a shiny new toy, he was so excited. She also remembered how hurt he had been when he told her how Susan always doubted his faithfulness. That was something Marge could never understand, because even when their marriage began to fall apart, she had never suspected that it was due to Warren being unfaithful.

"I don't want to lose her, Marge. I really love her."

"I know you do," she said, as she gently stroked his back. "But I think she loves you, too."

"I want to talk to her. I want to tell her how sorry I am. I tried to call her this morning but she hung up on me."

"Give her time, Warren. She needs time to sort this all out."

"Do you think she'll call me?" he asked, looking quite forlorn.

"She'll call you. Don't worry. I've seen the way she

looks at you. She's hurt and angry 'cause you didn't tell her, but I'm sure she still loves you."

"The only reason I didn't tell her was because I thought Susan was lying. I don't blame Alexandra for being angry with me. I just don't want her to think I've been lying to her."

"Yeah, I know. But listen, she'll come around. You'll probably hear from her today or tomorrow. Don't worry too much."

"Yeah, I'll try."

"You should probably try to get some rest, too. You really look like hell," she said as she playfully tousled his hair.

He looked over at her and could not help but smile. "Thanks."

She kissed him on his cheek.

"You're a good guy, Warren. Other than making Crystal, we weren't really good for each other, but I knew you would make some lucky lady very happy one day, and I think that lady is Alexandra. Just give her some time and don't worry. She'll come around. You just watch," Marge said confidently.

"I hope you're right."

"Hey, I'm always right," she said jokingly.

Marge had always had the power to make him laugh.

He smiled as he said, "Thanks for coming over, Marge."

"Hey, one hand washes the other."

Thirteen

After Marge left, Warren went upstairs and changed into some sweats, then went down to his gym to work out. He exercised for over an hour, and when he finished he felt better because he had relieved a lot of the tension he felt. However, he really did not feel like being alone.

He went upstairs to shower and shave, but before he did, he called Alexandra again. Her answering machine picked up after the fourth ring.

"Alexandra. Alexandra, it's Warren. Pick up if you're there."

He waited a few seconds, but when she did not answer, he left a message.

"Well, I guess you're not there. I was just calling to see how you're doing. I'm sorry for not telling you. I really didn't want you to find out like that. I hope you don't hate me, because I love you. I know you don't want to see me and I guess I can't blame you, but I just want you to know that I'm here. Whenever you decide that you want to talk about it, I'm here. That's all I wanted to say. I guess I'll talk to you another time. Bye, sweetheart. I love you."

When Warren got out of the shower, he immediately checked his answering machine to see if there were any messages. He was very disappointed that there were none. He had been hoping that Alexandra would call right back.

He got dressed and went down to his den and turned on the television. There was a football game on, and though he was an avid football fan, he could not keep his mind on the game.

He picked up the telephone again, but this time he dialed Frank.

"Yo, what's up, Warren?"

"Ain't nothin'. What you doin'?"

"Watching the game. Did you see that last play?"

"No, I'm not really here right now," Warren said with a light chuckle.

"What's up?"

"Did you see Susan last night?"

"Naw. Was she in the club?"

"Yeah. She's pregnant."

"Susan?"

"Yeah. She says it's mine."

"Is it?"

"I guess so. She's about five months, and I was still seeing her five months ago."

"Damn."

"Alexandra saw her."

"Aw, man. That's why she was. . . ."

"Yeah."

"Is she there?"

"No. She made me take her home and she said she doesn't want to see me."

"Damn, I'm sorry, man. Yo, you want me to come over?" Frank asked.

Warren really did not want to be alone and he had been hesitant to ask Frank if he would come over. But since he offered . . .

"Would you mind?"

"Naw, man. Give me about an hour."

"All right. Thanks."

"Don't mention it."

For the next forty-five minutes, Warren did not move from his chair. He heard Frank's car pull into the driveway and was glad his friend was finally there. He really needed to talk to someone who understood him.

When the bell rang, he rose from the chair slowly and dragged himself to the door. Knowing it was Frank, he did not bother to check before he opened it.

At first he thought he was seeing things. Could his need to see her be so bad that he was having visions of her?

"Hi, Warren."

She had come to him.

He was so choked up that he could not speak.

She stepped into the house and gently closed the door. When she turned to face him, there were tears in his eyes.

Alexandra put her arms around his waist and rested her head against his chest. He put his arms around her and held her tight as tears of joy slid down his cheeks. Soon, she was crying, too.

She was glad that she had spoken to Shari. She was even happier that she had listened to her. No matter what had happened, she could not deny that she still loved him.

"Alexandra. Oh, God," he sighed. "Thank you for coming back."

She turned her head up to him, and he kissed her with a passion that consumed them both. He had never been happier in his life. He thought he had lost her, but she had come back to him of her own accord.

"I'm sorry, Ally. I'm so sorry that I kept it from you."

"Shh, shh, Warren," she said, placing a finger to his

lips. "I don't want to talk about it now. I just want you to hold me."

"Oh, baby, I'll hold you," he said, squeezing her tighter. "I'll hold you and I'll never let you go."

They stood in the foyer, wrapped in each other's arms for about five minutes. Alexandra had always loved the feeling she got when he held her, and she felt so comfortable in his embrace that she could have easily dozed off where she stood.

Eventually, they moved into the den. Warren turned off the television. He had not been watching it anyway. They sat on the couch, snuggled close together without speaking, simply reveling in the warmth of each other's bodies.

As they sat there, the telephone rang.

Without really moving, Warren reached over to answer it.

"Hello."

"Hey, I'm outside on my car phone. Is that Alexandra's car?" he asked.

"Yeah."

"You all right?"

"Yeah, man. Everything's all right."

"Okay. I'll talk to you later."

"Later."

He reached over and returned the receiver to its cradle.

"Who was that?" Alexandra asked.

"Frank."

They sat in silence for the next few minutes.

"Warren, what are you going to do about the baby?"

He did not answer right away. He had considered that himself.

"If it really is my baby, I have to do the right thing by it. I don't want it to suffer for anything that Susan's done."

"Would you marry her?"

"No, Ally. I'll take care of my child, but I couldn't marry her because I don't love her."

"But you did. You told me so yourself."

"Yes, I did once, but she ruined it."

"What about us?"

"Baby." He made her sit upright so that he could look into her eyes as he spoke. "I love you and I want to be with you. I know how hard this is for you, and I know it's not going to get any easier, but I don't want to lose you. I want us to be together. I need you to help me get through this. I promise, no matter what happens, I'll never let you down. I'll never turn my back on you. I'll never stop loving you."

Her heart was breaking for both of them.

The next morning, Alexandra called in sick for work, and she and Warren spent the better part of the day in bed, making love.

When they got up, it was two-thirty in the afternoon and they went down to the exercise room and worked out together.

It seemed that with Susan's pregnancy now out in the open, they had drawn closer together, as if trying to shield themselves from anyone outside of their world that might hurt them.

Warren called Susan Monday night and told her he could see now, of course, that she had been telling the truth. He even apologized for believing she would make up a lie of such magnitude. He assured her that if the child was in fact his, he would be there to help her support and raise it. He made it clear, however, that her pregnancy by no means changed anything else between them.

On Wednesday evening, the night before Thanksgiving, Alexandra and Warren attended a play that Crystal's third-grade class put on for her school. When they arrived, Marge and Danny were already present. When Marge spotted Alexandra on Warren's arm, she smiled at him, happy to see that he was happy again.

They spent Thanksgiving together at Alexandra's parents' house in Philadelphia. Her brother David and his wife Michelle had come up from Virginia for the holiday. David and Warren spent hours reminiscing about their college days. Warren told David that he and Alexandra would come down and visit him for the weekend sometime in December.

Friday night, Warren and Alexandra went to Michaels Too as they usually did. Frank was there and he, too, was glad to see Alexandra and Warren together. He and Warren had been friends for about nine years. In that time, they had become very close, and Frank knew of all the bullshit that Warren had put up with while he and Susan were together. He knew that Warren was a good person and that deep down he would never do anything malicious to anyone. He was glad to know that his friend had found such an understanding woman in Alexandra and he hoped that everything would work out for them regardless of what was going on with Susan.

Before the night was over, Susan also made an appearance at Michaels Too. She knew Alexandra was well aware of her pregnancy now. Though he had not said so when he called her earlier that week, Susan was also sure that until last Friday, Warren had not told her about her condition. She was glad Alexandra had seemed so shaken when she saw her. Susan was positive that Alexandra would react negatively with Warren as a result, and she hoped she would have the good sense to send him packing.

She was shocked and appalled that things had not worked out the way she had hoped. When Susan walked into the dance hall, the first thing she noticed was Warren and Alexandra. They were on the dance floor, locked in each other's arms and kissing like there was no one else in the room. She stood there frozen to the spot watching them. Her blood began to boil. How dare he act like she did not exist? She was carrying his child.

Alexandra's back was to Susan but Warren felt eyes boring into him. He looked up and right into Susan's angry eyes. He stared at her for a long moment knowing that the last thing she expected to see was him and Alexandra, happy and still together.

Fourteen

As was customary, whenever Warren was at either of his restaurants, he was known to circulate so that he could greet his customers and let them know that he appreciated their patronage. He felt it was one of the things that kept frequent customers, of which he had many, coming back.

On this particular evening in the middle of December, during the dinner rush at Michaels, he noticed Susan and her best friend Tasha sitting at a table near the back of the restaurant.

His first instinct was to ignore them, but he quickly realized how childish that would be. He stepped over to their table and greeted them in the same gracious manner he would any of his other customers.

"Good evening, ladies. How have you been, Tasha? Long time, no see."

"I've been fine, Warren. How have you been?"

"Can't complain. How are you, Susan?"

"I'm fine."

"That's good. What brings you ladies in here this evening?"

"I had a craving for some blackened catfish and you know, Warren, no one makes it better than you," Susan said, her voice dripping with sarcasm.

"Well, you're right about that. I hope you enjoy it," he said, and started to turn away.

"Oh, Warren, by the way, I went to see my doctor a couple of weeks ago and I had an amniocentesis done."

"What's that?"

"A test that's done to determine whether the baby is healthy."

"And is it?"

"Yes. He told me everything was fine and that we're having a little boy," she said cheerfully.

Warren looked at her for a moment before he spoke.

When he did not answer, Susan asked, "Aren't you excited? I figured every man wants a son. Don't you?"

"The sex really doesn't matter to me, Susan. I'm just glad that you and the baby are all right. Now, if you'll excuse me, I have to make a phone call."

Fifteen

Warren's parents flew up from St. Petersburg, Florida, to spend the Christmas holiday with their children. Will and Wanda accompanied Warren to the airport to meet their parents on the morning of Christmas Eve. Ruby and Warren Michaels, Sr., would be staying with Warren while they were in town.

Alexandra had to work Christmas Eve but was planning to drive out to Huntington that evening to spend the holiday weekend with Warren and his family.

Warren had always been very close to his parents, as were Will and Wanda, but Warren had a very special closeness to his mother.

Ruby Michaels was a very young fifty-three-year-old. She had been a registered nurse for over twenty years. She was dark-skinned, like her children, and had bone-straight black hair that fell almost to her hips. Ruby was not very tall, only five four, but she was the backbone of the Michaels family.

She and BW (for Big Warren as she affectionately called her husband) had grown up together in Harlem, though her parents had been born in Belize, Central America. Warren, Sr., and Ruby's older brother Miguel had been best friends.

Warren, Sr., was sixty years old and a retired fire marshal. He was of a fairer complexion than his wife and children but they all favored him in appearance. He was a big man, standing six feet four inches and weighed a solid two hundred and seventy pounds. He and Ruby were both very athletic, and their penchant for healthy living had carried over to all three of their children.

Warren spoke to his mother at least once a week, so she was aware of his predicament with Susan. She was proud that regardless of the fact that he was no longer seeing Susan, he had owned up to his responsibility and was willing to support and help raise their child.

Alexandra arrived at Warren's house at a quarter after eight that evening. She was a bit nervous about meeting Warren's parents, and was very pleasantly surprised when she rang the bell and his mother opened the door and greeted her like she had known her for years.

"You must be Alexandra," Ruby said.

Smiling nervously, Alexandra said. "Yes, I am. You must be Mrs. Michaels."

"Ruby. Come in, honey. It's so very nice to meet you. I've heard so much about you."

"Thank you. It's nice to meet you, too," Alexandra said as she walked into the house.

She thought Warren's mother was a strikingly beautiful woman.

Mr. Michaels was sitting in the den watching television with Will.

"Hey, Alexandra. What's up, sweetie?" Will said as he got up and kissed her cheek.

"Hi, Will. How ya' doin'?"

"I'm okay. This is my dad. Daddy, this is Warren's girlfriend, Alexandra."

"Hello, Mr. Michaels. It's nice to meet you," Alexandra said as she extended her hand to greet Warren's father.

"Hi, Alexandra. It's nice to meet you, too. How are you?"

"I'm fine, thank you. How are you?"

"Not bad."

"How was your flight up?" she asked Ruby and her husband as she removed her coat.

"It was good," Ruby answered as she joined BW on the sofa.

"How long will you be staying?"

"We'll be here until after the New Year."

"Oh, good."

"Do I hear the love of my life?" Warren called as he walked down the hall toward the den.

Alexandra stepped into the hallway and smiled.

"Hi."

"Hey, baby," he said as he grabbed her and kissed her passionately, not caring that his parents were right there.

"Warren," she said, slightly embarrassed by his ardor.

"What? Oh, don't worry about them," he said, waving his parents off. "They're worse than me."

Everyone laughed.

"Did you meet everybody?" he then asked.

"Yes, I did. Hey, where's Wanda?" Alexandra suddenly asked.

"In the kitchen," Warren said.

"Well, let me go upstairs and put my stuff away," Alexandra said.

"Hurry up, baby. We were holding dinner for you," Warren said.

"Okay. I'll be right down."

Christmas with Warren's family was a lot of fun for Alexandra.

Ruby had made an incredible feast, which included

roast turkey and stuffing, baked ham, beans and rice, and a number of other delectable dishes. After dinner everyone sat in front of the tree and fireplace exchanging stories about past Christmases.

It was a tradition in the Michaels family to exchange gifts at the stroke of midnight on Christmas Day.

By twelve-thirty, all the gifts had been exchanged with the exception of Warren's gift to Alexandra. He had asked her a number of times what she wanted and she had never really been able to make up her mind.

With great anticipation, she slowly unwrapped her present as his family looked on. Her hands trembled as she opened the jewelry case that held her gift. She sucked in her breath in awe as she spied the object in the box. It was a two carat diamond tennis bracelet in an eighteen karat gold jacket. She could not believe her eyes.

She looked over at him as he sat next to her, praying to himself that she would like the gift.

"Warren," she whispered, not knowing what else to say.

She had never seen anything so beautiful in her life.

"Do you like it?" he asked softly.

"It's beautiful. It's so beautiful," she said as tears came to her eyes.

"Can I see?" Ruby asked.

Alexandra handed her the case.

Ruby, BW, Will, and Wanda oohed and aahed at the sight of the bracelet.

"It's beautiful," Ruby said, handing the case back to Alexandra. "Wear it in good health."

"Thank you, Ruby."

She took the bracelet out of the case. "It really is beautiful, Warren. I love it. Thank you."

"You're beautiful, Alexandra."

"Would you fasten it for me?"

As he fastened the bracelet on her arm, he said, "I'm glad you like it."

She reached over and hugged him. "I love you," she said, for his ears only.

"I love you, too, baby. Merry Christmas."

Christmas morning, though they all went to bed after two A.M., Alexandra was awake at seven-thirty. As she knelt on the floor in front of the toilet, she prayed that there was some logical explanation, other than the obvious one, for the nausea she had been having the last few mornings. She tried again to remember a time in the last month that she and Warren had not used protection. From the beginning, their lovemaking had always been extremely passionate and quite spontaneous, but since Susan's pregnancy had come to light, she and Warren had tried to be extra careful.

"Alexandra, are you okay?"

Warren was standing just on the other side of the door. He had heard her retching from the bed.

"Yeah," she called back.

He eased the door open just to make sure.

"What's the matter, baby?"

"I don't know. I just feel really sick to my stomach."

He did not know about her sickness the other mornings because he had not stayed with her.

He walked over to her and helped her to her feet.

"Do you think it's something you ate?" he asked with concern.

"I don't know. I just don't feel good."

"Do you wanna lay back down?"

"Yeah."

Warren led her slowly back into the bedroom after she had rinsed her mouth out and washed her face.

He laid her gently on the bed and sat beside her, caressing her face.

"Do you want me to get you anything? Would you like some tea or something?"

"No, thank you. I just want to lay here for a little while."

"All right, sweetheart. You rest."

Alexandra experienced the same symptoms for the next two mornings, prompting Warren to ask the inevitable question on Saturday.

"Are you pregnant?"

They were in the bathroom. She had just finished brushing her teeth.

"No," she said hastily.

"Are you sure?"

"I'm not pregnant, Warren."

"Did you get your period this month?"

She did not want to tell him, but her period was indeed late, now by two weeks.

"No, but it's not always regular. It's been late before without me being pregnant," she lied.

"Yeah, but were you sick like this in the morning?"

"It's probably just a virus," she said, trying to brush the matter off. "There's one going around at my office."

"Alexandra. I'm not stupid and I'm not blind. If you're pregnant, tell me. I want to know."

"I'm not pregnant, okay. I'm not," she said adamantly.

She moved past him and back into the bedroom. Warren did not miss the antagonistic tone in her voice.

He followed her into the bedroom. He sat in his lounge chair and watched her as she began rifling through her overnight bag, knowing that she was avoiding him.

"You sound as if you wouldn't want to have a baby with me," he said sadly.

She looked over at him, but shifted her eyes quickly so he could not read her thoughts.

"I don't think it would be a good idea at the time, that's all."

"Why not?"

"If you recall, Susan's already taken care of that."

He rose from the chair and started toward her.

"I didn't ask Susan to have my baby. I'd much rather it be you."

"Well, it's a little late for that now."

"Alexandra . . ."

"Look, Warren, what difference does it make? I'm not pregnant. I'm not having a baby, okay, so let's just drop it."

That night, Warren and Alexandra, along with Wanda and her photographer boyfriend, Mario, took Ruby and Warren, Sr., to dinner at Michaels Too. Alexandra had forgotten about the unpleasant conversation of the morning and was feeling very giddy for no apparent reason. Warren, however, was bothered by the fact that she was not being honest with him. He did not believe her when she told him she was not pregnant.

Warren had spoken to his mother about her morning sickness the day before, and though Ruby had not mentioned it to Alexandra, she kept a close watch on her. She liked Alexandra and thought highly of her for the way she was handling the situation with Susan. Though Warren had already told her, Ruby could see that he was very much in love with her. She was glad that Alexandra had not turned her back on him.

For dinner, Alexandra had ordered her favorite dish,

jumbo shrimp stuffed with deviled crabmeat. They were seated in a booth with Warren on the end and Alexandra next to him. When their meals arrived, Alexandra began to feel a bit queasy but tried to ignore the unsettled feeling she was having in her stomach. When her dinner was placed in front of her, however, she immediately felt as if she was going to throw up. The smell was horrible.

"Move! Move, Warren! Quick, I have to go!" she said as she covered her mouth.

Warren rose from his seat, shocked by her outburst. She had almost pushed him to the floor. She ran from the table in the direction of the ladies' room.

"Whoa, what's up?" Mario asked.

"Is Alexandra pregnant?" Wanda asked.

Warren looked at his mother before he answered. "She says she's not," he said sadly.

Everyone was silent for the next couple of seconds. The tension was thick enough to cut with a knife.

"I'll go check on her," Ruby said. "Let me out, BW."

When Ruby reached the ladies' room, Alexandra was at the sink wetting a paper towel. She had not quite made it and had slightly messed up her blouse.

"Are you okay, honey?" Ruby asked.

Alexandra was crying, mostly from embarrassment.

"I'm sorry. I don't know what's the matter with me," she sobbed.

"Here, let me see."

Ruby took the paper towel and gently dabbed the spot where Alexandra had soiled her blouse.

"How are you feeling?" Ruby asked.

"I was fine till they brought out the food. The smell just got to me. That's never happened before," she lamented.

"Have you ever been pregnant before?" Ruby asked.

"No. I don't think that's what's wrong, though."

Ruby knew the symptoms. Being a nurse and a

mother who had gone through morning sickness with each of her three children made her quite the expert.

"Have you missed any periods?"

"My period's not always regular."

"Alexandra, I can understand your reluctance to acknowledge what may be true, especially with Susan and all, but denying it is not going to change the facts. Warren is very worried about you, honey. Why don't you talk to him."

"And tell him what? I can't have a baby now. I just can't."

Wanda entered the ladies' room then.

"Alexandra, are you all right?"

"Yeah. I'm okay," she said as she wiped her eyes.

"Oh, your blouse is wet," Wanda noticed.

"It'll dry. Don't worry about it. It's not too bad," Ruby added.

"I guess we'd better go back," Alexandra said, not wanting to discuss her condition any longer.

Warren was very solemn through the remainder of their dinner. Alexandra ended up eating only some plain white rice and a couple of dinner rolls.

After dinner, they all went downstairs to the club to dance. Warren's mood had lightened a bit with Alexandra's coaxing.

They were all sitting at a table, laughing about a story Mario had told them about some kids he had been working with, when Susan approached their table. Neither Warren nor Alexandra had seen her approach, as they were sitting with the backs to the door.

"Mr. and Mrs. Michaels! Hi! Merry Christmas! It's good to see you again," Susan said brightly.

"Hello, Susan," Ruby answered, cordially.

"Hello," BW said.

"How are you?"

"We're fine, thank you," Ruby answered. "How are you?"

"Oh, I'm doing okay, considering."

Wanda, who was sitting next to her mother, did not acknowledge Susan but stared at her openly until Susan became very uncomfortable and turned to Warren.

"Hello, Warren. Merry Christmas."

"Hello, Susan," he said in a monotone.

"I'm sure Warren's already told you that *we're* having a baby," Susan said to his parents.

Alexandra sat where she was, stock-still, though her hands trembled and her heart was beating so loud she was surprised that it could not be heard over the music.

"He told us you were pregnant," Ruby said nonchalantly.

"Did he tell you we're having a boy? You're going to have a grandson come April."

"Is that right?"

Alexandra turned to Warren upon hearing this bit of information. He would not look at her.

"Excuse me," Alexandra said as she rose from her chair and walked away from the table.

Warren rose then, turning to Susan.

"Do you always have to be the center of attention, Susan?" he said angrily.

"What are you talking about?"

"Just stay away from my family, okay?" he said, then walked past her.

Susan wore a smirk as she watched Warren walk away. She thought to herself, *now I'm your family.*

When Alexandra left the table, she headed straight upstairs and to the coatroom. Warren caught up with her just as she was pulling her coat on.

"Alexandra! Where are you going?"

"I need some air."

"Baby, wait," he said as he grabbed her arm.

"No, Warren. I need some air. I'm going for a walk."

"Well, wait, I'll go with you."

"No. I want to be alone for a while."

"But it's so late. I don't want you—"

"Look, Warren, I feel like I'm about to explode right now, okay. Just let me go. I just want to be alone. I'll be back," she said, and turned away from him and walked out the door.

Warren stood where he was and watched her go. He felt as though he was losing her now for sure. He asked himself why Susan insisted on making his life miserable. *I told her I would take care of her baby, what more does she want from me?* he lamented. His blood began to boil. *If she thinks I'm going to stand still and let her destroy what I have with Alexandra, she's got another think coming.*

He turned then and headed back downstairs. He had to get Susan out of his club. The last thing he wanted was for Alexandra to come back and have to be faced with her again.

As he reached the bottom of the landing, he ran into his father.

"Warren."

"Excuse me, Dad, I have to do something," Warren said, trying to move past his father.

"No! Warren, wait," BW said as he restrained him.

"Daddy, I want her out of here!"

Warren was so angry that his eyes were watering. BW could see that if he did not stop his son now, someone was going to get hurt.

"Calm down, man, calm down. This is not the way to do it," he said.

"Dad . . ." Warren's voice was awash with emotion.

"Take it easy, son."

He held Warren until he felt his resistance ease. "Where's Alexandra?"

"She went outside. She said she wanted to be alone," Warren said dejectedly.

"Come on upstairs. Let's sit down for a moment," BW said, placing a comforting arm on his son's shoulder.

Though the restaurant was closed, Warren and his father walked through the darkened room and over to the bar. Warren sat on one of the stools.

"You want a drink?" BW asked as he stepped behind the bar.

"Yeah, I guess."

Warren Michaels, Sr., poured his son a shot of Absolut and one for himself.

"I don't understand it. I don't know why she's doing this to me," Warren said solemnly.

"Revenge."

"For what? I've never done anything to her. I've done too much for her, if you ask me. The entire time we were together, I treated her like a queen and she dogged me every chance she got. She was always accusing me of cheating on her and I never did. Never! She used to start stuff with me in here, just to make a scene so everyone would know that I was her man. Two years I put up with that nonsense. Two years too many, and now when I thought I'd finally gotten her out of my life, she's starting this. I don't deserve it."

"Warren, don't let this get the best of you. Misery loves company. Susan's miserable, Son, so she's got to make you miserable, too."

"She's carrying my baby. My son," Warren said reflectively.

"How do you feel about that?"

"I'm angry and I'm scared."

"No man wants to be forced into fatherhood, Son."

"But the way I feel . . . It's wrong. Every time I look at this kid, I'm gonna be reminded of what she's doing to me. Every time. That's not fair. It's not fair to me and it's not fair to this baby. I don't want to feel this way, but how can I help it? She's making it very difficult for me to be considerate of her feelings."

"Warren, when your son is born, you'll feel differently."

"No, Daddy, I won't. I know I won't. Alexandra is pregnant. She won't confirm it, but I know she is."

Warren was extremely sad about the idea that Alexandra might decide not to have his baby.

"Your mother seems to think Alexandra is very special. I'm sure you feel that way, too. Think about it, Warren, if she didn't care about you, she would have walked the moment she found out about Susan. But she didn't. She stuck by you because she loves you. Don't assume that she's going to turn her back on you now."

"I don't know what to do, Dad."

"Well, you have to try to look at the situation from her point of view. She probably feels like she's on the outside looking in. She has no control over what's going on with Susan, and you're in the middle of it, no matter what. She's not a part of it. Try to imagine all the things that must be going through her head right now, knowing that some other woman is going to be bringing your child into this world. You can't expect her to just go along with the program without there being some friction, no matter how much she loves you."

"I just feel like I'm losing her," Warren said sadly.

"Maybe not. Don't give up hope."

Alexandra did not go far when she left Michaels Too. Actually, she walked into the parking lot and stood near

Warren's car and cried. She was oblivious to the cold. Her heart was broken, and the pain from that seemed to block out all of her other senses.

Susan was having a boy. She was giving Warren a son. How could she compete with that? Every man wants a son.

Regardless of what he told her, she knew once he saw his little boy, Warren would forget all about how much he disliked Susan and do anything to be a part of his son's life.

Unconsciously, she began to caress her own abdomen. She was carrying his baby, too. She wanted to share the joy of being a part of his life forever but Susan was making sure there was no room left in his life for her. She felt so totally defeated.

How can I look at him now, knowing all of this? she wondered. She did not want it to appear that she was having a baby simply to try and outdo Susan. That would be what everyone thought if she decided to keep the baby. But how would he feel? Really. He said he wanted her to have his baby, but was that simply because of Susan? Would he try to use her to get back at Susan for what she was doing to him?

Aside from all of that, though, she wondered why he had not told her that Susan was having a boy. Did he think he was helping matters by keeping these things from her? Didn't he realize that every time she found out another piece of information about their alliance from Susan, it just added to the despair and disillusionment she had begun to feel since this whole thing came to light?

Did he think he was protecting her by keeping these little tidbits to himself? Though Alexandra had never looked at Susan's face when she came over to their table, she could hear the satisfaction in Susan's voice every time she surprised her with her little bits of news.

She had to decide if she could continue the masquerade she had been putting on ever since she found out about Susan. Could she continue to smile and act like she was not fazed by everything that was happening? Was it fair to Warren to pretend that she could take this all in stride? She loved him, more than she had ever loved anyone, but she was also hurting more than she ever had before because of him.

She stayed outside for almost thirty minutes. When she went back to the club, she felt as though she had her emotions pretty much in check.

She noticed Warren sitting at the bar in the restaurant with his father. She did not go over to him, instead she checked her coat again and went back downstairs.

Ruby, Wanda, and Mario were still sitting where she had left them.

"Hi," she said, as she sat down.

"You okay?" Ruby asked.

"Yeah."

"Was Warren with you?" Wanda asked.

"No, he's upstairs with your father."

"Alexandra, don't let Susan's antics bother you," Wanda said.

"I really don't want to talk about her, okay?" Alexandra said dolefully.

"That's all right, honey. I don't want to hear anything more about her myself," Ruby said in disgust.

Sixteen

Susan left the club about one-thirty and went straight home and to bed. She was up, however, at seven o'clock. She had slept terribly. Her little bundle had been moving all over the place, and as a result she was unable to get comfortable. Additionally, she had not been able to erase from her mind the look in Warren's eyes when he told her to stay away from his family.

He hates me, she thought. *He really hates me.*

This was not what she wanted. She did not expect him to be falling all over himself to be with her, but she did want them to at least be friendly. She needed him, after all. She knew she probably should not have approached him while he was with Alexandra, but she felt a deep resentment about their relationship. Though in the past when she had accused him of cheating on her, it had largely been speculation, she was positive that he was involved with Alexandra while they were still together.

Still, she figured that even though Warren was acting as though he was not happy about her pregnancy, he would probably be breaking his neck to see his son once he was born. After all, every man wants a son, she reasoned, regardless of what he said.

She got up from bed and went to the bathroom. She washed her face and brushed her teeth, though the taste of her toothpaste had become quite unbearable since she became pregnant.

She lumbered into her kitchen to fix herself a pot of herbal tea. She opened the cupboard and pulled down a can of sardines and the jar of peanut butter. She would have the two with a couple of slices of oat bran toast.

She was just finishing off the can of sardines when her doorbell suddenly rang. She looked up at the clock on the wall. Seven forty-five.

"Who the hell is that at this time of the morning?" she grumbled.

She was wearing a long flannel nightgown and fluffy slippers and her hair was unkempt, but she figured whoever had the audacity to ring her bell this early did not warrant her putting on her best face.

"Who is it?" she asked testily.

"Jeff" came the response.

"Who?"

"Jeff!"

Susan unlocked the door, but did not remove the chain catch. She looked through the three-and-a-half-inch space afforded by the chain at the man standing there.

"Hey, baby. Aren't you gonna let me in?" he asked with a devilish grin.

He looked even better than he had when she last saw him in July. He was wearing a tan sheepskin jacket and his close-cropped salt-and-pepper hair was covered by a brown wool baseball cap. He stood there in his tight-fitting jeans and cowboy boots with his devil-may-care attitude that she so disliked but could not resist. She hated the way he seemed to always pop up when she least expected, catching her in the most awkward situations. It was like he had a sixth sense or something.

She closed the door without responding and slowly

slid the chain out of the latch. She took a deep breath, then opened the door.

"What's up, sweetie? Merry Christmas and Happy New Year," he said.

He stepped into the apartment and put down the duffel bag he was carrying as if he belonged there.

Susan still had not acknowledged him, but she stood near the door and watched as he began to remove his coat and hat.

"How you doin', baby? You look like you've put on a little weight."

"What are you doing here?" she asked flatly.

"What do you mean, what am I doing here? What do you think I'm doing here? I told you I'd be coming in about this time when I spoke to you last month, didn't I? Have I ever lied to you? Have I ever told you I would do something and then didn't?"

Susan started to move away from the door and toward the living-room sofa. He grabbed her then and embraced her.

"Aren't you happy to see me? I thought you'd be . . . Hey, what's this?" he asked, suddenly noticing the bulge in her middle.

She had not told him of her condition when they spoke a month ago.

He held her at arm's length, looking at her in stunned disbelief.

"You're pregnant?"

"No. I swallowed a watermelon."

"When did this happen?"

"About five months ago," she answered as she stepped away from him.

"Five months ago? Why didn't you tell me? Is it mine?" he asked warily.

"No. It's not yours."

"Then whose is it?"

"Who do you think?"

"Warren?"

"Good guess." She plopped down on her sofa.

"Are you sure?"

She gave him a look of disapproval as she said, "Of course, I'm sure."

"So you're still seeing him, huh?" he said, a touch of sadness in his voice.

"No. We broke up."

Jeff came and sat next to her.

"Then why are you having his baby?"

"Because I want to," she answered, looking him squarely in the eye.

"Does he know?"

"Yes."

"Is he taking care of you?"

She looked down.

He very gently touched his hand to her chin and raised her head.

"You know, Susan, that I would do anything for you. If he's not willing to own up to his responsibility like a man and be a father to your child, you know I will."

"He said he would take care of his baby."

"But what about you?"

She did not answer.

"Why put yourself through that, Sue? You don't need any man whose not gonna do the right thing by you. You're too good for that, baby," Jeff said as he caressed her face. "I'll take care of you and your baby. I'll give you anything you need. Anything you want. All you have to do is say the word."

"And what about your wife?"

"You know I'm not with her anymore. I told you that when I was here in July."

Susan got up from the sofa and walked slowly to the

window. She took in the fantastic view of Central Park covered in snow as her eyes began to water.

Jeff rose from the sofa and stood behind her, embracing her gently.

"You know I love you, Sue. I always have."

She leaned against him, taking comfort in his warm embrace. With all of the madness that had been going on in her life in these last few months, it was nice to feel that there was one thing that had not changed. Jeff Foster was the one constant in her life, and she knew he would always be. And now, just as always, he was here for her when she felt as though her world was caving in. He was her rock, and though she genuinely cared for Warren, she realized she was still very much in love with Jeff.

"How long will you be here?"

"Until the second. I have a gig on New Year's Eve."

"Where are you staying?"

He smiled and turned her around to face him.

"Right here," he said, smiling.

She looked up at him and could not help but smile herself. He was so damn cocksure that she wanted to smack him.

She tried to move away from him but he restrained her.

"How have you been feeling?"

"Other than fat, okay, I guess."

"When's your next doctor's appointment?"

"Tomorrow."

"Good. I'll go with you."

"You don't have to."

"Yes, I do. Somebody's got to take care of you. Do you know what you're having?"

"A boy."

"Yeah? That's great! Are you gonna name him after me?" he asked with a sardonic smile.

She chuckled and said, "Maybe."

He hugged her close then.

"It's so good to see you, baby. I missed you. Did you miss me?"

She could not tell a lie.

"Yes."

He kissed her softly on her lips. As he held her, he could feel the life she carried moving against him.

"Active little fella you've got there."

"I know. He's always bouncing around when I'm trying to sleep."

"He's trying to get you ready for when he gets here. He wants to let you know that there'll be no sleeping on the job."

She laughed.

"You look beautiful, you know," he said softly.

"No, I don't. I look fat."

"No, you don't. You look beautiful."

He ran his hand through her hair, smoothing it back as he studied her face intensely.

"I want to make love to you," he sighed.

"Jeff, no."

"Why not?"

She moved away from him. She pressed her flannel nightgown against her body, defining the bulge in her stomach.

"Look at me!"

"I am."

"Jeff . . ."

"When's the last time you've been made love to?" he asked, cutting her off.

"That's not the point."

"Then what is?"

"I'm pregnant."

"Yeah, so?"

"Jeff . . ."

"I love you, baby. I want to show you how much."

He moved toward her.

"Listen, wouldn't it be nice to be pampered and cuddled and made to feel like you are the most beautiful woman in the world?"

She shook her head and smiled but did not comment.

"Come here," he said, reaching for her hand. "Wouldn't you like a nice massage? I'm sure with this extra weight you're carrying now, you must get backaches every now and then. Am I right?"

"Yeah, but what's that got to do with making love?" she asked.

"If I give you a massage, you know you're gonna want to make love to me," he said confidently as he wrapped her in his arms.

"Are you always so sure of yourself?"

"No."

"I'm fat, Jeff. I'm deformed," she argued.

"Stop saying that! You are not fat. And even if you were, so what? I love you! The person, not the shell, though I've never had any complaints about that, either," he quickly added with a smirk.

"Doesn't it bother you that I'm carrying Warren's child?"

"Of course, it does. I wish it was mine. As a matter of fact, I'm not convinced that it's not mine, regardless of what you say. I was with you five months ago. It could be mine. Besides, he's not here and you need someone to take care of you, Susan. I want to be that someone. I always have, you know that."

She did not respond.

He gently lifted her chin so she could look into his eyes.

"Sweetie, you are my angel," he said softly. "I've never loved anyone the way I love you and I know I never will. Give me a chance. Let me take care of you. Warren's a fool. He never deserved you anyway."

Susan could feel tears coming to her eyes as she looked into his big brown ones. She had always loved him, too. If it were not for his music and the fact that he was always on the road, they would be together now, she knew that. She wanted to believe they could have a life together, but knowing that in a few days he would be gone again, was too painful for her to put aside.

And when she thought about the little boy she was carrying, she cringed at the idea that Warren would not be there for her. He promised her he would be there for his child. She believed him. Being honest with herself, she had to acknowledge that Warren had never broken a promise he made to her. She had no reason to believe he suddenly would.

She was glad Jeff had come. She thought at first he would be angry at finding out that she was carrying Warren's child. She had not expected him to be so wonderful about the whole situation, but she did not know why she was surprised. He had always been there for her, willingly, no matter what the circumstances.

She put her arms around him and hugged him tight. She needed someone to love her and comfort her and just be there. She knew Jeff could and would do all that for her, and more.

Seventeen

Alexandra, too, was up at seven Sunday morning. Unlike Susan, though, she was once again bent over the toilet, battling another bout of morning sickness.

She had slept fitfully all night.

The family did not stay at Michaels Too very late. After Susan's sudden appearance and her unexpected announcement, everyone's mood was somewhat tainted.

Warren was on pins and needles as he and Alexandra got into bed that night. He was expecting a confrontation much like the one when she found out about Susan's pregnancy. But she never said a word. That unnerved him more than anything else.

The reason Alexandra slept so poorly was because she was confused about what she should do. She loved Warren deeply, but she could not ignore what was happening with him and Susan.

He obviously knew before last night that she was having a boy. Just as he knew before she actually saw for herself that Susan was pregnant. Why would he keep secrets from her if he really felt about Susan the way he claimed?

She figured the reason he did not tell her Susan was going to have a boy was because, whether he wanted to admit it or not, he was probably very excited about the prospect of having a son.

After she was sure that there was nothing else in her stomach to be thrown up, Alexandra shakily rose to her feet. She held on to the towel rack near the sink for support. She felt terrible. *How much longer am I going to have to endure this?* she wondered. She could not continue much longer. Though she had never discussed her condition with Warren, she had already decided that she would not keep this baby. Her only problem was that she was afraid to go through with the procedure.

She made her way to the sink and brushed her teeth to get the disgusting taste of her own vomit out of her mouth. As she looked at her reflection in the bathroom mirror, her eyes began to water. There were dark circles under her eyes from crying all night and not getting enough rest.

"What am I going to do?" she cried aloud.

She wanted to give Warren a son. Maybe this was a boy she was carrying. But how could she have this baby now?

She knew he was aware that she was pregnant, regardless of what she told him. After all, he was not stupid.

She felt betrayed, though she knew in her heart that he had not done this to spite her. She wanted to believe that he was as mortified about this whole situation as she was. But how could she believe him if he would not be honest with her?

She was angry with him, but she was afraid to express her true feelings for fear she would lose him.

Slowly, after more than fifteen minutes in the bathroom, she emerged and lumbered back into the bedroom. Warren was awake. He lay quietly on his side and watched as she made her way back to the bed.

She pulled the covers up to her chin and turned her back to him. Once again, her eyes began to tear.

Warren moved closer to her and gently put his arm

around her, pulling her closer. He kissed the back of her neck softly and whispered, "I love you, Ally."

She did not say a word.

He was afraid. He felt as though she was slipping away from him and that there was no way he could pull her back.

I should have told her about Susan, he thought. He cursed himself for not learning from the last time. He had almost lost her when she found out that Susan was pregnant. He was sure that whole ordeal could have been avoided if he had only been straight with her. And yet, knowing that, he again was not honest with her. *Why didn't I tell her when Susan came to the restaurant that day?* he asked himself.

"Baby, I'm sorry about last night," he said softly.

She lay there, as still as she could.

He could feel her body tense with his words.

At that moment, Alexandra hated him. How could he allow Susan to continually embarrass her the way she did? He had to know how embarrassing it was to be the last to find out that your man is having a baby with someone else. Then to be the last to know that the baby was a boy.

She abruptly threw the covers off and rose from the bed. She had to get away from him. She could not bear to be near him at that moment.

She was glad her car was there.

She went to the closet and got out a pair of jeans. She pulled them on quickly, then carelessly threw a sweatshirt on over the T-shirt she had worn to bed.

"Where are you going?" Warren asked as he sat up.

"Home."

He leapt from the bed immediately and stepped in front of her.

"Why?"

"Because I don't want to be here right now," she said angrily.

"Baby, I know I should have told you . . ."

"Why? Why should you have told me? You haven't told me anything else. I've had to find out everything else on my own, why should you have suddenly told me anything?"

"Ally, please don't leave," he pleaded.

She did not respond. She continued to don her clothing. She sat on the bed and pulled on a pair of sweat socks and hurriedly threw on her sneakers.

"Alexandra. Please? Don't go, baby."

She got up from the bed and stepped around him. She grabbed her pocketbook off his dresser as she headed toward the bedroom door. Warren grabbed her arm to stop her from leaving.

"Let go of me," she said, turning to him angrily.

Tears were rolling down her cheeks.

"Ally, I'm sorry."

"So am I. Now, let me go."

She did not raise her voice, nor did she sound demanding. Instead, her voice was cold and unfeeling. It sent a chill up Warren's spine.

He released her and she immediately turned and walked out of the bedroom. She headed for the stairs, descending quickly and stopped at the closet near the front door to remove her coat.

She hurriedly donned her coat and unlocked the front door, seemingly in one motion. She did not turn back once as she quickly exited, slamming the door behind her.

Warren sat on the bed with his head in his hands feeling totally defeated. He heard the door slam, signaling her departure, and could not ignore the symbolism behind it. She was not only walking out of his house, she was walking out of his life.

* * *

Ruby Michaels was also awake at seven A.M., though for very different reasons. She was very much in the habit of waking up early. She worked the seven-to-three shift at the hospital where she was employed, so she was usually at work by this time of morning.

She was in the kitchen, kneading dough to make her famous angel soft biscuits when she heard the front door slam. She wiped her hands on the dish towel lying on the counter and left the kitchen to investigate the noise.

When she reached the front door, she peeked out of the foyer window to see if anyone was outside. She saw Alexandra's car drive away.

She turned and went back upstairs and straight to Warren's room.

The door was open, and when she looked in she saw him sitting on the bed with his head in his hands.

"Warren, what happened, baby?" Ruby asked as she sat next to her son. She put her arm around his shoulder.

When he looked up at his mother, she could see the anguish in his eyes.

"I messed up, Mom. I've lost her."

"Shh, take it easy, baby," Ruby said in a soothing voice.

"How am I gonna get her back?"

"She needs time, honey. She just needs some time."

Ruby felt sorry for her son. She knew how much he loved Alexandra. Before she had even met her, Ruby had a clear picture of what she looked like, her personality, and everything else from the many conversations with Warren in which he constantly sang her praises.

"I should have told her myself."

"Why didn't you, Warren?" Ruby asked.

"I was afraid to."

"Honey, I know how difficult this is for you. I know Susan is putting you through the wringer with this whole mess, but if you really love Alexandra the way you say you do, you have to be honest with her and trust that she will understand and be empathetic to what's happening. If you continue to hide the truth from her, you're only leaving it open for Susan to step in and throw her own wrench into the works and screw everything up."

"I know, Mom. I know I should have told her. I don't know why I didn't. You would think I'd have learned from before. She came back then, but I know she's probably gone for good this time," Warren lamented.

"Don't give up on her so easily. She's stuck with you this far. Who's to say that she's given up on you. She probably just needs time to herself to try and sort out her feelings," Ruby told him.

"I hope you're right. I don't know what I'd do if I lost her now. I've never loved anyone like this before. She's very important to me."

"I know she is, sweetheart. Just have faith that everything will work out for the best. That's all we can do right now. Just have faith."

Eighteen

After sitting in her apartment alone for over five hours brooding about Warren and Susan and their unborn son, Alexandra decided that she needed to get out. She had to do something, anything, that would take her mind off Warren.

She called Shari at a little after one in the afternoon, hoping her friend would be interested in seeing a movie with her.

The call was answered with an impatient, "Yeah?"

"Shari?"

"Yeah. Alex?"

"Hi. What you doin'?"

"You just caught me stepping out of the shower."

"Oh. Do you feel like going to the movies?" Alexandra asked.

"I don't care. I'm not doing anything else today. I don't think I'm going to be seeing Vernon anymore."

"Why not? What happened?"

"I don't know. He's been acting real funny lately—ever since Christmas. I don't know what's up with him, but I don't have time to try and figure it out. How's Warren?" Shari then asked.

"I really don't want to talk about Warren," Alexandra said.

"What's the matter?"

"Susan's having a boy."

"How do you know?"

Alexandra replayed the events of the previous night.

"Damn," Shari sighed.

She also decided to share with Shari the secret she had been keeping to herself.

"I'm pregnant, Shari."

"What?"

"I'm pregnant."

"Oh, no. Are you sure?"

"Yeah. I've been getting sick every morning for the last week and my period is three weeks late."

"Does Warren know?"

"Yeah, even though I haven't told him. He knows I've been getting sick and he knows my period is late."

"What are you gonna do?"

"I don't know."

"What does he want you to do?"

"He wants me to have it. I know that and we haven't really even talked about it but I know that's what he wants. Probably just to get back at Susan."

"Damn, baby, is there anything I can do?" Shari asked with genuine concern.

"No," Alexandra said pitifully.

"Well, you know anytime you need me, just call me. Anything I can do, you've got it."

"Thanks, Shari."

"Hey, look, what movie do you wanna see?" Shari asked, trying to lighten the mood.

"I don't care. Anything. I just don't want to sit in this house all by myself today."

"You want me to meet you somewhere?"

"No, I'll come and get you. What time?"

"I'll be ready in twenty minutes. Whenever you're ready," Shari said.

"I'm leaving now."

"All right. See you in a few."

Alexandra didn't return to her apartment that evening until almost nine o'clock. She was glad that she had spent the day with Shari. She felt one hundred percent better than she had when they spoke earlier that afternoon. Not only had they gone to the movies but they did a little impromptu shopping, netting Alexandra a pair of boots and a new coat, and they also treated themselves to a very extravagant seafood dinner at the Lobster Pot.

After putting away her new coat and boots, she checked her answering machine for messages, expecting that there would be one from Warren.

There was. She sat down on her bed and listened.

"Hi, Ally. This is Warren. If you're there, would you please pick up?" There was a long pause. "Well, I guess you're not there and if you are, I can understand why you wouldn't want to talk to me right now. I know I should have told you about Susan. I'm sorry you had to find out like that. I hope you can forgive me for being such a coward about all of this. I want you to know that no matter what you think, I really do love you. I don't want to lose you. Please call me when you get this message. Even if it's to curse me out. I just want to hear your voice. Please call me?"

There was a long beep, signaling the end of the message.

Her eyes were watering and she could not ignore the fact that his voice sounded very shaky near the end of the recording.

She really wanted to call him, too, but something inside her told her to wait, to take her time and let him think about the consequences of not being honest with her.

She rewound the tape and listened to the message again.

As she got ready for bed, she thought about everything that had happened between them since she first learned of Susan's pregnancy. She considered the fact that he had known for a whole month before he ever said anything to her. Then she considered that had she not seen Susan with her protruding belly, he might have never said anything to her about it. Then she weighed that against the fact that though she had seen Susan, he still had not said anything until she actually asked.

It made her wonder if he was still seeing Susan behind her back. She knew he had spoken to her once to tell her he would support their child but was that all there was to their relationship? After all, he kept the knowledge of Susan's pregnancy from her and the fact that he had seen her when she informed him of the baby's sex. What was his reasoning behind not telling her?

She turned out her bedroom light and lay down, snuggling deep under the covers. But she was not the least bit sleepy. She was wide awake. She placed her hand on her stomach, unconsciously feeling for the fetus growing inside her. Was this, too, a male child? Could she really give birth to a child for Warren, knowing that only months before Susan would also have given birth to his child? Could she continue to pretend that she was not as devastated by this whole incident as she really was.

When she met him in August, he was obviously unhappy with Susan and must have been for some time; otherwise they would not have broken up so abruptly. Though he swore they had always used protection, she now had her doubts. He and Susan had been together for over two years. He had to know that she wanted to have a baby. After all, if that was not what she really wanted, Alexandra reasoned that there would be no way she would have his baby after they had already broken up. She did not believe that Susan was such a desperate woman that she would bring a child into this world for the sole purpose of trying to win Warren back. Surely, she could not think that he or any man was deserving of such glorification.

She knew Susan was older than Warren by a few years and that she had no children. She probably wanted to have a baby, very much. But Alexandra believed, too, that Susan probably still loved him. She figured that had to be why she decided to keep the baby. Maybe she thought they would get back together.

Alexandra did not sleep well that night, having lain awake until well after midnight. She arose at six and decided to go running, despite the fact that it was pitch black outside and, according to the radio announcer, twenty-five degrees. She silently chided herself for allowing all this mess with Warren and Susan to disrupt her normal routine of exercise and stress-free living. She had not gone running in over two weeks.

When she arrived at her office that morning, she dove right into her work so as not to allow herself time to dwell on Warren. She knew he would be calling her sometime today, probably this morning, since she had not returned his call last night.

It was a little after one, and she had just returned from the ladies' room before going to lunch when her assistant gave her the message that Warren had called. She started to call him back but decided against it. She had too much work to do to allow him to distract her with his pleas of forgiveness.

When she left her office that evening at six-fifteen, she was not surprised to see Warren waiting outside for her. She could not deny that she was happy to see him, despite all that had happened.

"Hi, Alexandra."

"Hello," she said, coolly.

He placed a hesitant kiss on her lips.

"How are you?"

"All right, I guess," she said.

"I hope you don't mind that I came by to get you."

"No."

"Are you hungry?" he asked as he moved to open the car door for her.

"I'm starving."

She got into the car and immediately fastened her seat belt. When he got back in the car he asked, "Anywhere in particular you want to eat?"

"No. It doesn't matter."

As he started the car, he looked over at her and smiled.

"You look very pretty today."

"Thank you," she softly responded.

As he wheeled the car into traffic, he asked, "Would you mind if I stayed with you tonight?"

"No," she answered without hesitation.

"Thank you."

They were silent for the next five minutes as they drove through the remaining rush hour traffic.

"I'm sorry about Saturday night. I should have told you about her then," Warren suddenly said.

"It doesn't really matter."

He looked over at her then and when she looked at him, she could see the sadness in his eyes.

"I love you, Alexandra. I don't want to lose you."

It was just after nine when they arrived at Alexandra's apartment that night after dinner. They did not talk much as they prepared for bed.

Though it was it still early in her pregnancy, Alexandra found that after a full day of working, she was very tired. When she crawled into bed, she groaned from the nagging pain in the small of her back.

"What's the matter, baby?"

"My back hurts."

"Would you like me to rub it for you?"

"That would be nice," she answered.

"Turn over."

Warren sat on the bed beside her and pulled her nightgown up so that he could rub her back.

Alexandra could not deny her incredible feeling of relief as he massaged her aching muscles. His hands were like magic.

He continued his gentle massage until she sighed, "That feels so good."

He leaned over and kissed her on the small of her back where he had been rubbing.

"I love you, Ally."

She turned over onto her back. As she looked into his eyes, she could clearly see the love he felt for her. She knew that he had never meant to hurt her and that he had always done everything with her happiness in mind.

"I love you, too, Warren."

"Can I take this off?"

"If you want to," she said.

He sat up and helped her out of her nightgown. He kissed her shoulders gently as he whispered words of endearment.

She held his head against her breast, running her fingers through his soft, wavy hair. He moaned from the sensations her gentle caresses caused within him. He looked up at her and she kissed his lips. As she held him, thoughts of losing him to Susan flooded her mind, and her eyes began to water.

"What's the matter, sweetheart?"

"Nothing," she lied.

"Why are you crying?"

"Because I don't want to lose you, either."

"Ally, I'm not going anywhere. I'm here for you. Always. I don't want to think about you not being a part of my life."

"Make love to me."

He rose from the bed and removed his underwear. She reached out to touch him. As her hand enfolded his erection, he sighed in delight.

He leaned over her and touched her breasts, one at a time, noticing the changes in her body already. He took one nipple in his mouth and sucked gently, causing shivers of pleasure to run through her. She arched her back involuntarily, rising to his touch.

She caressed his body, gently tracing lines in his back with her fingernails.

"I want to feel you inside me, Warren," she whispered seductively.

He was on fire for her. But the passion and desire to feel her warmth surround him was equally matched. She wanted to feel the fullness of him, to be one with him like no one else could. She wanted to own him completely, to know that he was hers and hers alone. She wanted to push whatever memory he had of being with Susan from his mind. She did not want him to think of anyone other than her. She was being selfish tonight. He was her man and she was all the woman he needed.

They made love fiercely, as though they were each trying to prove to the other that there was no room for anyone else.

When they were both spent, a good hour and a half later, they lay together, exhausted and soaking wet as though they had just stepped out of the shower.

"I don't want to share you with anyone, Warren," Alexandra said softly.

"You don't have to, baby. There's no one else for me."

They lay in silence for almost twenty minutes. Alexandra had begun to doze into a blissful sleep when Warren's voice brought her fully awake.

"Marry me, Alexandra."

She turned to face him, as she had been snuggled against him with her back to him. He lay there, looking at her with tears in his eyes.

"What?"

"Marry me."

She was saddened by his words. How could she marry him, knowing that Susan was having his baby? How could she tell him no without breaking his heart?

"I know what you're thinking, Ally. I know you're thinking about Susan. But you have to know that I want to be with you forever. I don't care about her."

"Warren, she's having your baby."

"I don't care. I love you."

"I care. We can't get married now. There's too much stuff happening. You can't ignore what's happening."

He did not answer her. He lay next to her in silence, praying that he would not lose her.

Nineteen

Warren stayed with Alexandra at her apartment in Brooklyn the next night also, though his parents were still in town and staying at his house on Long Island.

As usual, every New Year's Eve, Warren gave a big party at Michaels Too. The affair was semiformal and tickets for the event were priced at sixty dollars per person, one hundred dollars per couple. For the past two years, the turnout for this bash was phenomenal. Warren expected the same this year.

Alexandra worked until almost seven o'clock that evening. Warren was planning to pick her up at her apartment, take her out to Huntington to change and pick up his parents, then they would all leave together to go to the club.

Warren arrived at Alexandra's apartment approximately twenty minutes after she got home.

For the past two days, she had been a bit depressed thinking about Warren's marriage proposal and their situation overall.

When she opened the door to let him in, he grabbed her around her waist and kissed her, immediately telling her how excited he was about the evening ahead.

They walked back upstairs to her apartment, without Alexandra commenting about any of the things he was saying to her. After they were inside and she had closed the door, Warren asked, "Are you ready to go, baby?"

She sat down on the sofa and sighed.

"I don't feel well, Warren."

"What?"

"I don't feel well."

"What's the matter?" he asked with genuine concern. He sat beside her on the sofa.

"My head is killing me."

"Did you take anything?"

"No."

"Why don't you take a couple of aspirin. You can nap in the car on the way to my house. You'll probably feel better by then. You're probably just tired."

She knew her next words would upset him, so she spoke barely above a whisper. "I don't really feel like going tonight."

"What did you say?"

He knew he had to be hearing things. She could not be telling him that she was not going to spend New Year's Eve with him.

Alexandra rose from the couch and moved slowly across the room. "I just want to stay home tonight, Warren."

"Baby, it's New Year's Eve. How are we going to stay home tonight? The party's going to be spectacular. You don't want to miss this."

"You can go without me. I really don't feel well."

"How am I going to go without you?" he asked in disbelief as he, too, rose from the couch.

"Your mother and father will be there."

"I want you there."

She sighed. She really did not want to go. She was sure she would see Susan there, and she was the last person she wanted to see on this particular night.

Warren must have read her mind.

"You're worried about Susan being there, aren't you?" he asked.

"No."

He did not hear her answer. He took a few steps toward her.

"Look, Ally, she won't be there. I won't let her in. I won't let her ruin this night for us."

"It's not Susan," Alexandra lied. She turned her back to him. "I really don't feel well."

He was becoming angry. He tried, however, to keep his anger in check.

"How can I have a New Year's Eve party without you. Everyone will be asking for you, you know that. What am I supposed to tell them?"

"Tell them the truth; that I don't feel well."

"What am I supposed to tell my mother and father when I come home and you're not with me?"

"Tell them I decided to stay home."

"Just like that?"

"Look, Warren, I'm sure your party will be just as good whether I'm there or not. I can't believe that my absence will make such a big difference in the outcome of this party."

"What about me, Alexandra? Don't you care how I feel?" he asked.

She turned back to him then.

"What about how *I* feel? You've never taken my feelings into account. I said I don't feel well. Am I such a terrible person because I'd rather stay home and make myself well than to keep up appearances for your sake?"

"Keep up appearances? Is that what you think I want? You're my woman. I want to bring in the New Year with you, not with a bunch of strangers."

"Your mother and father will be there and so will Wanda and Will. They're not strangers."

He turned away briefly and sighed in exasperation before he faced her again.

"So that's it, right? You're not going to come with me?"

"No."

She would not look at him.

"Fine! Then stay here!"

He strode angrily to the door, then stopped and turned back to her. He did not want to leave without her. He did not want to be alone tonight.

"Please, Alexandra," he pleaded one final time. "Please come with me?"

"Have fun, Warren. I'll be here," she said.

The sadness in his eyes was suddenly masked by anger once again. He turned without another word to her and walked out, slamming the door behind him.

Alexandra stepped over to the window and looked out. She watched as he got into his car without so much as a glance up at her window and angrily peeled away from the curb.

She did not feel she could smile and pretend that she was happy to be there with him when only four nights ago everyone had witnessed Susan in all her pregnant glory cause a scene with Warren and her and his family.

He did not seem to care that every time she saw Susan it made her feel like a fool. Everyone knew she was supposed to be his woman and everyone knew that Susan was his ex and it was, of course, no secret that she was carrying his child. It had reached a point where she did not ever want to be at Michaels Too. As soon as she turned her back, she felt that everyone pointed and laughed at her and whispered that she was a fool to stay in a relationship with a man that had fathered someone else's child.

She stepped away from the window and turned out

the living-room light. She locked the apartment door and slowly dragged herself to her bedroom. With great effort, she removed her clothes until she was in her panties, then she crawled under the covers and cried herself to sleep.

Alexandra was awakened the next morning at six-thirty by the ringing of her doorbell. As she sat up in the bed, she was surprised that she had slept straight through the night.

She got up slowly and threw on her robe. She knew it was no one other than Warren ringing her bell at this time of the morning.

They had exchanged keys a while back, but Warren never used the key to her apartment unless he knew she wasn't there. She thought about asking him why he hadn't used it today, especially since it was so early. When she thought again, however, she was actually surprised that he would even come back there since he was so angry when he'd left her.

She opened the door to the apartment and walked down the stairs to let him in. When she opened the outer door, he stood there for a moment before he entered the house. She could tell he had been drinking.

"Hi," she said.

"What's up?"

As he entered the house, he looked at her with what she interpreted as indignation.

"Happy New Year. How was it?"

"What difference does it make to you?"

"I just thought I'd ask."

She stepped in front of him and started up the stairs. Warren followed, staggering slowly. He watched her walking in front of him and was involuntarily aroused by the sight of her swaying hips beneath her robe.

He wanted to be angry with her. He had had a terrible time last night. He could not remember ever having such a lousy time at his club. He spent most of the evening sitting alone at the bar. His mother and father tried to cheer him up repeatedly, but to no avail. His sister, too, had tried to bring him out of his dark mood. Even Alexandra's best friend Shari was surprised to see that he was there alone.

All night long, people were asking him, "Where's Alexandra? Where's Alexandra?"

At one point in the evening, he even felt like he would cry. He began feeling sorry for himself and he finally decided to drown his sorrows in the unlimited supply of champagne on hand for the celebration. By three-thirty, when the party ended, he was so intoxicated that his father had to drive them home.

He was at his house for an hour and a half when he got up from where he had slumped down in his den and decided to go to Alexandra. He was angry with her for leaving him to host his party alone but he could not deny how much he wanted to be with her.

When he entered the apartment, he closed the door and stood there with his coat on, glaring at her.

"Thanks to you, I had a terrible time last night," he spat.

"I'm sorry."

"Yeah, right. I bet you are."

She could tell that he was still a bit intoxicated. She wondered how he had driven all the way there in that condition.

He began to remove his coat. Alexandra did not feel like listening to him castigate her, so she started past him to return to her bedroom.

He grabbed her arm.

"What are you gonna do, walk out on me again?" he asked.

"If you came here to berate me, Warren, then you might as well leave, because I don't need to hear this."

"Don't you even care about me?" he asked.

"You don't seem to care about *me* very much. All you ever talk about is how you feel. You never take my feelings into consideration."

"I told you Susan wasn't going to be there and she wasn't."

"I don't give a damn about Susan!" Alexandra yelled. "I'm talking about you!" She pointed an accusing finger in his chest. "You've never once asked me what I feel about all of this. All you've ever said is 'I need you to do this' or 'I need you to do that.' Not once have you said, Alexandra, what do you want to do? What do you feel?"

By this time, she was crying.

"You act as though I asked her to have my baby," Warren yelled.

"You didn't have to ask her! You obviously didn't make any real efforts to prevent it. Susan didn't get pregnant by herself. You were just as much there as she was. Whose fault is this, Warren? What did *you* do to prevent this?"

"I don't give a damn about Susan!"

"That's beside the point. She's having your baby! If you were so much against this happening, you would have made sure that it didn't!"

Alexandra turned away from him and strode into the bedroom. She slammed the door behind her, shutting him out.

For the first time, he stopped and thought about the things she had said to him. She was right, of course. He was to blame for this. He could not fault anyone else, especially her.

In his intoxicated state, his feelings seemed magnified. He felt so sorry for himself at that moment that he sank to the floor, landing on his backside. He began to cry noiselessly.

When Alexandra stormed out of the living room, she was so angry with him that she actually considered telling him that she didn't want to see or hear from him again. But she knew if she did that in anger, she would only be spiting herself. She loved him, regardless of his shortcomings or the fact that he was having a baby with Susan.

As she sat on the bed with tears rolling down her cheeks, she heard a soft moan come from the other room. She rose from the bed, as her curiosity had gotten the best of her, and tiptoed to the door. She eased it open slowly and peeked out. She was stunned at the sight of Warren on the floor, up against her front door, sitting in the tuxedo he had worn the night before with his hair all askew. Her heart broke into a million pieces at that moment and she felt so sorry for him that she began to cry all over again. She hurried to his side and knelt beside him, hugging him close and cradling his head against her breast.

"Shh, shh. Warren. I'm sorry. I know you didn't mean for any of this to happen," she sobbed.

"I'm sorry, Ally. I'm sorry for hurting you. I love you so much, but I don't know what to do."

He wrapped his arms around her and held her tightly, as if his life depended on it.

"Shh, Warren, it's all right. It's all right, baby. Come on. Get up. Let's go lay down. You need to get some sleep. You haven't been asleep all night, have you?"

Warren shook his head no.

"Come on," she repeated. "Let's go lay down. It'll be all right. Everything'll be all right."

She helped him up from the floor. When they were standing, Warren took her in his arms and hugged her close.

"I'm so glad I've got you, Ally," he told her.

"I'm not going anywhere, Warren."

She walked him back to the bedroom and helped him get out of his clothes. She put him to bed, smoothed his hair out of his face and kissed him on his forehead.

"Will you lay with me?" he asked.

She took off her robe and lay next to him, snuggling close to him as he wrapped her in his arms.

When Warren woke up later that evening, Alexandra had prepared dinner for them. She was setting the table when he came into the living room, showered and shaved and very much rested.

"Hi, baby."

"Hi. How're you feeling?" she asked with genuine concern.

"Better."

"I made some curried chicken and peas and rice. Do you feel like eating?"

"Yeah. I'm starving."

"Sit down. I'll fix you a plate," she told him.

She started to move to the stove to serve up his food when he grabbed her hand.

"Thank you, Ally."

"For what?"

"Just for being you."

She smiled at him and kissed him softly on the lips.

"Sit down. Let me fix you something to eat," she said.

As they were eating dinner, Warren said, "My mom and dad are leaving tomorrow."

"What time?"

"Their plane leaves at eleven ten tomorrow morning."

"So you're going home tonight?" she asked.

"Yeah. Will you come with me?" Warren asked.

"I can't. My mother asked me to come out tomorrow.

My aunt and uncle are coming by, too. I'm leaving about eight o'clock."

"What time do you think you'll be back?"

"Six or seven."

"Will you stay with me tomorrow night?" Warren asked.

"Yes. I'll come straight out there, okay?"

"All right," he said and squeezed her hand.

"Would you do me a favor, Warren?"

"Sure, baby. What is it?"

"Would you tell your mother and father that I'm sorry for not being more hospitable while they were here?"

"What do you mean?"

"Well, since last Saturday when we saw Susan at Michaels, I haven't spoken to either of them."

"Hey, baby, they understand. They know how much that bothered you."

"Yeah, but I still should have at least called them or something," she said sadly.

"Baby . . ."

She cut him off. "And I'm sorry you had such a lousy time last night. I know how much it hurt you that I wasn't there," she said sincerely.

Warren got up from the table then. He reached for her hand and pulled her up from her seat.

"Alexandra, don't apologize. I can understand why you didn't want to be there. It's not like you can ignore all that's happened while you've been there. I'm just glad that you still want to be with me."

They embraced and their lips met in a passionate kiss.

Twenty

The following evening, Alexandra arrived at Warren's house just after seven-thirty. When she got there, she unlocked the door and walked in.

"Warren! Are you here?"

"I'm upstairs, baby."

She removed her coat and hung it up. As she climbed the stairs to the second floor, Warren was waiting for her at the top of the landing.

"Hi, sweetheart," he said with a big smile.

"Hi."

"How you doin', baby?"

He hugged her and gave her a big kiss.

"I'm tired. The traffic was crazy."

"What time did you leave? I didn't expect you this early," Warren said.

"I left there at three-thirty. Would you believe that? I should have been here by six."

"Damn, what happened?" he asked.

"I don't know. It was slow going all the way."

"You feel like going to the club tonight?"

"No, not really," she said with a childish pout.

"You sure?"

"Yeah. I don't feel like going back out. But you can go. I'll be here when you come back."

"You don't mind me leaving you here?"

"Of course not. I know you don't expect me to go with you each and every time you go to the club, do you?"

"No, but I don't want to leave you here by yourself."

"Why not?"

"Well, I mean, you know, if you wanna stay here, that's cool, but I thought maybe, you know, you'd want me to stay with you," he said boyishly.

"No, 'cause if you stay here, I know you're gonna try to mess with me and I'm going to sleep."

As he held her around her waist, pressing his pelvis against her, Warren said, "Now what makes you think that if I stayed with you, I'd be trying to mess with you?"

"Oh, I don't know. Maybe it's just this gun you've got on me now that makes me think that way." She started laughing. He could not help laughing himself.

"You know, Ally, I'm not leaving until about ten. Why don't we step into my bedroom and I'll give you a nice rubdown to take your mind off of that nasty traffic you just fought your way through to get here."

"But haven't you already taken a shower to go out?" she asked coyly.

"No, baby. I took a shower so I'd be nice and fresh when you got here."

"Hmmm, well, in that case, let's go in your bedroom so you can give me a nice rubdown to take my mind offa that nasty traffic I just fought my way through to get here. Then we can take a nice bubble bath to get you nice and fresh again to go out, okay?"

"Sounds good to me."

Warren left to go to Michaels Too at a few minutes to eleven. When he left, Alexandra was in bed and half asleep. They had made love for almost two and a half hours, then took a bath together in Warren's Jacuzzi.

He kissed her good night, promising to be home by three.

She was asleep soon after he left.

It was eleven forty-five when Alexandra was awakened by the telephone.

"Hello," she said in a sleepy voice when she picked up the receiver.

"Is Warren there?"

"No, he isn't. Who's calling?" she asked.

"This is Susan. Tell him I need to speak to him as soon as possible. It's about his son," she said.

"Warren doesn't have a son," Alexandra said, now fully awake.

"He will in a couple of months," Susan said in an unpleasant tone. "Just tell him to call me."

Alexandra did not respond. She simply hung up the phone.

What a lot of nerve she has to call here speaking to me in that tone of voice, Alexandra thought. *Who the hell does she think she is?*

She sat up in the bed. The anger that was rising in the pit of her stomach was making it impossible for her to get back to sleep.

Why would she be calling Warren at this time of the night in the first place? Alexandra wondered if this was a regular occurrence. After all, it had been a week since she had last stayed over at Warren's house. She wondered if Susan was in the habit of calling him at the restaurant, or even if she saw him on a regular basis.

The more she thought about it, the more she reasoned that Warren probably did see her. After all, he had lied to her about seeing Susan after he found out that she was pregnant.

Alexandra really did not want to believe that he was sneaking around with Susan behind her back, but what else was she to think?

She was so angry that she started to page Warren at the club and ask him what was going on, but she realized that would be senseless. It would be stupid to call him there ranting and raving about Susan's phone call.

She lay back down, but regardless of how she tried, she couldn't get back to sleep. Finally, after two hours, she decided to get up and go downstairs and wait for Warren to return. He said he would be home by three o'clock. It was after two now. He should be home soon.

She went into the den and turned on the wide-screen television. There was a movie on that she had never seen before but had heard about and was curious to see. She tried to concentrate on the screen but her mind kept wandering back to Warren and Susan. Was she letting her imagination get the best of her? Was she reading more into the phone call than there actually was? Why would she be calling him so late?

It was ten minutes after three when Warren came home. He was surprised to find Alexandra asleep on the couch in the den with the television blaring.

He turned off the television and squatted on the floor in front of her, gently nudging her awake.

"Ally. Alexandra. Wake up, baby. What are you doing down here? I left you upstairs in bed."

She opened her eyes and slowly came out of her troubled sleep.

"Hey, baby. Wake up," Warren cooed.

He kissed her softly on her lips and smiled at her.

"You didn't have to wait up for me."

Alexandra came fully awake after a few seconds and sat straight up on the couch. She looked at Warren for a moment with a disgusted glare, then turned her face away from him.

Warren did not miss the look and immediately wondered what he had done to have changed her mood so drastically from what it had been when he left earlier.

"What's the matter?" he asked as he sat next to her on the couch.

"Your girlfriend called," she said nastily.

"What? What are you talking about?"

"Susan!"

"Susan? She called here?"

"Yes, she called here. Don't act so surprised."

"Why not? She doesn't usually call here. What did she want?"

"She told me that it was very important that you get back to her. It had something to do with your son," Alexandra spat at him.

"So what are you angry with me about?" Warren asked.

Alexandra looked at him in disbelief.

"What do you think, Warren?"

"I don't know," he shrugged. "What did I do? I didn't ask her to call me."

"Oh, and she's never called you before, right?"

"No. The last time I spoke to her was that night at the club. I don't talk to her."

"Oh, no? Then how'd you find out that she was giving you a son? How'd you find out she was having a baby? What? Did she write you a letter?"

"Alexandra . . ."

"I'm so sick and damn tired of this, Warren. You have no idea," she said as she rose from the couch and stepped away from him.

"Well, what am I supposed to do about it? I have no control over what she does. I'm a pawn in this just like you are," he said, turning to her.

"No, Warren, you're not a pawn. You're a player. It's your baby she's carrying."

He rose from the couch.

"I didn't ask her to have my baby."

"I don't give a damn what you asked her!" Alexandra yelled at the top of her lungs.

Warren took a step toward her.

"Ally, take it easy, okay?"

"Take it easy? Take it easy? I'm tired of this! I'm tired of every time I go to your stupid club I'm finding out another piece of information about you and Susan and y'all's baby. I'm sick of you lying to me."

"I haven't lied to you," Warren said.

"What do you call it? I remember asking you one night in your club why you were so appalled at seeing Susan. I asked you if you had spoken to her. You told me no. If I'm not mistaken, that was about a month before *I* found out that she was having your baby. You already knew that's why you didn't want to see her. You thought she would tell me. What do you call that, Warren, an exaggeration?"

"Alexandra . . ."

"I'm tired of looking like a fool in front of your friends. I'm tired of people laughing at me when I turn my back. I hate this whole thing, Warren. I hate it!"

Warren stood there in stunned silence, not knowing what to tell her or how to calm her down.

Alexandra began to pace back and forth with nervous compulsion.

"I've been keeping all of this bottled up inside me for so long that its tearing me apart. And all you ever tell me is that you want me to stand by your side through it. You've never even inquired into my feelings about this. You've never even said to me, Alexandra, how do you feel about this? Then to make matters worse, now I'm pregnant. Do you know how that makes me feel?"

She was hysterical. Tears were streaming down her face. Her words were hitting him like bullets, tearing him apart inside. He stood there, stunned at her news of the baby trying to think of something, anything, that he could say to calm her. His heart was racing and he was dreading her next words.

"I've tried to be there for you, Warren. That's what you wanted me to do, but I'm not getting any support from you. I can't take this anymore. I can't keep pretending I'm all right with this, because I'm not. You want me to have a baby, too, so that you can prove something to Susan—"

"No," he interjected. "No, Ally, that's not what I want. I love you."

"I am pregnant but I'm not having this baby. I can't. Every time I look at you, Warren, all I can think about is that she's having your baby. Everyone knows. Then all of a sudden, they see me pregnant, too. You know what they're gonna say? 'Oh, she had that baby because Susan had one. Boy, that Warren sure gets around.' "

"Alexandra, no."

"I can't do this. I can't keep doing this. I can't make believe anymore. It's killing me, Warren. This is killing me," she sobbed and fell to the floor as though her legs had given out on her.

Warren wanted to go to her, to hold her and tell her that everything would be all right, but he couldn't move. He stood there, looking down at her, his own tears clouding his vision.

"Alexandra, I'm sorry."

He hated himself at that moment for not being able to think of anything else to say to her. How many times had he repeated those same meaningless words to her. What else could he say? What could he do? He had no control over what was happening. He felt helpless to do anything.

Finally, he moved to her. He knelt beside her, afraid to touch her. Afraid that she might flinch at his touch.

"Alexandra. I don't know what to do."

She turned her face away from him. She did not want

him to touch her. She did not want him to say anything. She wanted to wake up and find that this whole nightmare was just that, a nightmare. She could not deal with the reality of what was happening. She had never hurt so much before in her life.

"All I ever wanted to do was make you happy, Warren. That's why I came back. I thought I could be big enough not to let this get to me. Can you imagine how horrified I felt when I realized that I'm pregnant with your child, too?"

"Ally . . ."

"You don't understand how I feel. You don't care how I feel."

"Yes, I do."

"No, you don't. You might think you do, but you don't. You can't. Try and put yourself in my shoes for a moment and look at what I've been going through for the past two months. Just try. You don't know how many times I wanted to just walk away from you, from Susan, from this whole thing, but I didn't because I love you. I love you, Warren. But it hurts so much. It hurts too much."

Alexandra was curled up on her knees with her arms wrapped tightly across her abdomen, crying uncontrollably.

He could not stand to see her like this. He grabbed her, enfolding her in his arms, holding her as tight as he could, trying to comfort her and shield her from the pain he could now see clearer than ever before.

As he held her, she began to cry even harder. Though he had felt a number of times before that he was losing her, he knew now, without a doubt, that she was gone. He knew when she came out of this, she would tell him it was over between them. He did not want to hear those words. He wanted to keep holding her so he could protect himself from the words that he knew would cut him in two.

They stayed that way, with her wrapped in his embrace until she had cried herself out and she felt she had completely exhausted her supply of tears. He could feel the tension leaving her body and he loosened his hold on her. She rose from the floor and, without a word to him, walked into the hall and began to climb the stairs. She felt so exhausted and drained that all she wanted to do was sleep.

Warren followed her upstairs. He was more afraid of her silence than of anything she could possibly say to him.

Instead of going to his bedroom, Alexandra opened the door to the guest bedroom across the hall.

"Alexandra . . ."

"I just want to be alone, Warren. I just want to go to sleep," she said without turning to him. She entered the room and closed the door behind her.

Instead of going into his bedroom and going to bed himself, Warren stood in the hallway for a couple of minutes looking at the closed door Alexandra had just gone through. Finally, he sat down on the floor directly across from the guest room as if he was standing watch. In a sense, he was. He was afraid that if he turned his back for one second, she would be gone.

Alexandra slept for almost seven hours. When she emerged from the room to go to the bathroom, she was surprised to see Warren lying on the floor in the hallway, sleeping. She went to the bathroom and began making preparations to take a shower.

* * *

The sound of the water from the shower awakened Warren, and when he tried to get up from the floor, he paused because of a sharp pain in his back from the uncomfortable position he had slept in.

As Alexandra showered, tears fell from her eyes because she had decided that she would have to tell Warren that she could not see him anymore. She hated to do it but felt there was no other recourse. She could no longer pretend that it didn't hurt to be with him knowing that there was a part of him, a very important part of him being brought into this world by another woman. She knew that being the person he was, regardless of the fact that he was not happy about Susan having his baby, there would be no way he could keep himself away when their child was born. She knew he would do the right thing by his child, that he would always be there for him and be a part of his life. She reasoned that if the situation was different, if she had not been with him during Susan's pregnancy and instead had met him after his child had already been born, things could have been different for them. But knowing that she, too, was carrying his child and knowing that the discovery of Susan's pregnancy came after they were already together and had shared love and made love and devoted themselves to each other, it would be a mockery to continue. She cherished the love she had for Warren too much not to be completely honest with him about the way she felt. Her only hope was that he would try to understand her point of view and not hate her for what she felt she had to do.

When she emerged from the bathroom, Warren was in his bedroom. He had removed his clothes, as he had slept in them all night on that hard hall floor. He was sitting in his easy chair in nothing but his underwear when she entered the room. She had a towel wrapped around her body. She went straight to the bureau and opened one of the drawers and removed a pair of panties and slipped them on. She was afraid to look at him, but could feel his eyes upon her.

Suddenly, the telephone rang. The sound startled Alexandra, for the silence in the room had been deafening.

Warren did not move to answer the phone nor did Alexandra. After four rings the answering machine picked up the call. After a few seconds, there was a beep followed by a woman's voice.

"Warren, this is Susan. I need to talk to you as soon as possible. It's about your son. Call me back when you get this message, please. I'll be at home all day. Call me."

During the recording of Susan's message, Alexandra did not move. She did not even realize that she had become paralyzed by the sound of Susan's voice. Warren, however, noticed immediately. He simply sat where he was.

She dressed slowly, pulling on a sweatshirt and a pair of sweatpants and her sneakers.

When she was finished tying her sneakers, she sat on the bed with her back to him, not saying a word.

They sat as they were for almost five minutes. Finally, Alexandra admitted there was no sense in putting this off any longer.

"I'm going home, Warren."

She had not turned to face him.

He did not say a word. He knew what was coming. When he did not respond, Alexandra turned to him. She took a deep breath and sighed.

"I don't think we should see each other anymore. I can't keep lying to you and to myself that I can be here for you through this. It hurts too much. I wish things could be different but I don't see how they can be."

Though she felt her emotions slipping away from her, she tried hard to keep her composure.

"I love you, Warren. I hope you know that, but I can't stand the pain of not being . . . of knowing she's having your baby. I just can't take it anymore."

She bowed her head and cried quietly.

Warren sat where he was quietly. He felt as though he was dying. He knew this was going to happen and he had tried to prepare himself but he did not know it would be so painful. He had never felt anything so painful in his life.

Alexandra rose from the bed then and walked over to his chair. He looked up at her with pleading eyes, afraid to say a word because he knew there was nothing he could say to make her change her mind.

She knelt in front of him and took his hands. She brought them to her lips and held them there, crying all the while.

"I love you," she cried. "I always will."

He looked down at her not wanting to believe that she was actually leaving him. He still could not speak.

"I'll come back tomorrow to get my things if that's okay with you, but I have to go now. Good-bye, Warren."

She rose quickly, afraid that if she lingered too long she would change her mind, prolonging the agony she was already feeling.

It was then that he spoke.

"Ally, please don't leave. Please don't go."

He rose from the chair and reached for her, pulling her to him and holding her tightly in his arms. As much as she wanted to embrace him, she didn't. She did not want to give him any false hopes.

"Warren, please don't do this."

Self-pity overwhelmed him. It swallowed him up like a hungry animal. He released her suddenly as though he had received an electric shock. He turned on her.

"You don't love me! You don't care about me!"

"Yes, I do."

"No! You don't give a damn about me, Alexandra." He stepped away from her.

"Warren, please." She reached out to touch him.

"So, go! Go on! You wanna leave, then go!" He pointed toward the bedroom door as he yelled, "Get out of my house!"

"Warren, please don't do this."

"GET THE HELL OUT OF MY HOUSE!!!"

The look in his eyes and the sound of his voice frightened her.

He moved menacingly close to her and sneered, "I hate you, Alexandra."

She stood there in shock, not believing he was saying those words to her.

"Go on, what are you waiting for? Get out!" he yelled.

She turned then and ran from the room, crying even harder.

As she left his house and got into her car, she tried to stifle her tears but there seemed to be no end to them. *Could he really mean what he had said? Does he really hate me?* she agonized. She could understand his anger. She had expected that. But to hear him say that he hated her was something she had not expected, and that hurt more than anything else.

Twenty-one

At ten A.M. Sunday, Warren rang Alexandra's door-bell. She was shocked though pleased to see him. Her pleasure, however, was short-lived.

"Hi, Warren," she said with a hesitant smile.

Noticing her smile, he quickly stated, "Don't get excited. I just came to bring you your keys and your clothes."

He walked through the door and past her, ascending the stairs without pause. He entered her apartment and stood in the living room, holding a plastic bag full of her clothes.

"Where do you want these?" he asked coldly.

Her eyes had already begun to water.

"You can just put them down," she said softly.

He dropped the bag on her couch without circumstance. He immediately pulled a key ring out of his pocket and began to remove the three keys she had given him.

When he handed them to her, he said, "Where are my keys?"

She walked back to her bedroom to retrieve them. When she returned and handed them to him, he turned to the door to leave.

"What about your things?" she asked sheepishly.

"Keep 'em. I don't want 'em."

"Warren, why are you acting this way?" she asked as tears fell from her eyes.

He gave her a look filled with revulsion before he answered. "Save the tears, Alexandra, for somebody who gives a damn."

With that, he turned and walked out, slamming the door behind him.

She broke down then. This was not what she wanted. This was not the way she wanted things to be between them. She loved him, but it seemed that just that quickly, the love he had so insistently professed for her was gone without a trace.

How could he be so cold, so heartless? She wanted to be angry with him for the terrible things he said and the way he now scorned her, but the pain was too great. She wanted to run to him to tell him that she took back what she said. She wanted to tell him that they could be together if that was what he wanted. She wanted to tell him anything that would keep him from looking at her the way he had.

She collapsed onto the couch and cried from the excruciating pain in her heart.

When Warren slammed the car door, he sat there for a moment before putting the key in the ignition. He closed his eyes and, immediately, the vision of her face lined with tears appeared in his mind's eye. *Hurting her doesn't make the pain go away, you fool,* he chided himself. *It only makes it worse. What did you really expect? She hung in there longer than any other woman would have; longer than Susan would have had the shoe been on the other foot. How can you blame her?*

He thought about the unnecessarily cruel things he had said to Alexandra. He hadn't meant any of them. He loved her with every bit of his soul, and losing her hurt more than he could have ever imagined. He was sure this could have all been avoided if he had only been honest with her from the beginning.

He spied his reflection in the rearview mirror and muttered, "This is all your fault, Warren."

He knew he could not lay the blame anywhere else.

Finally, he placed the key in the ignition. As he pulled away from the curb, he reluctantly accepted his fate. She was out of his life now, though he knew he would carry this pain in his heart forever. Susan had won. There was nothing left for him to do except await the birth of his son.

Twenty-two

All day Saturday and Sunday, Shari tried to reach Alexandra. She had left two messages on her answering machine on Saturday and three on Sunday.

Because she had not returned her calls, Shari tried her at work Monday morning, ready to chew her out for not being around when she had such juicy news to tell her.

Friday night, Shari and a couple of the girls she worked with had met in the city to do some club hopping.

As usual, when Shari went out dancing, she was dressed in a very provocative outfit. Also, as usual, there were scores of men lined up to talk to her, dance with her, or buy her a drink. At one club, a young man who was there with his girlfriend tried to hit on her. Not knowing he was there with someone, Shari openly reciprocated his flirtatious advances. The girlfriend immediately confronted Shari and damn near challenged her to a fight.

Luckily, the girlfriend was not completely unreasonable, and when Shari gave her the particulars about her male companion, the two of them lit into him like all hell had broken loose. Shari could hardly wait to tell Alexandra.

When Alexandra's assistant answered the phone Monday morning, Shari was quite taken aback when she was informed that Alexandra had not reported to work that day, nor had she called in. It was already ten-thirty.

She tried her at home after that and once again, got her answering machine. She began to worry. She wondered where Alexandra was.

Monday evening when she got off from work, Shari decided to go by Michaels, since it wasn't that far from where she worked. She was quite upset with Alexandra for making her worry, and she intended to give her a piece of her mind. She figured if Alexandra was not there with Warren, he could at least tell her where she was.

When she entered the restaurant, it was the height of the dinner rush. The mâitre d' immediately inquired as to her seating requirements.

"Oh, no, I don't want a table. I was wondering if Warren Michaels is here."

"Oh, yes."

"Could I speak to him, please?" she asked pleasantly.

"Certainly. Have a seat. I'll get him for you," the mâitre d' offered.

She took a seat in the front of the restaurant as the mâitre d' went in search of Warren. As she sat there, she could not help but notice a very handsome man who had entered the restaurant. He was with a woman, but made it very obvious that he, too, had noticed Shari and appreciated what he saw.

"Hey, Shari," Warren said, somewhat solemnly, she noticed.

"Hi, Warren. How you doin'?" she asked.

"All right. What can I do for you?"

"I've been trying to get in touch with Alexandra. Is she at your house?"

"No."

"Do you know where she is? I've been calling her for the last two days and she wasn't at work today, either."

"No. I don't know where she is," he said nonchalantly.

Shari noticed the dispassionate manner in which he spoke and questioned him about it.

"Alexandra and I broke up," he explained. "I saw her yesterday morning. She was at home. I haven't heard from her since."

"You broke up?" Shari asked in amazement. She had not heard anything else he said."

"Yes. She told me she doesn't want to see me anymore."

She was stunned. She did not know what to say.

They stood there in silence for the next few seconds until Warren said, "Look, I'm real busy, Shari. I'll talk to you later."

He did not wait for her response. He simply turned and walked back into the restaurant.

When Shari left Michaels, she walked down the street in a daze. She was in shock. Warren said Alexandra had cut him off. Could that be true? It seemed so unfathomable. She knew how in love they were.

What had happened in the last two days that could have caused Alexandra to break up with him? Shari really had not had a chance to talk to her since before the New Year.

She had been very surprised when Alexandra did not come with Warren to Michaels Too for the party on New Year's Eve. She had gotten so wasted that night, however, that her ensuing hangover had her on her back just about the whole day on January first so she did not get the opportunity to call her that day to find out why she had not come.

When she tried to reach Alexandra on Friday, the second, she still got only her answering machine; then of course, that evening Shari went out with her coworkers.

When she finally got home Monday evening, Shari tried calling Alexandra again. Still, she got no answer, only her machine.

Now she was extremely worried. She started to call Alexandra's mother, but decided against it. She did not want to worry Mrs. Jenkins unnecessarily.

Shari decided to go by Alexandra's house. Maybe something had happened and she was inside and unable to get to the phone. She and Alexandra had traded keys to each other's apartments a long time ago in case of just such an emergency. If, when she got there, Alexandra still did not answer the bell, she would use the keys to get inside.

She did not bother to change her clothes, though she did change her shoes, putting on a pair of sneakers. She put her briefcase away and decided to take only her wallet and keys. She left the apartment after being there for only ten minutes and went in search of her best friend.

Warren had been surprised to see Shari that evening. He wondered where Alexandra was. He hoped she was okay. He would never forgive himself if she wasn't.

After leaning on the bell repeatedly and still not getting an answer, Shari used the spare key to enter Alexandra's building. She hurried up the stairs and knocked on the door, though this time she did not wait for an answer. She unlocked the door and went right in.

"Alexandra! Alex, are you here?"

The apartment was dark and stifling. The radiator, which always gave off too much heat, was going strong and every window in the apartment was closed. Alexandra usually had to open her windows in the winter to diffuse some of the warmth. When she turned on the light, the first thing she noticed was the bag of clothes thrown carelessly on the sofa. Some of the clothes had even spilled out of the top of the bag. It was not like Alexandra to leave anything lying around in her living room like that. There were dishes in the sink, which was also very uncharacteristic of Alexandra. She was disgusted by roaches and, Shari thought, a bit excessive in her habitual cleaning routine to keep them away.

"Alex!" Shari called again.

She headed for her bedroom. The door was closed. When she opened it, the heat from the room almost knocked her down. She hurried to the window to let some cool air in.

When she turned from the window and crossed the room again to turn on the light, she heard a muffled sound coming from the bed.

She hurriedly switched on the light and was shocked to find Alexandra, curled up in the fetal position on top of the covers wearing a sweat suit and her sneakers. Her clothes were soaking wet, obviously from sweating, and her hair was disheveled, as though it had not been combed in days.

The sudden flood of light in the room caused Alexandra to curl herself tighter into a ball and to cover her eyes with her hands, shielding herself from the brightness of the ceiling lamp.

Shari hurried to her side and sat on the bed, immediately embracing her. She cried with a mixture of relief and anguish at finding her best friend closed up in this room like this.

"Alexandra, oh, my God, Alex, what happened? I've been so worried about you. I'm so glad you're okay," Shari cried.

Alexandra broke down in the warmth of her friend's embrace and cradled her head against Shari's ample bosom and sobbed.

Shari held Alexandra in her arms and tried to comfort her, though she, too, was very distraught. She could feel Alexandra's pain and it truly broke her heart to see her friend this way.

"It's all right, Alex, everything's gonna be all right," Shari murmured.

"He hates me, Shari. He hates me," Alexandra wailed.

"No, he doesn't, baby. He didn't mean it. I know he didn't mean it. Come on, sit up," Shari urged softly.

She gently pulled Alexandra up into a sitting position but continued to hold her. Alexandra rested her head on Shari's shoulder, unable to quell the flow of her tears.

Shari sat with her, rocking her gently until she could feel a calm coming over her.

"I'm here and I'm not gonna leave you alone, all right?" Shari said softly as tears streamed down her face.

Shari tried with all of her might to control the anger she felt burning inside her. She wanted to tell Alexandra that Warren was not worth her suffering this way but she knew that was not what she needed to hear right now. She wanted to go to Warren and curse him and hurt him for the way he had hurt her best friend.

After a while, Alexandra sat up on her own, though she kept her face down and her body trembled with spasms as she tried to catch her breath.

"You okay?" Shari asked.

Alexandra could only shake her head no.

Shari sighed.

"I was so worried about you. I've been trying to call you since Saturday," she told Alexandra.

Through her sobs, Alexandra told Shari about the break up.

Shari put her arm around Alexandra's shoulder and said, "Don't worry about him, Alex."

"I didn't mean . . . I didn't want . . . him to think . . . that . . . I . . . don't love him. I do," she cried.

"I know you do."

"I just . . . didn't know what . . . else . . . to do."

"Come on, let's talk about that later, okay. I'm gonna run you a nice warm bubble bath so you can relax, okay?"

Alexandra nodded.

"Let me take off my coat. You lay down, honey. I'll be right back," Shari said.

Alexandra did as she was told. She was glad Shari was there. Though she had stayed closed up in her apartment for the last two days all by herself, she really had not wanted to be alone. She had just been too distraught to ask for anyone's help.

Shari ran a tub for Alexandra and added a capful of her lavender bath gel, which immediately foamed into rich suds. She went back into the bedroom to help her get undressed. She brushed her hair and braided it in a single braid which she pinned up on the crown of her head.

"When you get out of the tub, if you feel like it, I'll wash your hair, okay?"

"Okay."

"Are you gonna go to work tomorrow?" Shari asked.

"I don't think so."

"Did you call your job today?"

"No. They'll probably fire me," Alexandra groaned.

"No, they won't. I'll call them tomorrow for you."

"I'm gonna have to get an abortion, Shari," Alexandra said in a trembling voice.

Shari sat on the bed next to Alexandra and put her arm around her.

"Whenever you're ready to do that, let me know. I'll go with you."

"I'm scared."

"I know, baby, but I'll be there. You won't have to go through that alone," Shari told her.

PART THREE

Twenty-three

Over the next three months, Warren went about the running of his restaurants and night club as if they were his whole life.

He spent most weekdays at Michaels in the city, catering to his customers' every whim and desire. On Thursdays, Fridays, and Saturdays he supervised the goings-on at Michaels Too. This was really not a new phenomenon, however. Warren had always worked very closely with his managerial and subordinate staff at both of his establishments. However, since his breakup with Alexandra, his personality had changed. According to his employees, it was not a change for the better, for he had become unreasonable.

His employees had always appreciated the fact that he was so amenable to their feelings with regard to the people they served. As with any organization that serves the public, an obnoxious person will occasionally crop up. There had been a time when Warren would handle such situations diplomatically. If a customer was dissatisfied and his employee was at fault, they would be held accountable for their actions. If the patron was at fault, they would be dealt with in whatever manner the situation called for.

That, however, had suddenly changed. No longer was Warren of the notion that the customer could be wrong, about anything. They, after all, were the ones who put money in his pocket. Now the fault for anything that went wrong, in either of his restaurants, had to lie with the employee.

Frank Edmonds, manager of Michaels Too, noticed the change in Warren almost immediately. It was only the middle of January when Frank decided he had to speak to his friend about his new attitude.

He called Warren into the back office one evening after an altercation between one of his waitresses and a very rude customer during dinner.

"What's up, Warren?" Frank had asked.

"What do you mean, what's up?"

"You were wrong, man. That woman was acting up from the moment she walked in the door. You shouldn't have taken that out on Vera. You were wrong!"

"Vera knows that regardless of her customer's attitude, she is not supposed to stoop to their level. She is supposed to keep her head and ignore them if they say something to her she doesn't like."

"The woman called her names, Warren! She doesn't get paid to be spoken to like that. She didn't deserve that. She's one of the best waitresses you've got here and you know it!"

"I don't care. She should have just walked away," Warren said, turning his back to Frank.

Frank looked at the back of Warren's head for a few seconds before he said anything. He considered that this time Warren had a point, but besides that, something else was very wrong.

"Granted, Vera should have stepped off, but you've been unnecessarily hard on everybody lately. What's this about, man? It's not like you to be treating your people this way. What's goin' on?" Frank asked.

"I don't know what you're talking about, Frank."

"Yes, you do. This is about Alexandra, isn't it?"

"What?"

"Ever since you and Alex broke up, man, you've

changed. It's like you're angry at her and you're taking it out on the whole world. You've gotta stop this, man. It ain't right."

"Man, you don't know what you're talking about. Alexandra is history. I couldn't care less."

"Warren, who do you think you're talking to? You can tell that to somebody else, but this is me. You're not foolin' me. I know how you feel about her; and I know you're angry about what happened, but that's no reason for you to be taking that out on your people. They bust their butts for you . . ."

"Frank, save it, all right. I don't want to hear this."

"Yo, man . . ."

"I said, forget it!"

With his breakup from Alexandra, he also began flirting shamelessly with the women that frequented his club, not caring who saw or who was around.

He could be found any Friday or Saturday night leaving Michaels Too with a woman on his arm, and not necessarily the same woman twice. But this was a show. Once they left the club, Warren would simply drive them home and leave. Most times he would not even ask for their phone number. If a woman did give him a number, he never promised to call. Unconsciously, he compared each one to Alexandra and they never passed the test. He kept trying to convince himself that he did not need her, though he felt empty inside each time he dropped another woman off.

During this time, Warren also made an effort to see Susan occasionally. He was well aware that the day was fast approaching when she would give birth to his son.

Though he never said so, he had begun to look forward to this event.

Of course, he would much rather have Alexandra be the woman who bore his first and probably only male child, but he did not dwell on that. It was hard enough trying to forget the fact that she intended to abort the child she had conceived with him. The reality of that was very painful for him.

He spoke to Susan on the phone once a week but for a minimal amount of time. He only called to see how she was and how things were progressing. When he saw her, it was usually if he happened to drop by her office. He never visited her apartment and he never called in advance.

One Friday afternoon after leaving Michaels and on his way to Michaels Too in Queens, he decided to stop by Susan's office. He had just turned the corner onto the block where she worked when he spotted her standing in front of her building with a man. Warren pulled alongside a parked car a few doors down from where she stood and stopped. He watched as the man embraced her and gave her a very intimate kiss, then bent down, placing his hands on her belly, and kissed her swollen middle before he walked away. Susan then turned and entered the building. Warren sat in his car for a few minutes more before he drove off. He decided not to visit her that day and he never said anything to her about what he had seen. He did, however, wonder who the man was.

Twenty-four

It was unseasonably warm that Saturday evening, March 28, when Warren got the call. It was just after nine.

"Hi, Warren. This is Tasha. Susan had the baby."

"When?" he asked.

"About an hour ago. Eight twelve, to be exact. You know she had a boy," Tasha said.

"Yeah, I know. How are they doing?"

"Fine. Are you gonna come by tonight?"

"No, I can't tonight. What hospital is she in?"

"St. Mary's."

"All right. Thanks for calling," he said, and hung up.

He had been getting dressed to go to the club.

She had the baby, he thought. He wondered what he looked like. He wondered how much he weighed. He should have asked Tasha while she was still on the phone.

He was anxious about seeing him. He knew if he wanted to, he could go to the hospital tonight. They never refused the fathers when they came to see their offspring, regardless of what time it was. He decided to wait, however, until the next day. Besides, he did not want Susan to think he was excited about seeing her.

* * *

Susan had spoken to Jeff just two days earlier. He told her he would be in New York in two to three weeks. She was really looking forward to seeing him, too.

Ever since he learned of her condition last Christmas, Jeff made it his business to visit her at least twice a month if only for a day. He was still trying to convince her that she should give up on Warren and let him take care of her and her baby.

As she sat in her hospital bed that Sunday morning feeding her newborn son, she thought about Warren and Jeff.

Tasha had told her before she left the hospital the night before that she had called Warren to let him know that she had had the baby. She really had not expected to see him last night. Actually, she was not expecting to see him at the hospital at all.

She wondered if maybe it would be best to take Jeff up on his offer. She could not deny that she still loved him, she knew she always would, and there were no doubts about the way he felt for her. After all, she thought as she looked down at the beautiful little boy in her arms, he deserved the best chance at life that she could give him. She wanted her child to have a stable family life, with a mother and father around on a full-time basis. Jeff definitely seemed like the best candidate to provide that. He had recently been offered a position as the musical director at a middle school in Hackensack, New Jersey, and he was leaving it up to her to decide if he should take it.

But she also could not deny the way she still felt about Warren. She wondered if he would really continue to ignore the bond they had between them now.

"Hey."

She looked up in surprise. Warren stood at the door of her room, seemingly apprehensive about coming any closer.

"Hi," she said softly.

He took a couple of steps toward her bed. There was a chair next to the bed but he made no move to approach it.

"How you doin'?" he asked gingerly.

"I'm fine."

"That's him, huh?"

"Yeah."

Susan looked down at their son. She felt her eyes begin to water and she did not want Warren to see that. She really could not believe he had come.

Warren stepped closer to the bed and stood over her, looking down at the infant in her arms.

"Take the bottle out of his mouth so I can see him," he said.

She did as he asked.

Warren stared down at the infant and could feel his heart swelling with pride. He was a handsome baby. His head was covered with thick black curls, and though his eyes were closed, he could see his resemblance to Susan was uncanny.

"Is he okay? I mean . . . is everything, you know . . ."

"Yes, Warren. He has ten fingers and ten toes."

"Where'd he get all that hair?" Warren asked.

Susan looked up at him and smiled, "Do you really have to ask?"

Warren could not help but smile himself.

"Can I hold him?" he asked.

Susan felt herself falling for him all over again in that moment.

"Sure."

Warren reached over and took his son in his arms, cradling him against his chest. He moved back and sat in the chair by the bed.

He stared down at him, marveling at the wonder of life as he had when his daughter was born.

"What time was he born?"

"Eight-twelve last night," Susan answered.

"Eight-twelve. How much did he weigh?"

"Eight pounds, three ounces."

"That's a good size. How long is he?"

"Twenty-one and a half inches."

"What are you gonna name him?" Warren asked.

"William Jeffrey."

"William Jeffrey?"

"Yes. William was my father's name," she said.

"And Jeffrey?"

"I've always liked the name Jeffrey," she answered.

Warren looked at her for a moment but did not comment.

"Hey, William Jeffrey," he said, looking down at his son. "Do you like that name? Huh? You like that name?"

He could not help smiling at the little bundle. He placed one of his fingers in the baby's fist, looking closely at his hands.

"He's got some long fingers," Warren commented.

"And long feet," Susan added.

"Yeah?"

Warren gently laid him down on his lap and proceeded to remove his diaper.

"What are you doing?" Susan asked.

"I wanna make sure everything is all right," Warren exclaimed, as though she had no right to ask.

Susan looked at him and simply shook her head.

Warren stayed with them at the hospital until the nurses came to take all of the babies back to the nursery.

After William's bassinet was taken from the room, Warren asked, "How long do you have to stay in here?"

"Until Tuesday."

"Do you have a crib for him?"

"No. I didn't get a chance to get one. I wasn't expecting him so early," she said.

"Is there any special kind you want?"

"No, not really. Just a natural wood color."

"Is there anyone at your place to let someone in for it to be delivered?"

"No. Do you want to take my keys?"

"Yeah, maybe you should give them to me. I'll try to get one today. Is there anything else you need?"

"Diapers, bottles, everything really," she admitted. She reached for her purse on the bedside table and removed her house keys.

As he took them from her, he rose from the chair. "All right. I'm gonna cut out now. I'll try to get back here tonight. If I don't, I'll see you tomorrow."

He started toward the door.

"Oh, Warren, they told me in Admitting that if I wanted the baby to have your name, you would have to sign a release form," Susan informed him.

Warren paused a moment before answering her. The memory of Susan and her male friend invaded his thoughts. Though he had been positive Susan was pregnant with his son, there was now an iota of doubt lingering in the back of his mind because of what he had seen.

"Have him tested, then I'll be happy to sign the form," he said, matter-of-factly.

With that he left the room.

Susan felt as though he had punched her in the chest. Where did that come from? she wondered. He couldn't possibly know anything about Jeff, she told herself. She had always been very careful when he was in town. Besides, she could see, as clear as day, how excited Warren was about having a son. Why, then, would he suddenly try to act as though he wasn't?

Twenty-five

Unlike Warren, who, outwardly, appeared to have no problem getting on with his life after their breakup, Alexandra found that she no longer had the will or desire to date or attend any social functions.

Shari tried on many occasions to persuade her that she should forget about Warren and get on with her life, but Alexandra seemed to close herself off from everyone and everything except her job.

She still exercised every day; her need to stay physically fit had not waned in the least. In fact, it had magnified. She was up early every morning and, depending on the weather, she either did a fast walk around Prospect Park or an hour-long workout in her makeshift exercise room.

She spent long hours at her office, usually arriving by eight-thirty every morning as opposed to nine-thirty, and staying at least until seven o'clock every evening. When she got home from work, she would fix herself a light, albeit very healthy dinner, then either watch a little television or read a book before going to bed, always by eleven.

Occasionally, she would go to a movie with Shari on the weekend, but more often than not, she went alone.

Shari was under the impression that Alexandra was feeling sorry for herself because of the breakup. That was not the case at all. She was heartbroken about the whole incident with Warren and Susan, without a doubt, but she had made up her mind that what she needed to do was take some time to heal herself.

She decided that she needed a change. She had been thinking about buying a town house on Long Island for quite some time now. In February, she actively began house hunting.

She had made up her mind a long time ago that when she decided to settle down and start having babies, she would have to be able to provide them with a decent place to live that they could call their own. She wanted her children to have the luxury of a backyard to run around in whenever they wanted, without her having to worry about them being hurt by playing in the street.

By the end of March, Alexandra had found the house of her dreams. It was in a newly built development of town houses. It was a semiattached two-story unit, equipped with a driveway and garage. There was an ample lawn in front where she decided she would start a flower garden. A short flight of steps led to the front entrance.

Upon entering the house, there was a relatively large living room and dining room area. Though there was no door separating the dining room from the kitchen, it was partitioned off by a wall and overlooked the backyard. It was large with a separate eating alcove directly off it. In the corner of the alcove was a small bathroom with a toilet and sink. In between the kitchen and dining alcove, there was a door that opened onto a patio with a staircase that accessed the enclosed backyard.

The staircase leading to the second floor was near the front entrance and off the living room. Upstairs there were three bedrooms, completely carpeted in her own choice of colors. There was a full bathroom in the hallway at the top of the stairs, and the master bedroom had a private bath. The two walk-in closets in the master bedroom, were a major factor in Alexandra's decision to buy the house. She was an avid shopper and loved clothes, and needed the closet space this beautiful house afforded her. Each of the other two bedrooms had their own closets, also.

There was also a full basement that could be accessed either from a closed staircase off the living room or from the backyard. Alexandra was not concerned with the unfinished condition of the basement. Her imagination was going wild with the possibilities of what she could do with it.

Twenty-six

Despite the nasty disposition that Susan had taken on since he told her to have the baby tested to confirm his paternity, Warren made sure that he made time to see his son every day. Although William favored Susan, Warren began to look for characteristics about him that he shared with his older sister Crystal.

On Friday, Warren received a telephone call from his doctor. He was at Michaels in the city when the call came in.

When he hung up the telephone, he felt as though he had been punched in the stomach and all the air had been knocked out of him.

He had just been informed that William was not his son. The blood test had proven that. He was crushed by the news.

He left the restaurant almost immediately, moving as though he had been programmed. His doctor told him that Susan had already been notified. *She didn't even have the decency to call me and tell me,* he thought.

He went directly to her apartment. He could not believe she would do something like this to him. She had probably known all along.

He was numb when he rang her doorbell. He had

become very attached to William and she had let him, knowing there was a possibility that he was not his son. He was so hurt that he could not even be angry. There was no room in his heart for that.

When she opened the door, she did not say a word. She knew why he was there. When he entered the apartment, he was not surprised to see the man from outside her office there with her. He was holding William.

"Jeff, this is Warren. Warren, this is Jeff" she said indifferently.

The connection was made immediately. She had even named the baby after him.

Warren only wanted to know one thing.

"Why did you do this to me, Susan? What have I ever done to you to deserve this?"

She could not answer him. He turned away.

He wanted to hold William one last time but was repulsed by the idea of having to ask this man Jeff, who was obviously the baby's natural father, for that favor.

When he felt his composure returning, he turned back to them.

"You know, Susan, I hope you raise this little boy to be more considerate of people's feelings than you are. And I hope you don't subject him to your manipulative ways like you did me."

He looked at Jeff sitting there holding the infant who just yesterday he had claimed for his own.

"Congratulations, Jeff," he said with scorn.

He then turned and walked out of the apartment.

After Warren left, Jeff asked, "Sue, did you really believe the baby was his?"

"What are you talking about?" she asked defensively.

"You know what I mean, Susan. Was this a game you were playing with him?"

"Why would I do that?"

"Because of the way you told me he cut you off. I know you had feelings for this guy and I know how upset you were about what he did." Jeff paused a moment, watching her for a reaction before he continued. "To be perfectly honest with you, he doesn't seem like the bad person you've made him out to be. He's been taking care of you and William, hasn't he?"

"He owes me," she said spitefully.

"How do you figure?"

"He made a fool out of me in front of his friends and mine, too, at that party," she yelled. "You weren't there, you don't know what happened. I was always there for him. Always. I loved him and he just . . ."

She stopped in mid-sentence. The tears started then. She had always known there was a chance that Jeff was the father of her baby, but she had hoped against hope that it was Warren's. She hated the way he turned her away as if he had suddenly lost all feeling for her. She hated the way he had turned to another woman before she was even out the door.

She had been ready to do almost anything to get him back, which was why she purposely did not tell him about her pregnancy until it was too late to have it terminated. Knowing how he felt about his daughter and how he took care of her despite the relationship he had with his ex-wife, Susan knew he would be there for her until the end.

She had been crushed when her doctor called with the test results. She knew there was no way she would be able to hold onto him once the truth was out.

"Susan, you can't play with people's feelings like that," Jeff told her as he moved to her.

He had always felt that she was like a spoiled child who needed someone to look after her. He had seen her throw tantrums, or the reverse—use the silent treatment to get what she wanted. It had always puzzled him as to why she was so insistent on having Warren take on the responsibility of raising a child who he obviously did not want her to have, when he was there and willing to be whatever she wanted.

He should have known. She had not changed one bit in the twenty years he had known her. She was still that same selfish little girl.

"Listen, honey," he said as he tilted her chin so she could look into his eyes. "I'm here for you and I always will be. I love you, Susan. Let's put this behind us and start from here, okay? We have a beautiful little boy here that needs us. And I need you."

She looked into his eyes and realized that no matter what had happened in her life or what would happen in the years to come, she should be grateful for Jeff. She knew that not in a million years, would she ever meet another man like him.

Twenty-seven

On that same day, at approximately five forty-five in the evening, Alexandra was just leaving her job en route to an appointment with her real estate broker to go over some last minute details regarding her purchase of the town house.

It was a very warm day and she was carrying her jacket over her arm. She was just about to descend the stairs to the subway below when she heard someone call her name.

She stopped immediately, turning in the direction the voice had come from.

She recognized Warren's sister Wanda coming down the block in her direction.

Her initial impulse was to turn away and continue down the stairs as fast as she could, but she quickly realized how rude and ridiculous that would be.

She waited for Wanda to catch up to her as her heartbeat seemed to double its pace.

"Hi, Alexandra. How are you?" Wanda said, and at once hugged her and kissed her cheek.

"Hi, Wanda. I'm fine. How are you?" Alexandra said, smiling nervously.

"I'm okay. . . . What's this?" Wanda asked as she placed her hand on Alexandra's swollen middle.

She did not answer.

"Warren doesn't know you're still carrying the baby, does he?" Wanda asked.

"No, and I'd rather you didn't tell him," Alexandra said. "Though I know you will."

"Why don't you want him to know?"

"I really don't want to go into it."

"Okay. How're you feeling?"

"All right."

"When are you due?"

"In August."

"You look cute," Wanda said with a warm smile.

Alexandra could not help but smile. "Thanks."

"Listen, do you have my number?"

"No."

"Take it," Wanda said as she began digging in her pocketbook for a piece of paper.

She wrote her home and business telephone numbers on a piece of paper.

"Call me, Alexandra. If you need help or if there's anything that I can do, let me know. I'd like to keep in touch with you, okay?"

"Okay," Alexandra said, taking the slip of paper from her.

"Well, I'm not going to hold you. You look like you're in a rush." She hugged Alexandra again and said, "It's great seeing you. You really look great."

"Thank you, Wanda. You, too."

"Call me, okay?"

"Okay."

Alexandra watched as Wanda walked back down the block. She figured that in the next couple of days, she would probably be hearing from Warren.

In spite of the fact that she still loved him, she was not sure if that was something she should look forward to or dread.

Twenty-eight

Warren was at Michaels Too that Friday night by ten-thirty. He could not shake the feeling of disappointment at learning that William was not his son. He had begun to look forward to each new day with him.

When Wanda entered the dance hall she noticed Warren sitting at the bar with a woman she did not know standing almost on top of him. Not knowing that he had been celibate since his breakup with Alexandra, Wanda figured this was yet another woman he would be taking home tonight.

"What's up, Warren?" She did not acknowledge the woman.

"Hi," he said.

"What's the matter?" she asked, noticing how down he looked.

He sighed.

"You wouldn't believe it if I told you."

"What do you mean?"

Warren rose from the stool and told the woman, "Keep my seat warm."

"Don't worry," she purred.

He put his arm around Wanda's shoulder and took a few steps away from the bar with her in tow.

"What's up?" she asked.

"The baby's not mine."

"What?" Wanda asked, not immediately comprehending what he was saying.

"William's not my son."

Wanda looked at him in stunned silence as he related the details of Susan's deception. She wanted to console him. She knew how attached he had become to that baby. At the same time, she wanted to hurt Susan for what she had put him through in the last six months.

The one bright spot she could see was the news she had to tell him. She decided not to prolong it. He needed immediate cheering up.

"Guess who I saw today, Warren?"

"I really don't feel like taking a test right now, Wanda," he said sarcastically.

She looked at him and rolled her eyes.

"All right. Who did you see?" Warren asked in exasperation.

"Alexandra."

He was silent for a moment.

He huffed and said, "That's it?"

"No. That's not it. She's pregnant."

"What?"

"She's pregnant."

"Yeah, so?"

Despite his attempt at nonchalance, Wanda did not miss the glint in his eye at the mention of Alexandra's name.

"Warren, she's about five months pregnant. She didn't get rid of the baby after all," Wanda said, excitedly.

"Is this supposed to cheer me up, Wanda? The last thing I want to hear about is Alexandra and a baby she's having for someone else," he snapped, before he turned and walked away from her.

Twenty-nine

Two days later, Alexandra and Shari were in a restaurant in downtown Manhattan having dinner when they ran into Frank Edmonds. They had just finished seeing a movie, and at the last minute decided they wanted to get something to eat before they headed home.

Because the weather had been consistently warm in the last couple of weeks, Alexandra and Shari were dressed accordingly. As a result, Alexandra's condition was easily recognizable.

Shari noticed Frank first as she was sitting facing the entrance of the restaurant.

"Hey, Alex, isn't that Warren's friend?"

Alexandra turned to see who Shari was referring to and looked right at Frank as he, too, was looking in their direction.

"Alex!" he called cheerfully as he walked over to them. "How you doin', baby?"

He was very happy to see her. It had been four months since they had last seen each other.

"Hi, Frankie," Alexandra said with a smile.

He leaned over to kiss her cheek.

"How you been, Al? Damn, it's good to see you," Frank said.

"I've been okay. It's good to see you, too. You remember my friend Shari, don't you?"

"Most definitely," Frank said enthusiastically. "How have *you* been?"

"Good," Shari said with an appreciative smile.

"So what's up, Al?" Frank asked.

"Nothing and everything," she shrugged.

"I miss seeing you at the club."

"How's Warren?" Alexandra asked, avoiding the disapproving look Shari shot at her.

"He's all right."

"So what have you been up to?" Shari asked Frank, to change the subject.

"You know, working hard. That's about all."

Frank was standing over their table and suddenly noticed Alexandra's thick midsection.

"Hey, Al, are my eyes deceiving me?"

"What are you talking about?" she asked, but would not look him in the eye.

Shari looked at Frank then at Alexandra, then up at the ceiling.

Frank noticed Shari's look.

"Al, are you pregnant?"

Alexandra looked over at Shari and could feel her emotions threatening to overflow.

"Frank, I don't want Warren to know," she said.

"Why not? He can help you."

"I don't want his help. Besides, he's already got his hands full with Susan's baby. She had it, right?" Alexandra asked.

"Yeah, she had it, but it's not his."

"What?" Shari and Alexandra chorused.

"He just found out. He had a blood test done, you know, just to be sure. He really thought it was his. He was supporting the kid and everything. He got a call from his doctor two days ago. Told him there was no way the kid was his."

"I knew it! Didn't I tell you, Alex? I knew she was setting him up," Shari exclaimed.

Alexandra rose from her seat.

"Where're you going?" Shari asked.

"To the bathroom."

Frank and Shari watched her as she walked away.

Frank sat in Alexandra's seat.

"How's she doing, Shari?" he asked with genuine concern.

"All right, considering."

"Warren thought she was gonna have an abortion."

"She had planned to, but when the time came, she just couldn't go through with it."

"Damn," Frank sighed. "I'm sure now that he knows about Susan, he'll be real happy to hear about Alexandra."

"Don't tell him, Frank."

"Why not?" he asked, a puzzled looked on his face.

"Two reasons. First, it's not your place to tell him. I know you're his friend and everything, but it's up to her to tell him. Second, because he probably already knows."

"What makes you think that?"

"Because Alexandra ran into Wanda on Friday. I'm sure she's already told him."

"Yeah, probably. She can't hold water," Frank said.

As Alexandra entered the ladies' room, she thought about the things Frank had revealed.

She could not believe that Susan would do something so heartless. She felt bad for Warren.

Knowing him the way she did, she figured he had probably been with that baby every day since he was born. She knew how devoted he was to his daughter

Crystal. She was positive he would feel the same for any child of his.

As she stood at the sink washing her hands, she studied her reflection in the mirror.

Her hand instinctively went to her stomach. She was carrying his baby. Though she guessed he had been devastated at learning of Susan's deception, she could not help but feel relief that her worst nightmare had finally come to an end.

She was sure he must know by now that she was carrying his child. She knew that was something Wanda could not help but tell him. She was surprised, though, that she had not heard from him yet.

When Alexandra returned to the table, Frank rose from her seat.

"Frankie, do me a favor?" Alexandra asked before she sat down.

"Anything."

"Don't tell Warren."

"I won't."

"Don't even tell him that you saw me."

He put his arm around her shoulder and hugged her.

"Okay, but I want you to do me a favor," Frank said.

"What?"

"Call me. Keep in touch with me. I want to know that you're doing all right."

"Frank . . ."

"I'm serious, Al. If you need anything, anything at all, call me."

She smiled at him. "I promise."

He put a hand on her belly.

"I hope it's a boy," Frank said.

"Me, too."

Thirty

It was almost noon on Sunday and Warren was still in bed. He had not gotten home from the club until after four and though he was tired, he had been unable to sleep.

Thoughts of Alexandra filled his mind.

Though he tried not to think about it, Warren could not erase from his mind those two words from Wanda's lips.

"Alexandra's pregnant."

He had silently agonized for weeks after they broke up about her getting the abortion she had promised to have. He wondered what it was that made her change her mind. He also wondered why she had not told him.

Did she really believe she could raise a child by herself. *She does not realize what an enormous task child rearing is,* he thought.

Though he had told Wanda that, like Susan, Alexandra's baby probably was not his, he knew in fact that it was.

It had been difficult for him to hide the excitement he felt at hearing she was still pregnant. After learning that Susan had lied to him after all, it was almost like a silver lining had been placed around his cloud of gloom.

He thought about calling her but decided against it.

She must not want me to know since she didn't tell me, he figured. If that was the case, she probably would not talk to him, either. When he thought back to how he had reacted when she told him that Susan's pregnancy was too much for her to deal with, he could understand why she would not want to.

He had been a jerk. Plain and simple. But her leaving had hurt him more than anything he had ever felt.

Thirty-one

On Tuesday of that same week, Alexandra took the day off from work. She had a doctor's appointment that morning and planned to do a little shopping for her new house that afternoon.

She was happy when her doctor told her that everything was going well with the baby's development. She had her first sonogram taken that afternoon and was able to see a picture of the baby inside her. She could not wait until it was born. Her doctor asked her if she wanted to know the baby's sex, but she told him no. She would wait until it was born to find out. In her heart, however, she had a feeling it was a boy.

She decided to drive out to the mall at Roosevelt Field to do her shopping. She was there for almost five hours and ended up not buying a thing for her house but a lot of clothes for herself instead.

Though a number of the things she bought could not be worn immediately due to her condition, she was confident that she would be able to get into the outfits she purchased once she gave birth.

Warren wanted to strangle Wanda. Their young cousin Jeannie had flown up to New York from Birmingham, Alabama, to visit Wanda during her break from

school. Due to a special project she was involved in on
her job, however, Wanda was unable to get the day off
and had volunteered Warren to "baby-sit" Jeannie for
the day. Normally, this would not have been a problem
for him, but Jeannie was a thorn in his side. She had
had a crush on Warren since she was ten years old and
now, nine years later and believing herself to be quite
the woman, Jeannie was much more forward and her
advances were quite embarrassing to him. Aside from
that, she insisted on holding his arm in an iron grip so
that, as she said in her heavy southern drawl, "I'll be
safe on the mean streets of New York."

Wanda had promised to take her shopping that day,
so he was stuck with the task of escorting her around
the mall for four hours. Those were the longest four
hours of his life.

Alexandra was heading toward the exit when she
passed a store with an attractive leather pantsuit in the
window. She stopped to admire the suit and seriously
contemplated going into the store and buying it, but
decided that leather was too risky to buy without first
trying on.

The display window had a mirrored pillar in it, and
as she turned to resume her approach of the exit, she
caught a glimpse of a reflection that immediately gave
her pause. She turned quickly to see if her eyes were
deceiving her. They were not.

Across the corridor stood Warren with a teenager on
his arm. She could not believe it. The girl looked like
a sixteen- or seventeen-year-old. He stood there looking
very disinterested as she chatted animatedly about
something. Probably video game highlights, Alexandra
figured.

Suddenly, Warren turned his head away in what

looked to her like impatience. His eyes traveled in her direction but passed over her. He had seen her, however, because he quickly did a double take. His mouth dropped open and he stared at her in disbelief.

Alexandra had not moved, as she was just as surprised as he was. It looked to her that he started to take a step in her direction but his friend realized that he was no longer paying attention to her. She looked over in the direction Warren was looking but by then Alexandra had regained her senses and hurriedly continued on her way.

By the time she reached her car, she was very shaken up. She opened the door and climbed behind the wheel and just sat there for a few minutes until her heartbeat resumed its normal pace.

What was he doing with that young girl? she wondered. *He couldn't possibly be sleeping with her, could he?* The thought repulsed her.

Though she was positive that Wanda had already informed him about her condition, she could see how surprised he was to have seen for himself.

"Why did you come out here?" she asked herself aloud.

She knew Warren shopped at the stores in this mall. What had she been thinking about?

Thirty-two

For the rest of the evening, Warren would periodically slip into private contemplation for minutes at a time. It had been impossible for him to get Alexandra out of his mind after seeing her at the mall. A couple of times before he took her back to Wanda's house, Jeannie had even asked what was wrong with him.

He thought she looked beautiful. Even from a distance he could see how her face seemed to glow with the light of the life she carried in her womb. She was carrying well, too. Other than her belly, it appeared as if she had not gained a pound.

After lying awake for over two hours, he decided he would go see her. He thought about going to her house but figured she could easily slam the door in his face and that would be the end of it. He reasoned that if he met her at her job, she might, at least, give him the benefit of the doubt and talk to him. He knew how much she hated creating a scene.

Warren was in the lobby of Alexandra's office building at five-fifteen the following evening. He knew she did not leave before five-thirty, so he hoped he would be able to catch her before she left. He decided he would wait until about six o'clock if he had to.

He was nervous. It felt as though a swarm of butter-flies was fluttering in his stomach.

At five thirty-five, he saw her step off the elevator. She was talking to someone and paused just outside the elevator bank with them. They stood there for almost five minutes before they turned away from each other in the direction of the exits.

She had not even noticed him standing there. He hesitated before he turned to follow her.

As she went through the revolving door, he picked up his pace to catch her.

As he came out of the door, he called to her.

She turned immediately at hearing her name.

When she faced him, a chill went through his bones. She looked beautiful.

He stepped up to her.

"Hi," he said hesitantly.

"What are you doing here?" she asked antagonistically.

Warren was taken aback by her hostile tone of voice.

"I . . . I just wanted to talk to you," he said.

"I don't have anything to talk to you about," she said, and turned away from him.

"Alexandra, wait."

"What?" she said, turning back to him with impatience.

He looked at her for a moment, unable to speak. There were so many things he wanted to tell her, but the words just would not come.

Finally, he asked, "Why didn't you tell me?"

He reached out to her hesitantly, as though he wanted to touch her swollen belly.

"Why didn't you tell me?" he asked again, almost pleading.

"Why didn't I tell you? Why should I?"

"I could help you. I want to help you."

"I don't want your help, Warren," she said, coldly.

"But . . ."

"Look, I have to go. I have an appointment," she lied.

She turned away from him again and started to leave.

"Alexandra, you know how much I wanted you to have this baby," he called after her.

She stopped dead in her tracks and turned back to him. There were tears in her eyes.

"Should I have considered that? How many times did you consider my feelings when Susan was pregnant? Oh, yeah, and by the way, I specifically remember your last words to me were 'Tell somebody who gives a damn.' Why don't you take your own advice and leave me alone!"

With that she turned and hurriedly walked down the block and away from him.

He stood there and watched her go. He was heartbroken. He knew she would not be happy to see him but he did not expect such unbridled animosity.

What was he supposed to do now? How could he get close to her if she would not even talk to him? He wanted to be a part of his child's life. He wanted to be a part of her life again. He wanted them to be a family.

Thirty-three

Alexandra was still angry when she got home that evening. How dare he just pop up out of the blue and expect her to be happy to see him? What a lot of nerve he had. After the terribly mean things he'd said to her when they split up, did he really expect her to have forgotten simply because a couple of months had passed, she wondered.

Though she would not admit it out loud, she did still love him very much, but she could not forget how he had hurt her.

Shari was home for all of fifteen minutes when her intercom rang.

"Who is it?" she asked impatiently into the speaker. She did not like uninvited guests.

"Warren."

"Warren?"

She wondered what he wanted.

She pressed the button to open the lobby door.

About five minutes later, her doorbell rang.

She opened the door immediately, without asking who it was.

"Hey, Shari."

"Hello."

"I'm sorry for not calling first but I need to speak to you, if you don't mind," Warren said.

Shari stepped back and opened the door wider for him to enter.

"Come on in."

Warren stepped inside the apartment but stayed near the door.

"How've you been?" he asked.

"Fine. What's up?"

"I was wondering if . . . Well, I saw Alexandra today. My sister told me that she was still pregnant. I went down to her office, hoping to get a chance to talk to her, you know, 'cause I wanna help her with the baby, but she wouldn't talk to me. I was wondering if you could talk to her and tell her, that . . . well, that I'm really happy she decided to keep the baby and that I want to help."

Shari stood there for a moment looking at him without saying a word.

Her stare made him feel uncomfortable.

"You want me to talk to her," she finally said.

"Yeah, if you don't mind. I know how much you care about her, and so do I. I just want to help her."

She huffed in disbelief at his gall.

"You want me to plead your case to Alexandra," she said with a sneer.

Warren did not answer, and at once knew he had made a mistake in coming here.

Shari turned away from him and took a few steps across the room.

She shook her head and turned back to him.

"You've got a lot of damn nerve coming here. What makes you think I would talk to Alexandra for you? If my memory serves me correct, when last we spoke, I came into your restaurant looking for her and you were very cold to me, like I was wasting your time by even asking you about her whereabouts. Do you know how I found her? Would you like to know that?" she asked, not really looking for an answer, because she was going to tell him anyway.

"She was devastated by what you did. You think it was easy for her to break up with you? She loved you more than you deserved. She stuck by you for as long as she could once that mess with Susan came out, and it nearly killed her. You don't know how many times she came to me crying about Susan having your baby. And I used to tell her what a good man you were. That she shouldn't give up on you. But you didn't even have the decency to be straight with her. And you claimed you loved her. She had to find out about Susan from Susan. Now you want me to plead your case? I wouldn't blame her if she never spoke to you again. Did you even take her feelings into consideration when you told her how much you hated her?"

Warren was stunned by her barrage.

"I think you should leave," Shari said, moving to the door and opening it.

Warren moved to the door but paused before leaving. "I'm sorry, Shari."

"Yes, you are. Good-bye, Warren."

Thirty-four

On Friday of that same week, Alexandra was coming out of the ladies' room at her firm when she noticed Warren standing at the reception desk.

"Hi, Ally."

She did not say a word.

"I just came by to drop this off," Warren said, handing her an envelope.

"What is it?"

"Just . . . Just read it."

She looked at the envelope wondering what was inside.

"I'll see you," Warren said as he turned and walked through the door.

When she got back to her office, she closed the door and sat behind her desk. She was very hesitant about opening the envelope, but her curiosity soon got the best of her and she broke the seal on the envelope.

The letter was three handwritten pages long.

Dearest Alexandra,

Where do I begin? There are so many things I want to say to you. I guess the best place to start is with an apology. I'm sorry for all the pain I've caused you. I'm sorry for the tears you cried at my expense. I'm sorry for being so selfish as to have not recognized your pain in the midst of my own. And mostly, I'm sorry for being such a coward and not being honest with you from the start.

Next, I want to say how much I love you. From the day we met, I knew you were someone special and I knew that I wanted you to be a part of my life. As time passed and we came to know each other better, I realized that you were the woman I had been looking for all my life. You've made such a wonderful difference in my life.

When Susan came to me that day in October and told me that she was having my baby, I felt as if my world had fallen apart. I was afraid to tell you because I was unsure if your love for me was as strong as mine for you and I did not want to lose you. I felt that if you knew the truth, you would turn and leave, never to come back. I apologize for my lack of faith in you. I don't know why I thought that I could keep something so important from you.

When you came back to me of your own free will after finding out about her, I thanked God, because I truly thought that I had lost you forever. I promised myself that I would do everything in my power to keep you from being hurt that way again. When she informed me that she was having a boy, I was sure your knowledge of that would have you thinking that this was something I wanted or was looking forward to. I did not want you to have any doubts about my love for you, so I tried to keep that information from you.

I was horrified when she announced it to my parents that night at the club and felt again as if my world was closing in on me. Knowing at that time you were pregnant with my child and know-ing that you were trying to keep that from me be-cause of Susan, I was sure I was losing you. The mere thought of not having you as a part of my life was something I could not comprehend.

Forgive me for being so presumptuous with regard to your feelings.

You are correct when you say that I never truly considered your feelings. All I knew was that I needed you and I felt that should be enough for you to stay with me. It was selfish of me to not take the time to step back and look at what you were going through due to my carelessness. I know that I can never make that up to you.

I hope you know that I never meant it when I said I hated you. That was my anger at myself lashing out at you. You did not deserve that. I have always known that if you did not care for me, you would not have stayed with me for as long as you did.

When Susan's son was born, I was at first reluctant to contact her. I did not want to share parenthood with her and I also held and still hold her somewhat responsible for our breakup. I would be lying to you, however, if I told you that I was not excited when I saw that little boy for the first time.

Also, having decided that I would never be untruthful to you again, I have to tell you that I was very depressed when I learned in fact, that I was not his natural father. In the two short weeks of his life, I found that I had become attached to that little boy.

When Wanda told me that she had run into you and that you were still pregnant, I tried to pretend that I did not care. I'm sure she saw through my charade. I was overjoyed to learn that you had decided to bear my child. However, once again, it was my cowardice that kept me from calling you at that instant.

I know after the way I treated you when you told me you could no longer conceal nor bear the pain of my impending fatherhood, I have no right to expect you to be understanding of my feelings. I was wrong, pure and simple. I'm sure Shari has already told you about my unexpected visit to her apartment, when I asked her to speak to you in my defense. I'm also sure she told you that she gave me a very thorough sounding off and sent me packing. I cannot blame her. She has only your best interests at heart.

Whether you choose to believe it, Alexandra, I, too, have only your best interests at heart. I cannot deny, however, that there is a bit of selfishness in my plea to you.

I love you, more than I have ever loved anyone in my life and more than I will ever love anyone. I want to take care of you and our child. I want to be a part of the life of the child you are carrying. I want to be for you all the things I should have been before but was too selfish and too much of a coward to be.

I know I am asking for a lot, considering the way we parted in January, but please take a few moments to consider my words. They are from my heart.

People say it is better to have loved and lost than to have never loved at all, but the pain of having lost the love of one so beautiful as yourself is truly unbearable.

Please give me another chance. I know I have a long way to go to win back your love and trust but I promise you, unselfishly, that I will do whatever it takes to make you love me again.

Forever,
Warren

She was crying by the time she had finished reading the letter.

Why couldn't he tell me all of this to my face? she asked herself. Though his words were sweet and she was sure, sincere, she wondered why he didn't know how much more meaningful they would be if he told me this in person.

She folded the letter and placed it back in the envelope. *Does he really expect me to call him now?* she wondered. *Should I call him?* She asked herself that question over and over for the remainder of the day.

When she left that evening, she still was not sure what she should do.

Thirty-five

Almost two weeks had passed and Warren still had not heard from Alexandra. On a number of occasions, he had started to phone her and ask her if she had read his letter but always hung up the phone before it was answered.

Why hasn't she called me? he wondered. *What else does she want?* he asked himself.

He had poured out his heart in that letter. He had told her all the things he had been unable to say to her before. Why, then, had she not responded? He wondered if she really hated him for all the pain and sorrow he must have caused her. He had been surprised and quite saddened to learn from Shari that she had almost had a nervous breakdown when he turned on her. He never realized that her love for him was as strong as his for her.

He wanted to kick himself for being so blind and selfish. He had been so bent on making sure she did not leave him that he never even considered what she was going through because of her love for him.

He decided to take a chance and go by her office. He figured she would be more receptive about talking to him since he had written her the letter.

He bought her a dozen roses and waited outside her building. As he sat there in his car, he tried to decide exactly what he would say to her. He had to make sure he kept his cool. He was upset that she had not even responded to his letter, but he had to keep that emotion at bay.

His goal was to get her to talk to him, not to run away again. He was positive if she would talk to him, he could convince her that they belonged together.

He looked at his watch. A quarter to six. Where was she?

Ten more minutes passed before she came outside. When he spotted her, he was not sure if his eyes were playing tricks on him at first. It was almost as if he was looking at her through some sort of stop action lens.

She looked beautiful. Her hair was pinned up on her head, with soft curls falling down and surrounding her face. She had on an off-white dress, which though plainly styled, made her look quite angelic. She was laughing enthusiastically at something her companion had just said to her.

His heart sank into his stomach when the man turned in his direction. It was Frank.

They walked from the building, with Alexandra holding tightly to his arm. They went straight to his brown Cadillac Seville, which until that moment, he had not even noticed.

What's going on? What is she doing with Frank? he wondered. He felt a lump rise in his throat, one so big he could barely breathe. He did not want to believe that Frank would go behind his back this way. He was supposed to be his friend. How long had he been seeing her? He had never told him that he was in touch with Alexandra. Why would Frank keep that from him?

When they pulled away, Warren pulled away, too, but he kept his distance from them. He wondered where they were going.

All kinds of crazy thoughts ran through his mind as

he followed them. Could she really have chosen Frank over him? Would Frank really stab him in the back this way? They had been friends for years. He was Crystal's godfather. How could he do this to him?

About forty-five minutes after leaving her office, Frank pulled into Alexandra's block. Warren parked his car about five doors down from her building so they would not notice him. He felt some relief when he realized how foolish he was acting by following them. Frank was probably just driving her home. It did bother him, though, that he had not told him he was talking to Alexandra.

He watched as Frank got out of the car and opened the door to help Alexandra out. When he headed toward her gate, then through it, Warren felt that sinking feeling again.

He tried to think of a logical explanation for Frank going inside with her, but he could not come up with anything that satisfied his curiosity.

An hour passed before Frank emerged from Alexandra's building. Warren began a slow burn thinking of all the things Frank and Alexandra could be doing behind his back. He had swallowed his pride when he wrote her that letter and she probably just read it and threw it away. She was seeing Frank. That was why she did not want any help from him. And all this time, Frank had been smiling up in his face, knowing how he felt about her, and stabbing him in the back.

Frank got in his car and drove off. Warren started to get out of his car and ring Alexandra's bell and confront her with his discovery but he decided against that. He would deal with Frank first.

When Warren arrived at the club, Frank was not there yet. He was so angry, he could barely contain himself.

He walked over to the bar in the restaurant and stepped behind it. He began to make himself a drink. Absolut on the rocks. He thought for a moment, then dumped the ice out of the glass. Straight Absolut.

He threw the drink down in one gulp. Mitch, the bartender on duty at the time, looked at Warren strangely. He had never seen Warren drink Absolut or any other hard liquor for that matter.

"You all right, Warren?" Mitch asked.

"Yeah. Where's Frank?"

"He didn't get here yet."

"When he does, tell him I want to see him right away. I'll be in my office."

Warren fixed himself another Absolut straight and carried it to his office.

He sat behind his desk brooding over what he had seen between Alexandra and Frank earlier. How could they do this to him? Frank was supposed to be his friend and Alexandra . . . He loved her more than he had ever loved anyone. Why would they do this?

After about fifteen minutes, there was a knock on his door.

"Come in."

Frank opened the door.

"Hey, man. What's up? You wanted to see me?"

Warren looked at him for a moment before he spoke. He hated the way he stood there, looking all innocent and everything. He wanted to jump right at him and knock that stupid smile off his face.

He rose from his seat.

"I saw you today."

"You saw me?" Frank asked skeptically.

"Yeah. I saw you. You and Alexandra."

"Oh, yeah? Where were you?" he asked innocently. Warren wanted to hit him.

"How long have you been seeing her?" Warren moved closer to him.

"What?"

"You heard what I said. How long have you been seeing her?"

"Warren . . ."

"We're supposed to be friends and you're running around with her behind my back! How could you do that?"

"What are you talking about, man?"

"You know good and damn well what I'm talking about! I was there today when you came out of her building with her. I followed you to her house. What were you doing in her apartment for over an hour, man?"

Warren was yelling now. Frank stood there looking at him in amazement. He did not understand what was happening. Did Warren really think that he and Alexandra were . . .

"You're losing your mind, man," Frank said. "You're losing it. I'm not gonna stand here and listen to this."

Frank turned and started to leave the room.

"Don't walk away from me, Frank! I know what's going on!"

"You don't know a damn thing, Warren! Do you really think I would try to hit on Alexandra, knowing she's carrying your kid, man? I can't believe you would think that about me after all we've been through. You need to get your head together, man. You're losing your mind!" Frank exclaimed, and once again turned away from Warren.

Warren stood and watched as Frank put his hand on the doorknob and opened the door. He shook his head, suddenly coming to his senses.

"Frank, wait," he called.

Frank turned back to him. Warren could see his anger and hurt as clear as if they were standing before him.

"I'm sorry, man. I just . . . Why didn't you tell me you were in touch with her?" Warren asked.

Frank felt sorry for Warren. He could see the difficulty with which he was trying to keep his emotions in check.

"She asked me not to."

"But you're my friend."

"I'm her friend, too, Warren."

"Why doesn't she want to talk to me?" Warren asked in a trembling voice.

Frank looked away from him for a moment. He closed the door and stepped back into the room.

"Because you dogged her, man. See, you never told me what happened when y'all broke up, but she did. She told me all the things you said to her and you know she didn't deserve that. She stuck by you, man, longer than anyone else would have under the circumstances, and you dogged her. When she asked me not to tell you that I'd seen her, how was I supposed to go against her wishes? She's my friend, too. I'm trying to look out for her."

Warren sighed. "I apologized to her, man."

"When?"

"I wrote her a letter. I asked her to call me. What else am I supposed to do?"

"You wrote her a letter. Yeah, she told me about your letter. Did you write her a letter when you told her you hated her? Did you write her a letter when you ordered her out of your house? Be a man! You owe her an apology to her face. You talk about how you love her. Look her in the eye and tell her that you're sorry!"

"But . . ."

"No, buts, man. Go to her and tell her you're sorry. Don't ask for anything. Don't try to find out why she hasn't called you. Just apologize. You have to start from the beginning. You have to take it one step at a time."

Warren looked at his friend and realized that the words he spoke were heavy with the truth. He could not ignore them.

"She still loves you," Frank said softly.

"Do you think so?"

"No, I don't think so. I know so. She told me. But she wants an apology from you. Not on a piece of paper but from your lips to her ears, man."

Warren nodded his head, because at the moment he could not speak. He loved Alexandra so completely that at this point, he would do anything to get her back. That was all he wanted, to be with her again.

"I'll go talk to her," he said.

"Don't push, man. Just take it slow," Frank advised.

"Yeah, I will."

Thirty-six

Thursday evening when Shari got off from work, she went over to Alexandra's apartment to help her pack for her move into her new town house on Saturday.

Alexandra had already packed up everything in the kitchen and was working in her bedroom. Shari was packing up the books on Alexandra's living room bookshelf when the doorbell rang.

"I'll get it. Are you expecting company?" Shari called to Alexandra.

"No, but if it's somebody whose come to help, don't turn them away," Alexandra responded with a chuckle.

"Don't worry, honey," Shari laughed.

She opened the door and descended the stairs to answer the bell. She was very surprised to see Warren standing outside the door.

As she opened the outer door, she had a very sardonic smile plastered on her face.

"Hello, Warren."

He took a deep breath. He could vividly remember the sounding off he received from her the last time he saw her.

"Hey, Shari. Is Alexandra here?"

"Yeah, she's here. Come on in."

Warren entered the house cautiously.

Shari covertly looked him up and down. He was

dressed to the teeth in a navy-blue double breasted suit, white shirt, and an abstract print tie. There was a white pocket square in the breast pocket of his jacket. In his right hand he held a beautiful red rose.

"You cut your hair," Shari noticed.

"Oh, yeah," he said, and absentmindedly touched his head.

"It looks nice."

"Thank you."

"Come on upstairs," Shari offered.

Just that morning Warren had gone to the barber and had his long wavy locks cut very short. He felt it was time for a change.

When he entered the apartment behind Shari, he was shocked to see boxes everywhere. Where was she going?

"Who was that, Shari?" Alexandra asked as she came from the back. Before Shari could answer, however, Alexandra noticed Warren.

"Hi, Ally," he said humbly.

"Hi," she said, softly.

Not being able to contain his curiosity, he asked, "Where are you going?"

When she told him about her upcoming move, he said, "Oh. That's nice," his tone apprehensive.

Shari discreetly left the room to afford them some privacy.

They stood awkwardly in front of each other for a few seconds before Warren spoke again.

"Oh, this is for you." He handed her the rose.

Alexandra took it from his hand but did not speak.

"I, uh . . . I just came by because I wanted to apologize to you. I'm sorry for the way I hurt you and for being such a jerk about everything. I know I have no right to ask you for anything but I hope you can forgive me."

Alexandra could feel tears coming to her eyes. He looked so good standing before her, the picture of humility. She was glad he was not bombarding her with questions about why she never told him about the baby. Though she had been angry when he showed up at her office unexpectedly two weeks ago, she was glad he had come here today. She wanted to put her arms around him and tell him how much she still loved him but she did not want to be too hasty. *Take it slow, Alexandra,* she told herself.

"Thank you, Warren," she said, trying to maintain her composure.

They stood again in awkward silence.

Finally, Alexandra spoke.

"Why'd you cut your hair?"

"Oh, I don't know. Just something different, I guess."

When she did not respond, he asked, "You don't like it, huh?"

"Oh, no, it looks nice."

"Thanks," he said with a soft smile.

She was shy about being with him and he could see how nervous she was. But, he was nervous, too.

"Well, I'm not gonna hold you up any longer. I can see you've got a lot to do. I just wanted to tell you that."

He moved to the door and placed his hand on the knob.

"Do you need any help moving?" he asked as he turned back to her.

"No, thank you. I have a professional moving company coming."

"Oh, okay. Well, if you need my help with anything, just call me, all right?"

"All right."

He opened the door and stepped into the corridor. She moved into the doorway to see him off.

"I'll talk to you later," he said.

"Okay."

He moved to the stairs and started to descend. He stopped suddenly and turned back to her. He smiled up at her.

"You know, Alexandra, you look real pretty."

"Thank you," she said.

"Bye," he said, then continued down the stairs.

When Alexandra returned to the apartment, she could no longer control her emotions. Tears fell freely from her eyes.

She moved to the window to watch him as he got in his car and drove away.

She felt a sense of relief that he was gone, though she was glad he had come. She still loved him but she could not let him know that. Not yet. It had been very difficult being so close to him and staying cool. And she knew that though he had hurt her with his cruel words, they had not been from his heart. Being in constant contact with Frank, she was aware of the agony he, too, had gone through despite his attempt at coldness.

"You all right?" Shari asked as she came up behind her.

Alexandra turned to her. She was so choked up that she couldn't speak.

Shari embraced her. "He looks good doesn't he?"

Alexandra could only nod.

She cried on Shari's shoulder for a couple of minutes. Finally, "I still love him, Shari."

"I know you do, Alex. Deep down, he's a good man. Unfortunately, he's just like all the others when it comes to thinking straight, though. They're all babies. You know how confused they get," she said good-naturedly.

Alexandra chuckled and said, "I know."

Thirty-seven

Alexandra woke up the next morning with an incredible feeling of fulfillment. She had thought about Warren all night until she fell blissfully asleep and was thinking about him when she arose that morning.

After reading his letter two weeks ago, she had been tempted to call him, but felt he was still being a coward because he had not had the guts to tell her all he had written to her face.

That had made her angry. But her love for him was so strong that her emotions were all jumbled up. One minute she felt as though her life would end without him, and the next she wanted to hurt him, to pay him back for the way he had hurt her.

She noticed immediately how surprised he was to see her packing. She had wrestled with herself about whether she should tell him about her plans to move. Well, now he knew. She wondered how he felt about that.

She wanted to see him. She started to call him that morning but was too nervous to go through with it. *What would I say to him?* she asked herself. It was not as if there was anything special she wanted to tell him. She just wanted to talk to him, to hear his voice.

She tried to concentrate most of her time on getting as much of her last-minute packing done as possible.

Though her moving contract provided for the packing of her belongings, she really did not trust them to do it without breaking anything.

By three o'clock, she still could not get Warren off her mind. As she began to store her clothes in the storage boxes the moving company had supplied her with, she came across his clothes in her closet. That didn't help. Even after all these months, she could still smell his cologne on them.

She remembered that he had told her to do whatever she wanted with them, that he did not want them, but she could not bring herself to throw them away. It was as though his clothes had been the last little bit of him that she could still hold on to.

She made up her mind to use his clothing to her advantage.

At five-thirty that evening she walked into Michaels. She had not been there in over five months. She noticed that not much had changed about the place other than the staff.

The mâitre d' approached her almost as soon as she was through the door.

"Good evening, ma'am," he said cheerfully. "Will you be dining alone?"

"Oh, no, I was just wondering if Mr. Michaels is in?"

"Oh, certainly. Please, have a seat. I'll get him for you."

Alexandra was seated for maybe two minutes when she heard the sweet sound of his voice from behind.

"Alexandra! Hi!"

She rose immediately and smiled, though nervously.

"Hi, Warren."

"How are you?"

"I'm okay. How are you?"

"Good," he answered with a bright smile.

They stood there for a few seconds without speaking.

"Were you in the neighborhood?" he asked finally.

"No. I came down to, um . . . Well, I was packing some of my clothes yesterday evening after you left, and I realized that I still have some things of yours at my house. I was wondering if you wanted to come by and pick them up or what you wanted me to do with them."

As she spoke, Warren studied her face intently. His heart sang with joy as he realized that she did still love him. He could see it in her eyes.

"I'm surprised you didn't throw them away," he said with a smile.

"Oh, no, I couldn't do that. Not as much as I love clothes. I could never do that."

"Well, you're moving tomorrow, right?"

"Yeah. The movers are coming early tomorrow morning."

"Can I come by tonight to get them?"

"Sure, if you want."

She noticed the way he was looking at her and she could not help blushing.

"I think you look absolutely radiant with the glow of motherhood, Alexandra."

She said a shy, "Thank you."

He wanted to hold her in his arms so bad he could taste it. In order to control himself, he quickly shoved his hands in his pants pockets.

"Have you had dinner?" he suddenly asked.

"No."

"Why don't you have something to eat with me?"

"I can't. I have to make another stop before I go home. I'm meeting someone in a little while," she fibbed as she glanced at her watch.

"Oh, okay. Well, maybe another time."

"Yes."

"So, what time will you be home?"

"I should be back home by seven, seven-thirty."

"I'll come by about eight? Is that all right?"

"That's fine. I'll definitely be there by then," she assured him.

Warren was at Alexandra's house at eight o'clock sharp. He had actually been sitting outside in his car for about fifteen minutes, but he figured he should probably take things slow and try not to be too anxious.

"Hi," she said brightly as she let him in.

"Hi."

"Come on up."

"It looks like you have everything pretty much packed up, huh?" he said as they entered the apartment.

"For the most part, yeah. Sit down."

"Thanks."

"Do you want something to drink? I have a couple of Corona's."

"You do? What are you doing with Corona's. You're not drinking them, I hope," he said in a scolding manner.

She was tickled by his tone.

"No, I'm not drinking them. I've had them in there for months. They're ice cold."

"Well, in that case, yeah, I'll have one."

She removed a bottle from the refrigerator. As she was opening it, he asked her about her new house.

"Oh, it's really nice. It's brand new, so I don't have to worry about cleaning up after anyone. It's got three bedrooms and three bathrooms. Well, really, two and a half bathrooms and a backyard and a full basement."

"Thanks," he said as she handed him his beer. "Is it finished?"

"The basement? No, but I'm not worried about that.

I think I'm going to convert it into a gym. It's really big," she said.

"Sounds nice."

"It is. I'm excited."

"When are you due, Ally?"

"August twelfth."

"Really?"

She nodded her head.

They sat quietly for a few seconds.

"You know, I'm really glad you, um, you decided to have the baby," he said softly.

She bowed her head and murmured, "Me, too."

They sat quietly again because at that moment, there was no need for words between them.

After a while, Warren said, "Did I leave a lot of stuff here?"

"Not really. A few things."

She rose from the couch and started toward the back of the apartment.

"I put everything in a garment bag. I'll go get it," she said.

"Here, let me help you. I don't want you straining yourself."

He followed her into the bedroom.

She moved to the closet and grabbed the garment bag and began to lift it off the rod.

"Hey, no. Stop. I'll do that," he said as he grabbed the bag from her. "There's a lot of stuff in here."

"Well, not really in comparison to the stuff you have at home."

"Yeah, but too much for you to be carrying."

He laid the bag on the bed and began to unzip it.

"Damn, I did have a lot of stuff here," he said as he began to go through the bag. "I'm really surprised you didn't just dump it."

"Why? These things are perfectly good."

He looked at her and smiled.

"You're something else, you know."

"Yeah, I know," she said with a chuckle.

He laughed, too. "Well, thanks for taking such good care of my things."

"You're welcome."

She began to stretch. First her neck, then she bent over backward and forward to stretch her back.

"You all right?" Warren asked.

"My back hurts," she said, frowning.

"Probably doing too much."

"Yeah, probably."

He zipped the garment bag back up, then lifted it off the bed.

"Come on back in the living room. I'll rub your back for you, okay?"

"Okay."

When they reached the living room, she sat down on the sofa.

"Lay down," he told her.

She stretched out on her stomach on the sofa.

"Are you comfortable like that?"

"Yes."

Warren knelt on the floor beside her and began to massage her back. He could feel how tense she was the moment he touched her.

"Relax, Ally. Just relax."

He worked his fingers up her back, kneading her muscles until he could feel the tension going out of them. He loved this. He was in heaven. He wanted to bend over and kiss her on the back of her neck but was satisfied with just being able to touch her this way.

Warren massaged her back for almost twenty minutes, oblivious to the time. He was concentrating so hard that he did not even notice she had fallen asleep.

When he was finished, he asked, "How does that feel?"

But she was nestled in slumber. He leaned back on his haunches and watched her. She looked so beautiful, like a cherub. He reached over and gently brushed her hair from her face so he could take in her beauty. His eyes began to water as he thought of how he had hurt her after she had stood by him for so long. She was a precious jewel.

After a while he rose from where he was and went to her bedroom and retrieved a blanket. He covered her and leaned over to kiss her cheek.

"I love you, Ally," he whispered in her ear.

He picked up his garment bag from the chair he had placed it on and walked to the door. He knew she had a slam lock on her door, so he checked it to make sure it was engaged. He turned off the light and stepped out of the apartment, closing the door softly behind him.

Thirty-eight

Alexandra awoke the next morning at six-thirty. She was still on her living-room couch. When she realized that she must have fallen asleep on Warren, she felt terrible. *He must think I'm the rudest person alive*, she thought.

She got up and went straight to the bathroom. She hated the fact that she had fallen asleep in her clothes. She took them off and started the shower. She tied her hair up in a bun and stepped into the tub.

As she stood under the spray, she thought about Warren. He obviously had not lost his touch. She could remember when he used to give her massages regularly. His fingers had always had the power to lull her into such a state of relaxation that she would doze off. It was clear from last night that he still had magic in his touch. She felt bad, though, that she was not awake when he left.

She stayed in the shower for about ten minutes. She was glad that she had pretty much gotten everything packed up. Now all the movers had to do was load their truck.

She was excited about the prospect of moving into her own home. There were so many things she wanted to do with the place.

When she got out of the shower, she went into her

room and got dressed, putting on a pair of sweat pants and an oversized sweatshirt. She wanted to make sure she was ready for the movers when they showed up. She hoped they would be on time.

At seven-fifteen, her doorbell rang. When she noticed the time, she swore under her breath. They were forty-five minutes early.

She walked to the window and looked out but did not see a moving van. She opened the door and went downstairs to see who was ringing her bell.

She was shocked to see Warren standing outside the door when she got downstairs.

When she opened the door, she said, "Hi! What are you doing here this early?"

He, too, was wearing a sweatsuit and looked as though he was ready to work.

"I brought your breakfast. I noticed yesterday that you also emptied your fridge. I thought you might like a little something to start your day off right," he said as he walked in.

She laughed.

"Where did you get this from?" she asked, taking the bag from him.

"I made it," he said.

"You made it?"

"Yeah."

"But it's still warm," she noticed.

"I flew," he said with a smile.

"Thank you, Warren. I was just wondering what I was gonna eat. I hope you brought enough for yourself."

"No, I already ate. That's for you. Enjoy yourself."

Alexandra set the bag on the table and removed the container. When she lifted the lid, her nostrils were assailed with the smell of Canadian bacon, grits with melted butter, two eggs over easy, just the way she liked them, and a homemade biscuit.

"This looks great."

"Is there anything else you need packed?" Warren asked.

"No, actually, I think I got everything."

"Well, I'll start moving these things out of the way so the movers have no problem getting the big pieces out first."

"Thanks. Oh, Warren, I'm sorry I fell asleep on you last night."

"That's all right. You obviously needed the rest. You were probably pushing yourself too hard. Now I want you to take it easy today. I'll deal with the movers. You just relax, all right?"

She laughed. "All right."

To Alexandra's delight, the movers arrived on time and, with Warren's help, were able to get everything packed onto the truck before noon.

When everything was out of the apartment and she grabbed a broom to begin sweeping the place up, Warren stopped her, took the broom and swept the entire apartment himself.

He suggested that she should get into her car and lead the movers out to her new place. He promised he would meet her there when he was finished cleaning up. She tried to argue with him but he put his foot down. He did not want her doing any form of strenuous work while he was there.

Alexandra was tickled and more than a little flattered that he worried so much about her. She decided not to give him a hard time, but to go along with whatever he asked. After all, like he said, he was only trying to look after her.

* * *

The movers were so good at their job that they had everything moved in by four o'clock that afternoon. They had even arranged the furniture the way she asked. Warren was so impressed by their excellent job, that in addition to their agreed-upon fee, he gave them a generous tip.

When they were gone, Alexandra stood in the middle of the living room and looked around her with a big smile plastered on her face.

Warren smiled at her, knowing exactly what she was feeling.

"It's nice owning your own home, isn't it?" he said.

"Yes."

"It's a nice house. You've got a lot of room here."

"I know. That's what I like." She sighed with happiness.

"You wanna go get something to eat? I'm starving," he said.

"I know you must be. You haven't eaten since this morning, have you?"

"That's right."

"Yeah, come on. I'll treat you."

"No, that's all right, you don't have to do that."

"Yes, I do. You did a lot of work today, and you didn't have to. I really appreciate all of your help."

"Alexandra, I would do anything for you. You know that, don't you?"

She smiled at him but did not answer right away.

"Well, I still wanna buy you dinner. You don't have any objections to that, do you?"

"To a woman as beautiful as you. No, I don't have any objections."

"I'll drive," Alexandra offered.

"No, I'll drive."

"No, I'll drive. You relax for a change."

Alexandra drove them to a nearby Jamaican restaurant that she had discovered on one of her previous visits to her new home.

As they were walking toward the entrance, Warren said, "You know, Ally, maybe we should just get something to go. I'd really rather take a shower before I sit down in somebody's restaurant to eat. You know? I'm kinda sweaty."

"We can do that if you want. It doesn't matter."

Once they had gotten their meal, they stopped at a neighborhood store to get something to drink, then went back to Alexandra's house to eat.

They shared a meal of jerk chicken, curried goat, peas and rice, fried plantains, and a tossed salad.

They sat across from each other at Alexandra's dining-room table. When Warren had cleaned his plate, he leaned back in his chair and rubbed his stomach.

"That was delicious."

Alexandra smiled. "It sure was. I wanna eat some more but there's no room."

Warren smiled at her. He thought she looked so beautiful at that moment. He missed being with her this way.

"You know what, Ally?"

"What?"

"I've missed you."

Alexandra looked into his eyes for a moment before she lowered hers. Suddenly, she rose from the table and picked up her plate and his and took them to the sink. She turned on the water and immediately began to clean the two plates.

Warren rose from his chair, noticing her mood had suddenly changed. He walked over and stood behind her.

"What's wrong?"

"Nothing."

He reached around her and turned off the water, then took the utensils she was cleaning out of her hands and placed them back in the sink. He turned her to face him.

"Talk to me," he said softly as he placed his hands on her shoulders.

She looked into his eyes. "What do you want me to say?"

"Whatever's on your mind."

"You don't want to know what's on my mind, Warren."

"Yes, I do. Ally, I know how you feel. I know I've got a long way to go to make things right with you, but I want to. I'll do anything to make things right again."

She was silent for the next few seconds.

"Talk to me," he urged.

She thought for a moment and decided that she had to say what was on her mind. She knew it would be the only way they could really begin to mend their relationship. Besides, if she didn't ask him, it would eat at her for the rest of her life.

"How many women were you with while you were missing me?" she asked sarcastically.

He was surprised by her antagonistic tone. He looked at her for a moment before he answered. He released his hold on her and stepped back. He could see in her eyes that she was angry and he knew she was justified, but he had honestly, though naively, thought they had gotten past this.

"None."

She sucked her teeth and moved away from him.

"None?" she questioned in a cynical tone. "How dare you lie to me? I saw you with one who looked like she was still in high school. Did you forget that?"

"Ally, that was my cousin."

She cut her eyes at him. "Oh, give me a break."

"I swear, baby, that was my cousin." He went on to explain, and finished with, "I love you, Alexandra. I loved you then and I love you now."

"Spare me, Warren!" she said angrily. "You told me you hated me. Don't you remember that?"

"Because you hurt me."

"I hurt you? I hurt you!" she raged.

"Alexandra, I know what I did . . . the way I handled that was wrong. I know it was cowardly of me to try and keep all of that from you. I'm ashamed of what I did to you, but when you told me you didn't want to be with me anymore, that hurt. That hurt more than anything I've ever felt and I didn't know how to deal with it. I didn't mean what I said. I never meant it. I'll be honest with you, though. I wanted to hate you because it hurt too much to know that you didn't want me anymore. I tried not to think about you. I tried to do everything I could to not think about you."

He paused for a moment to collect his thoughts. When he continued, his tone was softer.

"I thought about dating a number of women but I couldn't. It would have been like rubbing salt in my wounds. Then when I found out that Susan had been stringing me along all that time, I felt like I was being paid back for what I'd done to you."

"Do you think it was easy for me to do what I did? Do you really think that was easy?"

"No. I know it wasn't. I was selfish, that's all. I was only thinking of myself."

They stared at each other for a few minutes without a word between them.

Finally, Alexandra plopped down on her sofa, seemingly exhausted.

"When Wanda told me she had seen you and that you were still pregnant, I was . . . I was overjoyed. I figured that you must still care for me if you were willing to have my baby."

"That wasn't the plan," she admitted.

He came and sat next to her on the sofa.

"I had every intention of not having it. I even went to a clinic. I was just too afraid to go through with it."

"Why didn't you tell me?" he asked hesitantly.

She looked over at him and asked, "How was I supposed to tell you? After what you'd said to me, I didn't want anything to do with you. I didn't even want to have your baby."

"Are you sorry that you're having it?"

"No. Not now. I decided that I wasn't going to punish my baby for what had happened between us. That's one of the reasons I decided to buy this house. I felt like I needed a change. I wanted to start all over again. When I saw Wanda that day, I started to run from her because I didn't want you to know that I was still pregnant."

"I know I owe you the world for the way you stuck by me with Susan. I'll do anything you want to make that up to you. But aside from that, I want to be a part of our baby's life, Ally. I want to take care of you and him."

They were silent for a few minutes, each absorbed in what the other had said.

"Does he move around a lot?" Warren finally asked.

"Yeah. He's moving right now."

"Can I feel?"

She nodded her head.

He gently placed his hand on her stomach. He felt the baby moving inside her, and a chill went up his spine. He kept his hand there for almost five minutes. It was almost as if he could not move it away.

"He's an active little guy, isn't he?" Warren finally said with a smile.

"Oh, yeah, that he is."

"Do you know if it's a boy or a girl?"

"No, but I have a feeling it's a boy. A football player," she said with a chuckle.

"A quarterback."

They gazed into each other's eyes, and no words were needed between them. At that moment, their love for each other was as clear as a freshly washed pane of glass.

Warren removed his hand from Alexandra's tummy and gently caressed her face. He leaned closer to her so that he could kiss her. To his delight, she did not pull away. Though he wanted to take her in his arms and devour her, he merely placed a tender kiss on her lips.

They sat there, frozen in that position for what seemed like hours. Warren was so pleased to be able to be close to her this way that he could have screamed, but he stayed cool. Alexandra, on the other hand, felt her eyes begin to water and made no move to wipe her tears away. She was glad that he was there with her. She had missed him, too. When Warren noticed her tears, he gently kissed them away.

"I love you, Ally."

She wanted to tell him that she loved him, too, but the words would not come. She was afraid of being hurt again. She had never doubted his love, not even when Susan tried to destroy it, but the hurt was still fresh in her heart and mind and she sensed that if she confessed her true feelings, she would tear down the wall of protection she felt she needed between them.

"I'm gonna get ready to go," Warren conceded.

He knew she still had doubts about him. He could feel them.

He rose from the couch and stretched his arms up over his head.

"Boy, I'm beat."

"Thank you for helping me, Warren," she said softly.

"You don't have to thank me. I'll come by tomorrow to help you start putting this stuff away."

"You've already done so much."

"No, I haven't. I owe you."

Alexandra rose from the couch and stood before him.
He caressed her cheek before he turned to the door.
"I'll see you tomorrow, all right?"

She nodded.

"Good night, beautiful." He suddenly bent over in
front of her and touched her stomach again. "Good
night, baby. See you tomorrow."

Alexandra laughed softly.

When he straightened up, he kissed her softly on her
cheek. "See ya."

She stood at the door and watched him as he drove
away. As she closed the door and turned to look at her
new house, she felt a twinge of sadness. She did not
want to spend her first night there alone.

Thirty-nine

She was up at eight o'clock that next morning. She took a shower and got dressed and plunged right into the job of getting her new house in order.

As she went about her tasks, she thought about the conversation she and Warren had last night. She knew he was sincere in everything he had told her. He wrote in his letter that he had decided to be truthful with her about everything, and he had been. Though it was hard to hold her true feelings for him inside, she knew it would be for the best if she took her time. She missed being with him and had yearned for the day when they might be together again.

He was at her door at nine-thirty.

"Good morning," he said cheerfully, kissing her on the lips as he stepped into the house.

"How are you?" he asked.

"Good. How are you?"

"All right."

"I didn't expect you this early. You didn't go to the club last night, did you?"

"Yeah, I went."

"What are you doing here so early? You must be exhausted."

"No, as a matter of fact, I feel quite . . . perky," he said with a grin.

"You know what I realized?"

"What?"

"I don't have any food here. I have to go food shopping."

"Let's go."

"You don't mind?"

"Of course not. Come on," he said as he stepped back to the door and placed his hand on the knob.

"Okay, let me go get my purse."

She hurriedly headed toward the stairs and began to run up them.

"Hey you, slow down. I'm not going anywhere. Take your time."

He did not want her to do anything that would jeopardize her safety or the baby's. If it was up to him, he would literally carry her everywhere she needed to go. He knew, however, that she would never go for that.

They returned from the supermarket two hours later. They had stopped on the way to get something to eat since neither of them had had breakfast that morning.

Alexandra was in the kitchen putting her groceries away and Warren was putting her stereo system together when the doorbell rang.

"Are you expecting company?" he asked her.

"No, but maybe it's my new neighbors coming to welcome me. That's the kind of stuff they do when you have a house, right?"

Warren laughed and said, "Yeah, that's the kind of stuff they do."

Alexandra went to open the door.

"Hi!" Shari sung. "We were in the neighborhood so we thought we'd stop by," Shari lied.

"Hi, Al."

"Hi, Frank," Alexandra said with a quizzical smile.

He kissed her cheek and said, "Nice house you've got here."

"Thank you."

Alexandra looked at Shari with a questioning glance. How did these two get together? she wondered.

"Hi, Warren," Shari said.

"Hey, Shari. Hey, Frank," Warren said with the same questioning look.

"I wasn't expecting you so early, Shari, and I wasn't expecting you, Frank, at all."

"Yeah, well, Shari told me she was coming over. I didn't think you'd mind if I tagged along."

"Of course, I don't mind. But can I ask y'all something? What . . . ? How'd . . . ?" Alexandra started.

"Come on, Frank, let me show you the house," Shari said, grabbing his arm before Alexandra could begin her grilling.

As Shari pulled Frank up the stairs, Alexandra and Warren looked at each other with a frown.

"Did we miss something?" Warren asked.

"I guess we did," Alexandra commented.

When Shari was finished showing Frank the house, they returned to the kitchen where Alexandra was still putting away her groceries.

"This is really a nice place you have, Al."

"Thanks, Frankie. I'm glad you like it."

"So, what do you want me to do?"

"You didn't come to work, did you?"

"Of course."

"Well, in that case, take your pick. As you can see, there are plenty of boxes that need emptying."

Frank looked around for a moment then said, "Where are your books? I'll start shelving them."

"See those four boxes over there," Alexandra said, pointing.

"All right," Frank said, and headed in that direction.

"Oh, Frankie?"

"Yeah."

"You're gonna hate me, but I like to keep my books in alphabetical order," Alexandra said with a grimace.

Frank smiled and said, "Don't worry, Al, so do I."

Shari volunteered her services next. "Okay, what can I do?"

Alexandra grabbed her hand. "You can help me upstairs. I have some things that have to be put away up there."

Warren looked at Alexandra skeptically, knowing that she was going to give Shari the third degree about her and Frank. He had to admit, though, he wanted to know what was going on, too.

As soon as they were up the stairs, Warren asked, "So, Frank, what's up with you and Shari?"

Alexandra pulled Shari into her bedroom and closed the door behind them.

"What is going on with you and Frank?"

"What? What are you talking about?" Shari asked, feigning innocence.

"Don't even try it, Shari. I want the scoop."

Shari blushed.

"Are you blushing?" Alexandra asked, incredulously.

"Yeah, so what? Look, I don't know what happened. It just happened."

"What?" Alexandra asked impatiently.

"Okay, sit down," Shari said, grabbing Alexandra's hand and leading her to the bed. "Friday night, I went to Michaels Too, you know, just to hang out."

"With who?"

"By myself. Frank was at the door, and for some reason he was looking better than he ever had before. Well, I was downstairs sitting at the bar having a drink when he came over and we started talking. He asked me if I was hungry and though I really wasn't, I told him I was.

He took me upstairs and bought me dinner. After dinner, we just hung out. You know, he bought me drinks and we talked. About everything. We were sitting downstairs and I was telling him something about you and Warren, I don't even remember what, but he took my hand and said, 'I don't want to hear about them. I wanna hear about you.' "

Alexandra giggled like a little girl.

Shari smiled and continued.

"Well, anyway, he ended up driving me home and we sat in his car outside my building for almost two hours, talking and laughing and stuff. I didn't want to go upstairs and he didn't want to leave. Finally, the sun was coming up so we decided to say good night or good morning. We made plans to have dinner that night."

"Did he kiss you?" Alexandra asked eagerly.

"Yeah, but it was just a kiss on the cheek," Shari admitted. "When he picked me up last night, though, he brought a dozen long-stemmed roses. He took me to this really elegant Japanese restaurant where you have to take off your shoes and sit on the floor and everything. It was really nice. Then we went to this little jazz club and we danced and talked and you know, just had fun. You know, Al, he's like the sweetest man I've ever known. He's so romantic. He was telling me things like . . . He said I reminded him of an African princess and, you know, I've heard all kinds of stuff from all kinds of guys who would just tell me anything, trying to impress me, but with Frank, it wasn't like it was a line. It was . . . I could tell he was sincere, you know. I don't know, I've never felt like this before. He makes me feel like . . . like I'm special. When he took me home last night, I asked him to come in. We sat on the couch and had some wine and listened to a couple of CD's and just talked. I can talk to him about anything and he listens, like he really cares."

"Frankie is a sweetheart," Alexandra concurred.

"Yeah, he is."

"Did he spend the night?"

"I was nervous with him," Shari started. "I wanted to make love to him, but I didn't want him to think that I was easy, you know, or that I would just go bed for the hell of it, though we both know I have before. But I didn't want it to be like that with him. We were sitting there and he kissed me, really for the first time. And he was so gentle. I just melted in his arms. You know, I feel like I'm under a spell or something. Nothing's ever felt this right. Never. I'm in love with him, Alexandra. It's crazy, I know, but that's how I feel. I don't want to be with anyone else."

Alexandra sat and listened to Shari telling of her feelings for Frank with the biggest smile. She was happy for Shari and for Frank. She knew what a sweet person Frank was and she thought he would be good for Shari.

"He was fantastic, Alex. The best lover I've ever had. I mean, we made love until we couldn't move. I could not get enough of him and vice versa." Shari was beaming. She hugged herself and sighed, "I'm in love."

Alexandra leaned over and put her arms around Shari, hugging her, too.

"I'm happy for you, Shari. I'm really happy for you. I think you and Frank make a great couple and you deserve someone special like him and he deserves someone as wonderful as you."

"I'm gonna marry him, Alexandra. I don't know when, but I'm gonna marry him. I'm not gonna let him get away," Shari said emphatically.

"I heard that."

"Did Warren stay with you last night?"

"No, he went home. I don't want to go too fast. I'm trying to be cool, but all this talk about making love has me a bit warm, if you know what I mean. I haven't had any since January second."

"Damn, you even know the date," Shari laughed.

"Yeah, it's marked on my calendar."

Both girls laughed at that.

"Come on let's go back downstairs. I know they know we're talking about them," Shari said.

"Yeah, I'm sure."

They rose from the bed and headed toward the door.

"I'm really happy for you, Shari."

By six o'clock, they all decided that they had unpacked enough boxes for one day.

Warren volunteered to make dinner for them.

They sat around Alexandra's dining-room table and ate Warren's special homemade spaghetti and meatballs, garlic bread, and a tossed green salad.

Earlier in the day, Frank ran out to the store, and as they sat down to dinner, he popped open a bottle of Moët and toasted Alexandra in her new home.

"Al, I just want to say that I'm proud of you, honey. You've been through a lot of shit in the last few months and you've come through it all with flying colors. I wish you all the best in your new home and lots of love and happiness and, of course, a healthy baby."

"Thank you, Frankie," Alexandra blushed.

Warren was a bit embarrassed by Frank's candidness, but he figured they were all friends and they all knew what he had put her through.

"Cheers," Frank said.

"Cheers," Shari and Warren echoed.

They all sipped from their glasses.

After Alexandra took her first sip, Warren said, "Ally, you don't need to drink any more of that. It's not good for the baby."

"Warren, one glass of champagne is not going to hurt the baby. It's not like I do this all the time. Please, let me indulge myself," Alexandra coaxed.

"Yeah, Warren, don't be such a spoil sport," Frank teased.

"Damn, what is this, gang up on Warren night? I just slaved over a hot stove to cook dinner for you people," Warren said, good-naturedly.

"Oh, shut up!" Frank, Shari, and Alexandra chorused.

They all laughed.

After dinner, they all praised Warren's meal.

"Damn, that was smokin'. What are you doing tomorrow night? I'ma be hungry about this same time," Frank joked.

Warren laughed.

"Yeah? That's nice," he said.

"That was good, Warren. You make some mean spaghetti and meatballs," Shari declared.

"Thanks, Shari. I'm glad you enjoyed it."

"Oh, I did. Especially since I didn't have to cook it."

"Right," Alexandra agreed.

"Okay, so who's gonna do the dishes?" Warren asked. "And don't look at me."

"I'll do 'em," Shari offered.

"Oh, thanks, Shari," Alexandra said, gratefully.

"That's all right. You're on your own tomorrow, though," she said with a smile.

They all pitched in and helped Shari clean up the kitchen, then moved back to the living room to relax.

At about nine o'clock, Shari and Frank left, leaving Warren and Alexandra alone.

"That was fun. I'm glad they came over," Alexandra said to Warren, with a smile.

"Yeah, it was fun. I'm still a little shocked about Shari and Frank, though."

"Yeah, I know, but I'm happy for them. Shari's really crazy about him. I mean she's really . . ."

"Yeah? Frank, too."

"They make a nice couple."

Warren nodded his head in agreement.

Alexandra moved back to the sofa and plopped down on it.

"Whew, I'm tired," she sighed.

"Yeah, I'm not surprised. Hey, I'ma get ready to go, too, so you can get some rest."

"Okay. Thanks for everything, Warren. You've really been a big help to me."

"I haven't done enough, Alexandra. If it's okay with you, I'll come by tomorrow night and try to finish getting the rest of your stuff unpacked."

"You don't have to."

"Yeah, I do. I don't want you pushing yourself. You should take it easy."

She smiled at him. Regardless of everything that had happened between them, he was still one of the sweetest men she had ever known.

"If you want to come by tomorrow, it's all right with me. I wasn't going to mess with any more of this stuff until next weekend anyway."

"Well, when I come by tomorrow, you just show me where you want everything and I'll take care of it."

"Thanks."

Warren walked to the door. Alexandra rose from the couch and followed.

"Thanks for dinner," she told him.

"My pleasure, lovely." He bent over and kissed her belly. "Good night, handsome."

"She may resent that," Alexandra said with a smile.

"No, he won't," Warren laughed. He kissed her softly on the mouth. "Sleep tight, princess. I'll see you tomorrow."

* * *

Over the next few weeks, Warren became somewhat of a fixture in Alexandra's life again. He visited her every evening, even if it was for a few minutes. He went with her to her doctor appointments and told her to keep him abreast of her appointment dates because he would make himself available so he could go with her. Aside from his concern for her well-being because of her condition, Warren began to court her again. He took her to dinner and plays; he sent her flowers and bought her gifts. Through all of this, though, he never pressured her about her feelings for him, and though he dreamed of the day he would be able to hold her and kiss her and make love to her again, he never mentioned any of that to her.

One evening after having a wonderful dinner and attending a great jazz concert, Warren came in for a brief moment. He had a beer when they got there, as Alexandra kept them on hand now for him.

They were sitting together on the couch when she let out a big yawn.

Warren smiled as he rose from the couch and walked to the kitchen to throw out his beer bottle. When he returned to the living room he said, "I'm gonna cut out, baby."

"Oh, you are?" she asked, a bit dismayed.

"Yeah. Don't get up, though. I'll see myself out."

Warren stepped over to the sofa and leaned over her to kiss her good night.

"Are you working tomorrow?" he asked.

"Yeah."

"Well, then you should get some sleep."

"Yeah, I guess," she said spiritlessly.

Warren noticed her solemn mood and questioned it. "What's the matter?"

She looked down at her hands in her lap and could not stop the tears she felt coming to her eyes.

When he heard her sniffle, he sat next to her and took her hands.

"Honey, what's wrong?" he asked again.

Sheepishly, she looked up at him. It was difficult for her to say what was in her heart because of everything that had happened between them. Though he had been a perfect angel in the past few weeks they had spent together, she did not want to be hurt again but she did not want to lose him either.

"I don't want you to leave, Warren."

He did not respond. He really did not know how to. He did know, however, that he did not want to leave, either. Was she trying to tell him that she still loved him, he wondered. He hoped so.

As he looked into her tear-filled eyes, he longed to kiss her tears away. He wondered if he was being too presumptuous by thinking that she would want to kiss him as much as he wanted to kiss her.

After a few seconds of quiet contemplation, he decided to take his chances. He leaned closer to her and gently pressed his lips to hers.

To his sheer delight, she immediately released his hands and embraced him as she pushed her tongue into his mouth and kissed him hungrily.

He returned her embrace with eagerness, as he had longed for this day, seemingly forever.

"Oh, Warren, I love you so much," she cried when their lips parted. "I love you."

He continued to hold her, deliriously happy that she would be his again.

"I love you, Alexandra," he sighed breathlessly.

"I want you to stay with me. I don't want to be alone tonight."

"I won't leave you, sweetheart. I'll never leave you," Warren promised.

Two hours later, Alexandra lay snuggled close in Warren's welcoming embrace.

She was deliriously happy. Being with him again this way made her feel like that. During their lovemaking, she had been nearly insatiable. At first, Warren was very cautious because he was trying to be considerate of the fact that she was pregnant and he did not want to hurt her, but Alexandra made it very difficult for him to be tame.

He, too, was overjoyed to be able to love her again. It had been far too long. He was eager to give her all of his love but held back for as long as he could or, more aptly, for as long as Alexandra allowed. She assured him that he would not hurt her. She told him that she did not want him to love her cautiously, or gently, for that matter. She wanted him to love her the way they used to love, with abandon. She attacked him fiercely and he loved every minute of it. When he saw that she was able to take him completely, he gave in to her and pulled out all the stops.

As Alexandra lay with her head on his muscular chest, she stroked the soft hair that covered his torso. She was overwhelmed with the love she felt for him and had to fight to hold back the urge to scream out her joy lest he think she was losing her mind. She thought about the love they had between them before Susan's attempts to tear them apart. She thought about the love she still felt for him after learning that she was pregnant. She also thought about the love she felt for him when she told him good-bye.

"Warren," she softly uttered. She was not sure if he was still awake.

"Yes, baby."

"I'm really sorry about what Susan did to you. I know that must have really hurt you."

Warren hugged her closer. He thanked God, at that moment, for her love.

Alexandra raised her head so that she could look into his eyes in the darkness of the room.

"I hope I can give you a son."

He smiled at her. He gently kissed her forehead. "You've already given me everything I need, Alexandra. I have you. That's all I need."

Forty

One month later . . .

Shari and Frank were still going strong. They had become inseparable.

Alexandra and Warren, though extremely happy for their friends, were still a bit stunned at how intense their love seemed to be for each other. Warren often told Alexandra that Frank "walked, talked and breathed Shari," and Alexandra said the same was true of Shari's feelings for Frank.

As a result of their respective relationships, Alexandra and Warren did not see Shari and Frank as often as they had before. Frank, of course, was still managing Michaels Too, but Warren now spent less time there in the evenings and more time at Michaels in the city because it allowed him to be with Alexandra more as she approached her due date.

Though in actuality, Alexandra was still six weeks away from her due date, Warren was very protective of her. He refused to allow her to do anything he thought would be the slightest bit strenuous. At times, Alexandra became quite annoyed with Warren's smothering, but more often than not, she kept it to herself. She knew the only reason he behaved the way he did was because he cared and, truthfully, how could she be angry with that?

Because she had not seen Shari in over a month, Alexandra had really been looking forward to getting together with her that last Saturday during June. She told Shari when she spoke to her that morning that she was glad to be able to get away from Warren for a few hours.

"He's driving me crazy," she had said.

"Aw, don't complain. You should be flattered that he's making such a fuss over you," Shari told her.

"I am, but sometimes he acts as though I can't do anything for myself. That gets a little tiring."

"Well, you'd better enjoy it while you can, 'cause once that baby gets here, you won't be able to find him," Shari said with a chuckle.

"You're probably right."

"So, listen, I'll come and get you at about one, okay?"

"I'll drive," Alexandra offered.

"No, you won't. I'm driving. All I need is for you to go into labor behind the wheel. And don't give me any arguments."

"Yes, ma'am."

The girls took in a movie and did a bit of shopping. Shari bought Frank some silk boxer shorts and Alexandra bought Warren three pairs of multicolored bikini briefs. And they each bought a pair of shoes.

Over dinner, they exchanged stories about their sexcapades. Alexandra had Shari laughing as she told her how she had broken Warren out of the habit of making love to her with caution. Shari boasted of Frank's strength and stamina, stating that "when it comes to making love, my man holds the patent on originality."

They discussed Alexandra's baby and Shari asked her about names.

"Well, if it's a boy—"

"Please don't say you're gonna name it Warren the third," Shari exclaimed, cutting Alexandra off.

"No. I'm gonna name him Stefan Anthony. If it's a girl, I'm gonna name her Alexis Noelle."

"That's pretty," Shari said with a smile. "I really thought you were gonna name her after me, though."

"I'll name the next one after you."

It was almost seven-thirty before they decided to leave the restaurant. They were at the door when Alexandra decided she had better use the ladies' room because they had a half-hour drive ahead of them.

Shari sat in the foyer of the restaurant and waited for Alexandra. When she rejoined her there, Alexandra sighed, "Chile, I woulda been in trouble if I hadn't stopped. This baby is pressing down on my bladder somethin' terrible."

"Well, at least you went. That should hold you for about a half an hour, right?" Shari laughed.

Alexandra joined her.

As they walked through the door of the restaurant to the street, they were still laughing about some of the disadvantages of pregnancy.

Neither of them saw the man running toward them like a bat out of hell, clutching the pocketbook of a woman he had just snatched it from. The man did not see them, either, and slammed right into Alexandra, knocking her to the ground and falling with her.

Shari screamed when she saw Alexandra go down, and as the man hurriedly scrambled to his feet, Shari dropped to her knees to help her friend.

Alexandra tried to get up, almost as a reflex, but Shari would not let her move.

"Take it easy, honey. Lie still," she urged. "Somebody call a doctor! She's pregnant!" Shari yelled to the quickly gathering crowd.

"I'm all right, Shari," Alexandra said with a moan.

She did not realize that she was bleeding.

There was a cut on her left cheek where her face had hit the ground.

"No, you lie still! I'm taking you to the hospital."

"But, Shari . . ."

"No, buts. You're going whether you feel all right or not. I want to make sure. I don't want anything to happen to you or my godchild."

Miraculously, an ambulance was there in less than twenty minutes.

By the time they arrived at the hospital emergency room, Alexandra was unconscious and hemorrhaging. As the paramedics hurriedly wheeled her stretcher into the hospital, Shari stayed with them, running alongside for as long as she could until the hospital personnel stopped her as they entered a private treatment room.

She noticed the blood on Alexandra's pants, and a chill went through her bones. Shari prayed that she would be all right and would not lose her baby.

She headed straight for the public phone in the waiting room and swore out loud when she got no answer at Alexandra's house, nor at Warren's, and was told that he was not at Michaels. She finally called Frank at Michaels Too, telling him what had happened and insisting that he find Warren and bring him to the hospital immediately.

An hour passed before Warren and Frank arrived, and though she had tried to speak to the nurses on duty numerous times, she was given no information on Alexandra's condition.

Frank had tried to reach Warren for almost a half hour without success before Warren walked in the door of Michaels Too. He was standing at the bar with the telephone receiver to his ear when he spied him. He immediately hung up and called out across the crowded restaurant.

"Warren!"

Forty-one

They were on the highway heading toward Manhattan. Frank was doing sixty-five on a fairly crowded straightaway.

"Can't you drive this thing any faster?" Warren yelled at Frank.

"Warren, take it easy, man. I'm going as fast as I can," Frank said.

Tears were rolling down Warren's face, and Frank knew he had not meant to yell at him. He was worried about Alexandra and his baby. He could understand. Frank was worried about them, too.

He had not told Warren everything that Shari told him. He did not tell him that she had been hemorrhaging when they took her into the emergency room. He did not feel that Warren needed to know that. He was upset enough as it was.

"I should have been with her," Warren moaned. "I should have been with her."

"Warren, man, you couldn't have known that this would happen."

"If I had been with her, it wouldn't have happened!"

"You don't know that."

"Yes, I do."

They sat in silence for the next fifteen minutes as Frank maneuvered in and out of traffic.

"I can't lose her, Frank. I can't," Warren groaned.

Frank did not know how to comfort Warren so he remained silent.

"I've put her through so much," he said. "I was careless and Susan took advantage of that." He paused before he went on. "You know, I was real skeptical about how I would feel about Susan's baby, but when I saw that little boy and held him in my arms it was like . . . I don't know, I can't describe it, but I was happy to have a son. When I found out that he wasn't mine, I was crushed. Now, with this happening, I don't know what I'd do if I lost Alexandra and this baby, Frank."

"You won't, Warren. You won't. They'll be all right, you'll see," Frank said, praying it was true.

When they finally arrived at the hospital, Shari was near the emergency room entrance waiting for them.

Warren jumped out of the car before Frank had even stopped it completely.

"Shari! Where is she?"

"They took her up to maternity," Shari informed them.

As he ran past her, he called back, "What floor?"

"Five."

Frank poked his head out of the car and Shari called to him, "Go park the car. I'll wait here for you."

Warren rushed right to the elevators to take him upstairs to the maternity ward. As he stood on the empty elevator, he watched anxiously as the floor numbers repetitiously dimmed and lit with each passing floor. He prayed silently for Alexandra and his unborn child.

After what seemed an eternity, the doors opened to the fifth-floor corridor. He almost crashed into a doctor who stood on the other side of the elevator door as he hurriedly exited.

"Excuse me," he said breathlessly as he brushed past the woman.

He hurried to the nurses' station and, without skipping a beat, interrupted three nurses in the middle of a conversation.

"I'm looking for Alexandra Jenkins."

The more senior of the three women looked at him over the rim of her glasses and said, "Excuse me!"

"Alexandra Jenkins. She was brought in here a while ago by some paramedics. She's pregnant!"

"Well, I would hope so since this is the maternity ward," the nurse said.

"Is she here?" Warren asked, becoming all the more impatient.

"Who are you?"

"Her husband!"

One of the other nurses, who had stepped away from the group and was examining some records on the desk, answered.

"She's in surgery."

"Surgery?"

"Oh, God," Warren sighed.

Seeing how distraught he was, the nurse said, "If you'll have a seat in the waiting room, I'll let you know as soon as I have any information on her condition."

"How long has she been in there?" Warren questioned.

"I'm really not sure, sir."

"She didn't lose the baby, did she?"

"I don't know. I'm sorry. I don't have any information. You'll just have to wait. Sorry."

At that moment Warren turned away from the desk, exasperated that he could not learn anything about Alexandra's condition.

Shari and Frank were just rounding the corner.

"Warren, where is she?" Shari called as soon as she spotted him.

"In surgery," he answered in a trembling voice.

"Oh, no," Shari cried.

"I'm sorry but you'll have to go to the waiting room. You can't stand here," one of the nurses told them.

"What happened?" Shari asked as Frank tried to usher them toward the waiting room.

"I don't know. Nobody can tell me anything," Warren said.

"She'll be all right," Frank said optimistically as he placed a comforting arm around Warren's shoulders, and squeezed Shari's hand.

Warren, Frank, and Shari were in the waiting room for over an hour. They took turns pacing from one end of the room to the other. At one point, Warren became so fed up with waiting that he started to storm out to the nurses' station to demand they give him some information about Alexandra.

Frank stopped him, and Warren broke down. He was so afraid of losing Alexandra, especially after all they had been through and after coming so far together.

Shari, too, broke down after seeing Warren so distraught. Unlike Warren, she knew how bad Alexandra had been bleeding when they brought her in.

It was just past eleven that evening when a nurse entered the waiting room looking for them.

"Mr. Jenkins?"

Warren jumped right up.

"Yes!"

"Your wife's out of surgery. They've taken her to recovery."

"How is she?"

"Right now she's in stable but guarded condition. She lost a lot of blood due to the hemorrhaging."

"Oh, no," he sighed.

"She's still under the influence of the anesthesia and probably won't be awake until early morning."

"What about the baby?"

"The baby's fine. It was delivered by Cesarean section. She had a boy."

Warren sighed with relief.

"Can I see him?"

"Sure. He's in the nursery."

"Can I see her?" he asked.

"She's still asleep."

"I just want to look at her. Please?"

"I'll ask the doctor. In the meantime, you can see your son."

"Thank you."

Warren turned to Frank and Shari who were standing right behind him.

He smiled halfheartedly and said, "She had a boy."

Shari put her arms around him and hugged him.

"Congratulations," Frank said over Shari's shoulder.

"I want to see Ally," Warren said.

"She'll be okay," Shari said confidently. "I know she will. Come on, let's go see the baby."

She pulled them along like an anxious little girl.

When they stepped up to the window of the nursery, they did not spot Alexandra's baby first off.

"Where is he?" Warren asked.

"I don't know," Frank said. "Are you sure he's in this room?"

There were several rooms filled with bassinets.

Shari had moved to the next window and found a lone bassinet sitting in the middle of the floor, away from the window.

This baby was in an incubator. It was smaller than the other babies, but other than that, it looked fine.

"I found him!" she called to them.

Warren immediately moved over to her. When he saw the infant, a chill went through him.

He noticed how tiny he was, and it frightened him at first.

Suddenly, a nurse entered the room from another entrance.

Shari tapped on the glass, and though the nurse could not hear her, she called, "Can you move him closer to the window?"

The nurse shook her head no, and moved toward the glass. She was about to draw the shade on the window.

"Visiting hours are over!" they read her lips as saying.

"That's my son!" Warren said, tapping his chest.

She pointed at Warren, "Yours?"

"Yes."

She pulled the blinds down. A few seconds later, the door to their immediate left opened and the nurse walked out.

"Only the father can come in," she said. "You have to put this on, though."

"Why is he in the incubator?" Shari asked.

"He's a preemie. He only weighs five pounds and two ounces. Until they're five eight, they have to be incubated. But don't worry. He's fine. His breathing and heart rate are normal, otherwise he'd be on a respirator."

Warren had donned the gown the nurse had given him and was ready to see his son.

When he stepped into the nursery and moved over to the bassinet, he stood over it watching his son as he slept. He studied the infant as best he could from his vantage point. The baby was lying on his stomach with his knees tucked under him and his backside sticking up. His tiny fists were held close to his face and he looked peaceful.

Warren smiled, and tears came to his eyes as he watched him. He did not want to disturb him but he wanted to hold him.

"Can I pick him up?" he asked the nurse.

The nurse stepped over to the incubator and removed the top. Warren reached in and petted the baby.

"What are you going to name him?" the nurse asked.

"Stefan Anthony Michaels," Warren said, proudly.

The nurse smiled. "That's a nice name."

Warren noticed the resemblance to Alexandra. He thought he was a beautiful baby. He could tell, though, that he would take his coloring after him. He was already a rich brown complexion and his head was covered with straight jet-black hair.

"Hey, little man," Warren cooed. "How you doin'? How you doin', little man?"

Warren was in the nursery with Stefan for over an hour. He had completely forgotten that Shari and Frank were waiting for him.

When he rejoined them in the waiting room, Shari was asleep with her head on Frank's shoulder.

"Damn, Frank, I'm sorry I had you guys waiting out here so long," Warren said immediately.

"That's all right. How is he?"

Warren sat down next to Frank and said, "Aw, man, he's beautiful. He's . . . beautiful."

Frank smiled but remained silent. He was happy for Warren.

Shari woke up then.

"Hi, Warren," she said with a yawn. "How is he?"

"He's great. They haven't said anything about Ally, have they?" Warren asked.

"No," Shari and Frank answered together.

"I'll be right back," Warren said, and left them again, in search of information about Alexandra's condition.

To his disappointment, he was told that she would not be allowed any visitors until she was out of Recovery.

Warren told Shari and Frank, "Y'all might as well go home and get some rest because they said she'll be in there all night."

"What about you?" Shari asked.

"I'm not leaving until I can see her."

"Then we'll stay, too," Frank said.

305

Forty-two

Warren returned to the nursery twice that night while they waited to see Alexandra. He had been unable to sleep. He was too excited about Stefan and too nervous about Alexandra.

At seven-fifteen the next morning, Warren returned to the nurses' station to inquire about Alexandra. To his delight, they informed him that she was doing well and she had just been moved into a private room.

He hurried back to the waiting room to tell Shari and Frank the good news.

He startled both of them out of their sleep.

"What happened?" Shari asked, alarmed at being brought out of her sleep so abruptly.

"They moved her. She's out of Recovery."

Frank stretched and yawned as he said, "That's good."

"Have you seen her yet?" Shari asked.

"No, not yet. I'm going right now. Are y'all coming?"

"Okay, we'll be in. You go ahead."

"All right," Warren said, and turned away from them. He turned back, suddenly, and with a big smile, said, "They said she's doing okay, too."

Frank and Shari both smiled.

When Warren reached Alexandra's room, he tiptoed over to her bed. He stood over her and smiled as his eyes began to water. He touched her hand gently and she opened her eyes.

"Hi, baby," he said softly.

"Hi."

He leaned over and kissed her gently on her lips. He caressed her cheek as he asked, "How're you feeling, sweetheart?"

"Sore."

"I know. I'm so glad to see you. God, I'm so glad to see you," he said as he sat on the bed and leaned over to hug her. "I was so worried about you."

"I'm sorry."

"No. No, baby. I love you. I love you so much," Warren murmured as he gently placed kisses all over her face.

"Warren. What about the baby? Is the baby okay?" she asked, fright in her eyes.

"He's fine," Warren said with a reassuring smile. "We have a son, and he's beautiful. He's beautiful, Ally."

She broke down then, crying with relief.

"Oh, God, thank you. I was so scared," she cried.

"Don't worry. He's in an incubator because he's so small, but he's healthy and he's strong," Warren told her with a smile.

Alexandra laughed through her tears.

"I want to see him," she said.

"Okay. Shari and Frank are here."

"What time is it?" she asked.

Warren looked at the watch on his wrist and answered, "Ten to eight."

"Oh, my God. I've been here all night? The last thing I remember is this guy crashing into me outside the restaurant."

"Yeah, the creep had stolen someone's pocketbook."

"Oh, no. Have you been here all night?"

"Yeah. I wasn't leaving until I knew you were all right."

"Have Shari and Frank been here all night, too?"

"Yeah."

"Oh, my God. Where are they?"

"They'll be here in a minute," Warren said as he gazed lovingly into her eyes. "You look so beautiful."

Alexandra ran a hand across the crown of her head and frowned. "I'm sure I don't."

"Yes, you do."

He leaned over and kissed her again.

"I love you," he whispered.

"I love you, too," she said. "Warren, what does he look like?"

"Oh, he's gorgeous, Ally. I think he's gonna take his coloring after me. He's a little chocolate baby. He's got a head full of straight black hair. He has your eyes and your nose. Oh, baby, I can't wait until you see him. You're gonna be so proud of yourself."

Just then Frank and Shari entered the room.

"Alex?"

"Hi, Shari. Hi, Frank," she said with a wide grin.

They both leaned over to kiss her.

"How're you feeling, honey?" Shari asked.

"Oh," she sighed. "Like I've been through the wringer."

"Well, you look gorgeous," Frank said.

"I wish y'all would stop lying to me."

"We're not lying, baby. You do look gorgeous," Warren added.

"I don't feel gorgeous."

"You will when you see your son," Shari said.

"Did you see him?" she asked Shari.

"The desk nurse knew we'd been here all night, so she was sympathetic when we told her we were his godparents. They let us see him just now."

"That was nice of her," Warren said.

"Yeah. He's beautiful, Alexandra," Frank said.

"Yes, he is," Shari agreed.

"I can't wait to see him," Alexandra groaned.

"You'll see him soon, baby. They'll probably be bringing him in any minute to eat."

"They probably won't let me breast feed him while I'm in here. I'm on this medication," Alexandra said.

"That's all right, baby. There's time for that. Besides, that'll give me a chance to feed him," Warren told her.

She smiled at him.

"Listen, Al. We're not gonna stay. I know you must be tired," Frank said.

"Me? *You* must be exhausted. Thanks for sticking around, guys," she said sincerely.

"I wasn't going anywhere until I knew you were all right. Besides, Warren needed the company," Shari said.

"Yeah, a lot of company we were. We slept just about the whole night," Frank added.

"Oh my goodness. You guys are true friends. Thanks. I love you both."

"We love you, too, Al," Frank said, and placed a kiss on her forehead.

Shari kissed her cheek. "We'll be back later, okay? See ya, Warren," Shari said.

"All right, Shari. Thanks for everything."

"Anytime."

"Thanks, Frankie," Warren said as he and Frank shook hands.

"No thing. Congratulations."

Warren and Alexandra sat smiling at each other for a moment after Shari and Frank left.

"They're great!" Alexandra said.

"Yes, they are."

"Thank you, Warren."

"For what?"

"For Stefan."

"Thank you. You are the most beautiful woman in the world. I don't want to ever live without you again, Alexandra."

He kissed her lips softly.

As he looked into her eyes, he whispered, "Promise me something?"

"What?"

"Promise me that you'll always love me and that we'll always be together."

"I promise to love you forever and I'll never leave you and I won't let you leave me. I need you in my life, Warren."

"Marry me, Alexandra."

"Of course I'll marry you. That was a part of the plan," she said with a smug smile.

He laughed as he put his arms around her and placed a very sensuous kiss on her mouth.

About the Author

Cheryl Faye has been writing as a hobby for over twenty years. For her, it is the best form of relaxation. Aside from romantic fiction, she also writes poetry and short stories. She is the mother of two sons and lives in Jersey City, New Jersey.

Look for these upcoming Arabesque titles:

September 1996

WHISPERED PROMISES by Brenda Jackson
AGAINST ALL ODDS by Gwynne Forster
ALL FOR LOVE by Raynetta Manees

October 1996

THE GRASS AIN'T GREENER by Monique Gilmore
IF ONLY YOU KNEW by Carla Fredd
SUNDANCE by Leslie Esdaile

November 1996

AFTER ALL by Lynn Emery
ABANDON by Neffetiti Austin
NOW OR NEVER by Carmen Green

ROMANCES ABOUT AFRICAN-AMERICANS!
YOU'LL FALL IN LOVE
WITH ARABESQUE BOOKS FROM PINNACLE

SERENADE   (0024, $4.99)
by Sandra Kitt

Alexandra Morrow was too young and naive when she first fell in love with musician, Parker Harrison—and vowed never to be so vulnerable again. Now Parker is back and although she tries to resist him, he strolls back into her life as smoothly as the jazz rhapsodies for which he is known. Though not the dreamy innocent she was before, Alexandra finds her defenses quickly crumbling and her mind, body and soul slowly opening up to her one and only love, who shows her that dreams do come true.

FOREVER YOURS   (0025, $4.50)
by Francis Ray

Victoria Chandler must find a husband quickly or her grandparents will call in the loans that support her chain of lingerie boutiques. She arranges a mock marriage to tall, dark and handsome ranch owner Kane Taggart. The marriage will only last one year, and her business will be secure, and Kane will be able to walk away with no strings attached. The only problem is that Kane has other plans for Victoria. He'll cast a spell that will make her his forever after.

A SWEET REFRAIN   (0041, $4.99)
by Margie Walker

Fifteen years before, jazz musician Nathaniel Padell walked out on Jenine to seek fame and fortune in New York City. But now the handsome widower is back with a baby girl in tow. Jenine is still irresistibly attracted to Nat and enchanted by his daughter. Yet even as love is rekindled, an unexpected danger threatens Nat's child. Now, Jenine must fight for Nat before someone stops the music forever!

Available wherever paperbacks are sold, or order direct from the Publisher. Send cover price plus 50¢ per copy for mailing and handling to Penguin USA, P.O. Box 999, c/o Dept. 17109, Bergenfield, NJ 07621. Residents of New York and Tennessee must include sales tax. DO NOT SEND CASH.

INFORMATIVE—
COMPELLING—
SCINTILLATING—
NON-FICTION FROM PINNACLE TELLS THE TRUTH:

BORN TOO SOON   (751, $4.50)
by Elizabeth Mehren
This is the poignant story of Elizabeth's daughter Emily's premature
birth. As the parents of one of the 275,000 babies born prematurely
each year in this country, she and her husband were plunged into the
world of the Neonatal Intensive Care unit. With stunning candor, Elizabeth Mehren relates her gripping story of unshakable faith and hope—
and of courage that comes in tiny little packages.

THE PROSTATE PROBLEM   (745, $4.50)
by Chet Cunningham
An essential, easy-to-use guide to the treatment and prevention of the
illness that's in the headlines. This book explains in clear, practical terms
all the facts. Complete with a glossary of medical terms, and a com-
prehensive list of health organizations and support groups, this illus-
trated handbook will help men combat prostate disorder and lead longer,
healthier lives.

THE ACADEMY AWARDS HANDBOOK   (887, $4.50)
An interesting and easy-to-use guide for movie fans everywhere, the
book features a year-to-year listing of all the Oscar nominations in every
category, all the winners, an expert analysis of who wins and why, a
complete index to get information quickly, and even a 99% foolproof
method to pick this year's winners!

WHAT WAS HOT   (894, $4.50)
by Julian Biddle
Journey through 40 years of the trends and fads, famous and infamous
figures, and momentous milestones in American history. From hoola
hoops to rap music, greasers to yuppies, Elvis to Madonna—it's all here,
trivia for all ages. An entertaining and evocative overview of the milestones in America from the 1950's to the 1990's!

*Available wherever paperbacks are sold, or order direct from the
Publisher. Send cover price plus 50¢ per copy for mailing and
handling to Penguin USA, P.O. Box 999, c/o Dept. 17109, Bergenfield, NJ 07621. Residents of New York and Tennessee must
include sales tax. DO NOT SEND CASH.*

IF ROMANCE BE THE FRUIT OF LIFE—
READ ON—
BREATH-QUICKENING HISTORICALS FROM PINNACLE

WILDCAT (722, $4.99)
by Rochelle Wayne

No man alive could break Diana Preston's fiery spirit . . . until seductive Vince Gannon galloped onto Diana's sprawling family ranch. Vince, a man with dark secrets, would sweep her into his world of danger and desire. And Diana couldn't deny the powerful yearnings that branded her as his own, for all time!

THE HIGHWAY MAN (765, $4.50)
by Nadine Crenshaw

When a trumped-up murder charge forced beautiful Jane Fitzpatrick to flee her home, she was found and sheltered by the highwayman—a man as dark and dangerous as the secrets that haunted him. As their hiding place became a place of shared dreams—and soaring desires—Jane knew she'd found the love she'd been yearning for!

SILKEN SPURS (756, $4.99)
by Jane Archer

Beautiful Harmony Harper, leader of a notorious outlaw gang, rode the desert plains of New Mexico in search of justice and vengeance. Now she has captured powerful and privileged Thor Clarke-Jargon, who is everything Harmony has ever hated—and all she will ever want. And after Harmony has taken the handsome adventurer hostage, she herself has become a captive—of her own desires!

WYOMING ECSTASY (740, $4.50)
by Gina Robins

Feisty criminal investigator, July MacKenzie, solicits the partnership of the legendary half-breed gunslinger-detective Nacona Blue. After being turned down, July—never one to accept the meaning of the word no—finds a way to convince Nacona to be her partner . . . first in business—then in passion. Across the wilds of Wyoming, and always one step ahead of trouble, July surrenders to passion's searing demands!
